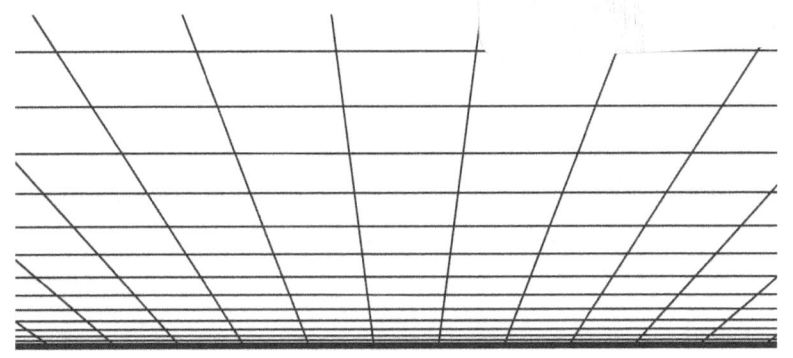

REVIVING ZEKE
PROJECT DEEP
BOOK FOUR

BECCA JAMESON

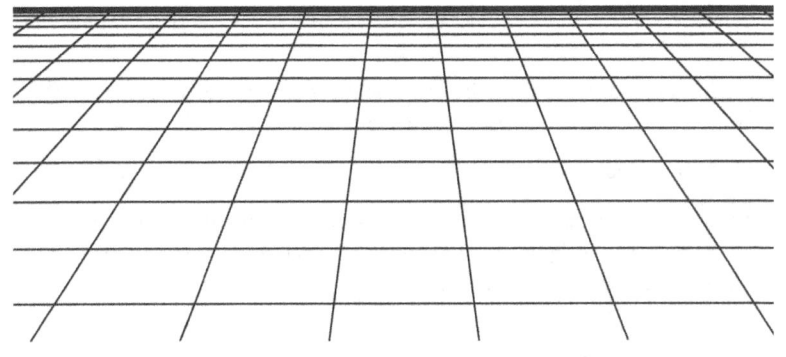

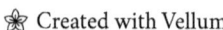

ACKNOWLEDGMENTS

I really have to thank everyone who listened to me ramble on and on about this series for months while I worked out the plot and figured out where we were going. It's a totally new genre for me. (Well, I mean except for the fact that it's still erotic romance! Let's not get carried away.) So, it took a lot of planning.

The concept came to me in the early hours of the morning in a dream when I wasn't quite awake yet. (Okay, gotta pause again here to say that "early" is a relative term. I don't do "early." Nothing in my world is actually "early." I just mean whatever time the last hour of my sleep occurred. Probably more like ten in the morning.)

In my dream, there were these scientists in a government bunker. They were studying diseases. They got sick. They had to be cryonically preserved… And from there, a series was launched. I spent a great deal of time studying cryonics and learning the difference between cryonics, cryobiology, and cryogenics--which are very different things.

I worked very hard to ensure that my terminology was correct with respect to the field of cryonics, though I obviously took a great deal of artistic liberty when reviving the preserved since alas, as far as we know, no one has been reanimated to this date.

Many thanks to Christa Soule for plotting with me when we were in the early stages, and then when we were in the middle stages, and still to this day.

Thanks to my husband and countless friends who listened to me and added their two cents.

CHAPTER 1

"Put me to work. I don't care if you want me to take out the trash, vacuum the floors, clean toilets, or find a cure for Ebola, but I'll lose my mind soon if you don't give me a task."

Michelle lifted her gaze from the paperwork she was going over with her boss, General Temple Levenson, in the general's office. Standing in the doorway, scowling, was one of the latest patients to be reanimated by the Project DEEP team—Zeke Holleran.

Of the eight people who had been revived so far, Zeke was Michelle's least favorite. He seemed permanently angry. Sure, he was ridiculously good looking, but his brow was always furrowed, and he rarely spoke to anyone.

Temple leaned back in her chair. "You've been awake only three weeks. You should be concentrating on standing, walking, using a fork."

He narrowed his gaze. "I think I've got those things down, Temple. I realize you haven't seen me for ten years, but do you remember me sitting around with my feet up?"

She chuckled. "No. Definitely not." Temple was the link between every member of both teams—the old and the new. She had been there from the beginning, so Zeke knew her as well or better than anyone who had been hired in the bunker in the last few years.

"Look, I realize you have no system in place to pay any of us yet, but you're going to have a mutiny on your hands soon if you don't figure out something for us to do. We're scientists. We may be behind on the latest developments, but we each need to figure out if we're willing to put in the work or change professions. The only way that's going to happen is if you give out some assignments."

Michelle could see his point. If she were in his shoes, she would be crawling out of her skin.

"Do you still feel solid as an immunologist? Any memory problems?" Temple glanced from Zeke to Michelle.

Oh no. Hell, no. Please, God, no.

"I'm solid." Zeke lifted a brow.

"And you're sure you want to continue with Project DEEP? You realize you have options. No one is required to stay. We can relocate you. Provide you with a new identity so you can start over."

"Not a chance. This is my life."

Temple nodded slowly. "Well, it's only been three weeks. You don't have to decide anything today, but if you want to get back to work, why don't you shadow Michelle? She's also an immunologist. She can bring you up to speed."

Zeke shifted his gaze toward Michelle, seeming to just that moment notice she was in the room. He was still frowning, but she refused to take it personally. He knew nothing about her, and he scowled like that at everyone.

That didn't mean she wanted to work with him. *Shit.*

Zeke hesitated. Was he scrutinizing her?

She stood straighter to her full height of five nine and crossed her arms as if this were a standoff. "Join me any time you'd like. I know you're still gaining strength. I'll understand if you want to start slow. Maybe a few hours a day?" She knew she sounded snarky, and she fully intended to. Jesus, the man could melt iron with his looks.

"I'm not having trouble staying awake, for God's sake. I'm just not quite up to a marathon."

"Well, everything around here is a marathon. That's why I'm suggesting you not attempt to enter the competition. Ease in. See what you remember and where the holes are. Then we can take it from there."

"Excellent," Temple interrupted. "Now, I've got a meeting in the conference room. I trust you two can continue this tête-à-tête elsewhere?" She glanced at Michelle as she stood, eyebrows lifted. She gave her a more pointed glare as she shuffled toward the door.

Great. Now Temple didn't think Michelle could play nice. Then again, Michelle wasn't at all sure she was capable herself.

She followed Temple out of the office as Zeke backed into the hallway also. Temple walked away, and Michelle pasted on a smile. "You want to start tomorrow?"

"Now's fine. Show me what you're working on." He swept a hand in the direction of the wing of the bunker where most of the medical personnel worked. At least he was a gentleman.

He followed her while she tried to imagine how she was going to live through this ordeal. She was backed up with projects that needed attention. Meanwhile, the bunker was quickly filling with newly reanimated staff whose skills were ten years behind. Next week, there would be four more joining the group.

The bunker was getting crowded, and tensions were high because no one was supposed to leave the bunker without permission.

The only way anyone could leave the bunker was if they chose to take a new name and relocate to start a new life. So far, no one had opted to leave. As more of them awoke, Michelle had little doubt some of them would decide they didn't want any part of this chaos.

When Michelle rounded the doorway leading to the main lab, she found several coworkers already buried in work.

"For some reason, the lab looks smaller than it did the last time I was here," Zeke murmured.

"Well, I wasn't here ten years ago, but Tushar, Trish, and Emily have all confirmed there have been few changes to anything. With the exception of the additional attached housing units, this section of the bunker hasn't undergone much of an overhaul."

"Oh, trust me. I would remember. I was just here a month ago in my mind."

"Right." She nodded as she led him to a workstation. She was aware of how each of the reanimated scientists perceived the passage of time, but it was still eerie. As far as the original team was concerned, they'd been in a sort of coma with no awareness that a decade had gone by.

Zeke picked up a notebook she'd been using before she went to see Temple. "How can you even read this?" he asked, scowling.

She inhaled slowly, forcing herself not to slap him. If he said one more condescending thing, she wasn't sure she could hold back. "I don't need to. Everything important is in the computer. I just keep a notebook next to me to jot something down if I need to."

"The computer..." He glanced at the laptop open on the desk area.

The room was bustling with six other people working and talking over each other. Sometimes Michelle felt like she worked for a major newspaper always on the cusp of an important story instead of in a government bunker.

Project DEEP was the thankfully short abbreviation for Disease & Epidemic Eradication & Prevention. Not a soul used that term. Half of them couldn't even remember it.

"Yeah, I've also come to realize your team didn't rely as heavily on computers ten years ago."

"We used computers, of course, but I've never trusted them enough to rely on them not eating my data or losing it somehow in the ether," he grumbled.

"They've improved a lot in the last decade. We back up everything multiple times into a cloud and onto external hard drives. It's all safe."

He lifted a brow. "I'm clear on how the computer works. We backed up everything even in the dark ages a decade ago, but if I can't hold it in my hands, it doesn't feel safe."

Was he going to argue with her like this constantly? She was losing her patience, and they hadn't even started yet. Great. This was going to be so much fun. "You might like to take a refresher course on computers to get up to speed. Kate, Grayson, and Colton were going to sit down with our tech guy and brush up." The three people she was referring to had been reanimated at the same time as Zeke. They were coworkers of Zeke's.

Zeke ignored her offer. Perhaps he didn't play nice with others even a decade ago. "I'll just stick to paper for now."

"Okay. Suit yourself."

"What's most urgent?" he asked, taking a seat in the rolling chair as he lifted the printout of a spreadsheet to scrutinize. He didn't look her in the eye. It was annoying as hell and somewhat rude or condescending. She wasn't sure which.

If this guy even so much as insinuated that she wasn't as good as him because she was a woman, she truly would kill him with her bare hands. She wasn't sure why she got that particular vibe, but it stuck. "Myasthenia Gravis," she said.

He nodded slowly, peering into the microscope in front of him and then glancing around at the samples on the desk. "It makes me kind of sick to my stomach to realize how little advancement has been made in the last ten years in some areas of research," he told the microscope.

She chose to pretend he wasn't criticizing her in particular or even the Project DEEP team. *He's just making an observation. Don't take it personally.*

"Why is this disease at the forefront right now?" he asked the desk.

She wanted to grab his chin and force him to make eye contact with her. Instead, she took a deep breath and answered his question. They were going to be working closely. She needed to find a way to stifle this animosity. "There has been an unusual surge in occurrences in the last few years. No one knows the causes, and we're still no closer to a cure."

"I see."

"I'll give you some time to look over the data." she stated, hoping to get away from him so she could breathe again. It was too bad he was so foul. If his brow weren't knitted together and he actually smiled and relaxed his shoulders, women would do a double-take when they walked by.

At a glance, he was attractive. Six feet tall. Green eyes she'd only glimpsed. Broad shoulders. Brown wavy hair. He could even be sexy. But instead, he was a bit of an ass.

"Let me know if you need anything. Or ask anyone in the room. We're all friendly." *Except you.*

Keeping his head tipped down, he lifted his gaze alone to meet hers. It was the first time he made eye contact with her. "I have a PhD in immunology from Harvard. I think I'll be fine."

"Good for you," she returned. "I have a matching PhD from Emory that is ten years newer than yours." Without another word, she turned around and left the room, praying she could make it to someplace private before she stomped her feet in frustration.

CHAPTER 2

Zeke kicked himself internally as he watched Michelle gracefully saunter from the room. There had been no need for him to be such an asshole. Nothing about his current situation was her fault. In fact, it was a wonder she hadn't slapped him in the last fifteen minutes.

She probably thought he was a total dick with the way he'd behaved since Temple set them up to work together. And that wasn't far from the truth. But not for the reasons she might suspect.

His sour personality had nothing to do with her personally. Not professionally anyway. No part of him doubted her abilities or her education. The reason he couldn't stand to look at her was because she was eerily similar to his ex-wife—a woman who left him soon after they moved to Falling Rock, Colorado. Long brown hair. Dark chocolate eyes. Tanned skin. High cheekbones. Slight build. Even her long legs that went on forever reminded him of his ex-wife. It was uncanny, and he was afraid if he stared at her very long, he might growl.

Zeke met Meredith in the last year of his doctorate on a night he should have been studying. He had taken an evening off from studying or catching up on sleep to attend another student's wedding, and had met Meredith at the reception.

From the moment he met her, he should have seen the signs. Red flags everywhere. So many of them waving in the air, it was a wonder he could even see through them.

Meredith, it turned out, had been far more interested in money than she was in love. And she incorrectly assumed Zeke would be a rich man who would spoil her for the rest of her life. What she didn't count on at the time was that Zeke had already made a commitment to the government to move to Falling Rock, Colorado, after he finished his PhD, where he would work long hours for little thanks in a dark bunker.

Zeke's new wife knew all that before she said I do, but she hid her distaste for his plans and pretended she was on board. She was greedy. She made a mistake.

Meredith was left in a small apartment in a smaller town with no friends, no family, and very little money. She had lasted about two months before she left him. So much for her vows of for better or for worse, for richer or for poorer.

Zeke shook thoughts of his ex-wife from his head and concentrated on the specimen in the microscope instead. He was in over his head with his demand to be put to work. Not only was his stupid PhD from Harvard completely useless today, but he was going to have to work long hours every night to play catch-up.

"Hey, Zeke."

He lifted his gaze at the familiar voice and found Kate leaning her hip against the desk next to him. She was smiling, and she crossed her arms and rolled her eyes. Kate had been revived at the same time as himself. "After ten years of hibernation, it wouldn't kill you to smile," she joked.

Everyone on his team knew he didn't find life particularly amusing. He might have been slightly more carefree as a young child, but hard work on a virus he eventually succumbed to and a bum marriage had put him in a permanently bad mood. "My muscle memory hasn't changed," he teased back, letting the corners of his lips tip up in the only form of a smile he ever used.

Kate had been one of the few people who'd ever coaxed even that much out of him. Not because he was interested in her as more than a friend, but because she had his number and knew how to push his buttons to get him to lighten up like no one else. "Apparently not. Listen, Grayson, Colton, and I are meeting with the tech guys to bring us up to date on the latest technology. Join us." She didn't ask. She was telling him.

He sighed. He'd insisted he didn't need any help when Michelle suggested it. He'd been a fool, however. Obviously computers had changed so much in the last decade he hardly recognized a thing on the screen. "Yeah. I should do that. When are you meeting?"

"Four this afternoon. In the conference room. We'll meet a few hours every afternoon until we've got it."

He nodded. "Sounds good. I'll see you there."

Kate bounced from the room in her usual energetic way that apparently hadn't been affected by preservation. When she disappeared, Zeke shifted his attention to Michelle, who was staring at him over the top of a pair of reading glasses.

He immediately noticed two things. One, she had caught him halfway smiling at Kate. And two, she looked like a completely different person in the glasses, especially now that he was looking at her directly. The long braid hanging over one shoulder was also distinct from Meredith. His ex would never have been caught dead without her hair curled and styled and her makeup perfectly in place.

Michelle had on minimal makeup and had probably pulled her hair back haphazardly that morning without giving a shit what anyone thought. Tendrils hung loose around her face, teasing her cheeks. He visualized tucking the errant strands behind her ears.

Jesus, Zeke. He jerked his gaze away from her and picked up the data sheet in front of him to pretend to study it. His face was flushed from being caught staring. He felt like a ten-year-old boy. In fact, his social skills where women were concerned hadn't changed much in the last twenty years since he *was* a ten-year-old boy.

While he attempted to control the shaking of his hands, it occurred to him that Michelle had other qualities Meredith couldn't compete with. She was competent, educated, and intelligent. Why was he comparing the two women anyway? For fuck's sake. Were his defense mechanisms so automatic that any woman who even had brown hair triggered his grumpiness?

Who was he kidding? His defense mechanisms were going bonkers because Michelle was hot and he hadn't expected to react to anyone physically within the first few weeks of being *brought back to life*. Tall. Slender. Great legs. Mesmerizing chocolate eyes. And those glasses... They made her look downright studious. Which she was of course. But it was sexy on her. Meredith had never given off a vibe of intelligence.

Zeke shook his wandering thoughts from his mind. What was wrong with him?

He didn't date anyone ever. Not just coworkers. He'd spent the next four years after Meredith left bitter and alone, sequestered in the bunker, trying to save people's lives. In the end, his own life had been one of them.

Since waking up, Zeke had felt out of body. Something was... off. He couldn't put his finger on it, but he felt a little like he was floating around watching himself, instead of participating. Apparently he was not alone. The others who had awakened before him expressed similar reactions. Emily had been the first person reanimated. Tushar and Trish—the married couple who headed up the original team—had been two and three. And then Dade.

Zeke took a breath as he thought about Dade. His best friend. A man who had been hiding in a remote cabin, fighting for his life. He'd had the genetic marker for another type of anemia that decided to kick into gear as soon as he received the cure for the first type of anemia they all had contracted a decade ago—AP12.

Life was fucking unfair. Even though Zeke had only been reanimated three weeks ago, he was aware of everything Ryan Anand had done to try to save Dade's life. Luckily, Zeke had been able to see his friend for a few hours last week before Dade had received the cure for AP12 and an experimental stem cell therapy that stood less than a 50 percent chance of saving his life. What kind of fucked-up world allowed a man to be brought back from preservation only to kill him with some other disease?

Perhaps half of the reason Zeke was so bitter had to do with Dade. Everyone in the bunker was sullen over the possibility of losing Dade. Both the old team who knew him well and the new team who didn't want to lose a single person.

Zeke found his gaze wandering to Michelle again. She wasn't looking at him this time. She was talking to two coworkers who were members of the more recent Project DEEP team. They were handpicked from their respective military academies for this project just as Michelle had been, as well as every member of the original team beginning almost three decades ago.

As Zeke watched Michelle smile at them, nodding in agreement to something he couldn't hear, he sat up straighter. A deep buried piece of him was coming to life. Unbidden. He shifted his weight in the chair, his breath caught in his lungs. Apparently, all parts of his body were well and truly in good working order.

He forced himself to look away, glancing around the room at the others, wondering if he might experience the same hitch in his breath as he did when looking at Michelle. Maybe being reanimated jump-started his libido in some unusual way.

Surely his physical reaction to her was an anomaly. After years of denying himself any woman at all, perhaps the current down time he was experiencing had made him more aware of their existence. He glanced around the room. Crap, not the case at all.

Michelle was the only woman in the bunker who had caught his attention.

Dammit.

~

Michelle followed Zeke around the room out of her peripheral vision for the next several hours. She found herself pissed at him and unable to shake the feeling, even as the afternoon progressed. After giving her nothing but a scowl and a bad attitude, he had not only smiled at Kate but agreed to take computer lessons with her after flat-out denying the need for any extra help when Michelle suggested it.

There was no reason for her to be so affected. Who the hell cared if the man didn't like her? She knew nothing about him. In fact, he and Kate had worked together for a few years before they'd been preserved. They had history. As friends? Or more?

Michelle shook the questions from her mind. She should not give a rat's ass.

When Zeke left the room at four to go meet with the others, she breathed a sigh of relief. It was absurd to let the man get under her skin. She wasn't sure if her frustration had to do with the fact that she didn't like people to so summarily dismiss her, or if she hated the idea of Zeke in particular disliking her.

Either way, the feeling was foreign. Michelle was well-liked among her peers. She was friendly and outgoing in a profession where many people were cocky or self-absorbed. She hadn't been raised to think she was better than anyone around her, and she never had.

Did Zeke think he was better than her? He acted as if that were the case when he tossed out his credentials, as if spending a few years at Harvard excused him from being polite for life.

If his animosity extended to all humans, fine. She would deal with it. But if he didn't like her in particular... A chill shook her body.

She was going to have to put on her charm and force him to like her. Though Lord knew she couldn't imagine why she cared. No matter how much she'd tried to shake it, her first reaction was always wanting new people to like her. It was ingrained in her. Had been from a young age. A southern thing, always wanting to please people and make them happy. As a child she had learned to kill people with kindness until they had no choice but to like her.

Eventually, she'd realized she spent way too much time trying to fit into other people's mold, keeping herself from being who she was meant to be. She had changed a lot since leaving her childhood home to seek advanced degrees. And now here she was, suddenly reverting back to her old self, thinking she needed to impress Zeke so he would like her. The idea pissed her off.

"Hey." Emily Zorich startled her from behind, making Michelle jump in her seat.

She spun around to find the room empty except for Emily. She must have really been deep in thought. She was usually more observant than she'd been today. All her brain cells had taken a leave of absence from the moment Temple suggested she work with the disagreeable Zeke Holleran.

"You okay?" Emily asked, frowning.

"Yeah." Michelle sighed, setting her glasses on the table and then swiping a hand down her face. "Exhausted, I guess. I didn't hear you come in."

Emily leaned her butt against the edge of the desk. "I heard Temple assigned you to work with Zeke."

"Yep." She pursed her lips, not wanting Emily to realize how much of her day had been squandered out of perseverating over Zeke from every imaginable angle.

Emily smirked. "How's that going?"

"Fine." Michelle returned her attention to the computer, moving her mouse around to shut it down for the night. "I didn't see him much. He spent most of the day familiarizing himself with the research and then went with a few others to get some computer training."

Emily was silent for long enough that Michelle finally glanced at her to find her still smirking. "In my experience, a person doesn't have to spend much time with Zeke before they want to throttle him. I figured you could use some advice and moral support."

Michelle let her shoulders fall as she blew out a breath. "Yeah. You're right. It took about two minutes. What's his deal? I should have thought to ask you. You've known him a long time." Michelle and Emily had gotten close since Emily's reanimation eight months ago. It was hard to remember that Emily had worked with Zeke prior to their vitrification.

"He's always been a serious guy, but any sort of happiness he might have felt earlier in life fled with his bitchy ex-wife."

Michelle flinched. "He was married?"

Emily nodded. "Not for very long. She was a gold digger who lasted about two months in Falling Rock before she divorced him."

"Damn. That's harsh." It also explained a lot.

"I don't think he trusts women."

"Got it." Michelle sat up straighter. "Well, he's met his match because if he thinks I'm going to cower to him, he's lost his mind. I spent way too much of my childhood deferring to the male species and killing myself to ensure I made them happy. Been there. Done that. Not going back. If he thinks I'll put up with that shit, he's wrong."

Emily smiled. "Good. Don't let him intimidate you. He's a nice guy under the gruff exterior. I promise. I've met that guy. We all have. But he doesn't come out often, and he doesn't stay long."

"I saw a glimpse of it with Kate earlier. I think he might have even smiled at her."

"Smiled?" Emily laughed. "I hate that I missed such a

phenomenon." She shoved off the edge of the desk. "Come on. Let's go eat. I haven't had dinner yet. I'm sure you haven't either. I think they made spaghetti tonight in the cafeteria."

Michelle's stomach growled. She was starving. As she stood, she touched Emily's arm. "Thanks for the pep talk. Zeke challenge accepted." She hoped she conveyed a twinkle in her eye as she met Emily's gaze. She would not let Zeke get to her. She was determined to win him over. But she'd do it her way, not by cowering to him, but by proving her own competence. If he couldn't see her value without her having to bend over backward to please him, that was his problem, not hers.

Day two working with Michelle started off on the same tone as day one. Zeke got up early and made his way quickly from the cafeteria to the lab. He beat everyone there, including Michelle, and already had the computer up and running when she arrived. In fact, she startled him when she leaned her hip against the desk next to him and crossed her arms.

He lifted his gaze to find her posture defensive, her expression wary. Good.

"You're up early," she pointed out.

"You get a medal for astuteness," he bit out before he could stop himself. He had no good reason to be a dick. He just couldn't stop himself. He'd been rather sour before vitrification, and it would seem nothing had changed in his attitude while he'd hibernated. Though inwardly he cringed at his unnecessary sarcasm.

Ignoring his snide comment, Michelle turned toward the screen. "One afternoon of tech support and you're a pro?" she asked, though he couldn't tell if she was trying to be snarky or complimenting him.

"I'm a quick study." He continued to push the mouse around,

returning his gaze to the screen, but her proximity was unnerving. Something about her made him sit up straighter. It was as if he could feel her heat even with several inches between them.

"No notepads today?" she tossed at him next.

"Nope." He realized how ridiculous he had been yesterday, insisting he would not need her modern technological advances because pen and paper were the only notes he would ever fully trust.

He'd been wrong; a fact he'd fully embraced after a few hours of listening to the advances in both hard drives, backups, and the cloud where any and all documents could be stored and retrieved. It would seem that if nothing else, the last decade had made it possible to easily ensure not a damn piece of information was every truly lost.

Michelle turned more fully toward the screen, but when she did so, her arm brushed his and a shock startled both of them. She flinched, rubbing the spot on her arm. "Sorry."

He sat stiff and frozen, trying to ignore the unwelcome effect of her presence. She needed to move away from him so he couldn't smell her vanilla shampoo or so closely watch her full lips move as she licked them.

She was cute. She was confident. And for whatever reason, he couldn't stop reacting to how attractive she was.

When she lifted her glasses from her free hand and settled them on her nose to see his screen better, he watched her profile. "You did all this since you got here this morning?"

"Just organizing the data so I can make sense of it," he retorted, leaning a few inches away from her. She made him nervous. He didn't want to accidentally brush against her again.

He needed her to move out of his space.

He needed to walk away and step closer to someone else on staff to prove to himself that his arousal had nothing to do with her specifically. Instead, something about reanimation must cause the pheromones to get out of control.

He should ask someone about it. Maybe Ryan. Or how about Tushar. Ryan's dad had come out of preservation five months ago. If Ryan didn't know, Tushar would.

What the hell was he thinking? No way on God's green earth was he going to approach another man from his team or any other team to ask them if they felt some sort of irrational attraction toward a woman after returning to the living.

"Are you done scrutinizing my work?" He glared at her, willing her to walk away. "It's my second day. Surely I don't need a performance review yet."

She jerked her gaze from his screen to his face. "For your information, I'm simply impressed with what you've accomplished, but evidently you're either not a morning person, or you can't take a compliment. Either way, you should consider an attitude adjustment." She turned on her heels and walked away. Or stalked rather. Or maybe stomped.

Either way, he cringed. *Great.*

Michelle made her way to the other side of the lab without tripping over anything, even though her vision was blurred with fury. She also managed not to grab any breakable items on the way to launch against the wall.

Don't let him get to you. She would be the bigger person in this scenario if it killed her. She had no idea what crawled up his ass or when it happened, but he'd met his match if he thought she would cower to him.

Her hands were shaking when she lowered into her chair and reached for her mouse. She took several deep breaths to control her emotions. When she'd first entered the room and found Zeke already hard at work, she'd watched him for several moments from the doorway.

He'd been so focused he hadn't noticed her. Before

approaching him, he'd also appeared to be human. More than human. Attractive. Tall. Lean. Confident. Someone had trimmed his dark hair in the last few weeks, making him look professional and clean cut.

Her heart rate had picked up a beat at first glance, just as it had yesterday, before she remembered he was sour most of the time.

She had no idea what had possessed her to approach him this morning, as if he might have experienced a personality shift in the night, but such had not been the case. If anything, he was more foul than yesterday.

Did he reserve that animosity for *her*?

According to Emily, Michelle would be overthinking things if she took his mood swings personally. He'd had a bad temperament for four years apparently. She didn't think it was reasonable or fair for him to treat people with such disdain just because his ex-wife had left him, but then again, there was no way to be certain he hadn't been rather ill-tempered even before he married the woman.

Michelle closed her eyes and continued to breathe deeply. It pissed her off that his presence at her back alone affected her so strongly. She tried to convince herself her reaction was fury, but she knew better. She seriously couldn't stand the fact that anyone would so openly feel disdain toward her. It dragged back unwelcome memories of her childhood.

Why should she care? For years she'd managed to bury that side of her, the side that felt the need to please people at all costs. It took too much energy, and most people weren't worth the effort.

Why did Zeke get under her skin, then?

She knew the answer, but she was loathe to admit to herself that some ridiculous part of her was attracted to him. As a man. Perhaps it was just his looks alone. Or maybe it was the challenge. Either way, he was about as closed off from any sort of human advances as anyone could be, so she needed to shake the absurd draw and move on with her life.

CHAPTER 3

One week later...

Zeke was fiddling with the newest smartphone as he leaned back in his desk chair, feet propped up on the desk. He nearly fell off the chair Michelle walked into the lab.

He sensed her immediately and dropped his feet to the floor, turning to face her. It was late in the evening. He'd assumed everyone was done for the day and wouldn't return. But Michelle never seemed to sleep. She had a work ethic that rivaled his own.

She didn't give him more than a passing glance as she headed to the other side of the room, but she did speak, probably because it would have been awkward not to. "I heard you got a smartphone. I assume you've already loaded it with a hundred aps and informed the designer how to improve it for the next version."

He couldn't be sure about her tone of voice. Perhaps a combination of teasing and taunting. Maybe even a hint of envy. He laughed, because he couldn't stop himself quickly enough. No matter how she intended her message to come across, her snarky comment had amused him. Which was saying something. "Not yet, but I did google his information," he joked in return.

She faced him, eyes rolling. "Of course you did."

"I had the latest phone before I was preserved, but it wasn't nearly as cool as this one. If you need me to program anything into your phone, let me know," he returned.

She lifted her eyes toward the ceiling next. "Were you born this cocky?"

"Nope. It's a trait I picked up a few years ago." She didn't need to know he'd gotten bitter and defensive after his divorce. Nor did she need to realize he reserved most of his animosity for her alone. And he sure as shit wasn't going to tell her why. He didn't think he could articulate it if he wanted to anyway.

Without saying another word, she turned around and faced her desk. She notably didn't sit in the swivel chair that was pushed under the computer. Instead, she bent forward and moved the mouse around as if she didn't intend to stay more than a minute.

She wore scrubs. They all did. Nearly every day. There was no reason to bother to dress in anything else. It was easier in the lab, plus no one who was recently reanimated had much in the way of clothing at all. Scrubs in all sizes and colors were in the supply closet.

Michelle's ass, however, was prominently featured as she bent forward. Her damn fine glutes drawing his attention. Since when did he notice or give two shits about women's butts?

Suddenly, Michelle blurted out a string of uncharacteristic cuss words. She spun around to meet his gaze, forcing him to jerk his attention higher and causing him to hope she hadn't noticed he'd been ogling her from behind. "Who else has been in here?" she asked.

"What do you mean?" He set his phone on the desk next to him and sat up straighter, hands on his thighs.

"How long have you been in the lab? Did you ever leave?" She ran a hand through her hair, making him nervous alongside her.

"I went to dinner, then I came back. The only people I've seen were the janitor and Temple."

Michelle pressed her palm into her forehead as though she suddenly had a headache.

"What's the matter?" he asked as he stood and strode across the room.

She spun back around as he approached and stared at the screen. "The data I've been entering all day is gone."

That made the hairs on the back of his neck stand on end. "Are you sure?"

She yanked out her chair as she shot him a glare. A glare that could melt ice. She didn't respond, and that was probably a good thing. He hadn't earned any brownie points with her by questioning her.

She lowered to her chair and started opening files. She checked the backup. She searched the hard drive. All while he watched over her shoulder. "Fuck," she muttered, and then she looked up at him again. "Just Temple and a janitor?"

He nodded. "I wasn't here the entire time, though. When I got here, no one was in the room. Everyone was at dinner."

"Someone wasn't fucking at dinner," she retorted.

"Apparently not," he agreed. "Mind if I have a look?" he asked, half afraid she might actually take a swing at him if he suggested his week-old computer skills might be superior to hers. The only thing that would be worse would be if he proved his expertise was better by finding the missing file.

She pushed to standing and made a dramatic gesture with the swipe of her arm, indicating he should sit. "Be my guest."

A week ago she had lurked over him in a similar fashion. The results weren't different today. She stood too close, distracting him with her vanilla scent and her soft breathing.

He quickly looked through all the same files she'd just scanned. "Is this the document you were working on?" he asked, pointing at the screen. The crazy thing was he could see it was open and whatever data she'd entered at some other time was there, but nothing from today.

"That's the one."

No way in hell would he insinuate she hadn't saved it. And besides, it shouldn't have mattered. It backed itself up every few minutes and should have been on the hard drive and in the cloud. There was no evidence she had come to work today at all. And yet, he'd personally seen here working all day at this desk.

"Dammit," she shouted, spinning around, hands on her head.

"Has this happened before?" he asked, his concern growing by the moment as he continued to look through possible backup files.

She chuckled sardonically. "Shit happens in this lab all the time. Welcome back to DEEP. It's a new decade."

He shuddered as he released the mouse and turned to face her. "I'm starting to get that." There was a chance the computer had a glitch, but from what he'd been hearing from Ryan and Tushar, the number of unexplained incidents and accidents in this lab were far too many to be coincidences.

Zeke felt sorry for Michelle. She would beat herself up over this, doubting her abilities when he knew damn good and well she was a perfectionist who didn't make mistakes of this magnitude.

No way in hell would he touch her, but he had the urge to pull her into his arms and comfort her. He wasn't sure if she was on the edge of tears or a rampage of anger. Probably both.

"It's like someone doesn't want us to cure Myasthenia Gravis. We're so close, and every time we take a step forward, we end up two steps backward."

"You mean accidents happen more often related to that particular study?" Zeke stood. He hated sitting with Michelle staring down at him for some reason. She wasn't a short woman, but at five nine she was still three inches shorter than him.

"Yes. But it could simply be that we spend more time on that disease than others right now."

"Why that one?" He cocked his head to one side. "I mean, I know there have been more incidents of it in recent years, but there are thousands of diseases out there that need our attention. What's special about Myasthenia Gravis?"

She shrugged. "How the hell should I know? I just do what I'm told and focus on whatever trickles down to me."

He nodded.

"And now I've lost an entire day's work for no apparent reason." She rubbed her arms, shivering. As she turned around to leave the room, she murmured, "Gives me the creeps."

Zeke watched her leave and then turned back to her chair and stared at her computer. He made note of the files she'd been using, grabbed a laptop, and headed for his suite.

Michelle slept fitfully, got up early, showered, and headed for the cafeteria. She grabbed a bagel and an apple and hurried to the lab. It was going to take her all day to make up for yesterday's lost work, and she also needed to tell Ryan what happened when he showed up.

As soon as she opened the file she'd been using, she froze. "What the hell?" She dropped the bagel on the desk and leaned closer, opening several other files.

She glanced behind her, half expecting to find Zeke at his desk even though he hadn't been in the room when she entered. No one was. It was not even six in the morning.

She returned to the first file and scrolled through it. The only thing that kept her from assuming she'd lost her mind entirely and completely fabricated the missing data the night before was that it was organized differently today.

It was all there, but whoever entered it the second time used a different method. A better one.

She gritted her teeth. "Zeke."

For a moment she sat there staring at it. He had to have stayed up for hours entering all the information, not to mention creating a slightly different spreadsheet. This one was more interactive and useful than the one she'd been using.

She played around in it for a few minutes, her emotions all over the place. On the one hand, she was excited to see the improved system. On the other hand, she was pissed that Zeke had figured out a better method instead of her.

Zeke Holleran was the only person she'd worked with since coming to the bunker who got under her skin so badly that she didn't feel like a team player most days. She'd never been this competitive with the rest of the staff. They were all on the same team. Didn't even matter if they were from the old team or the new team. Their job was the same. Cure diseases. If someone came up with easier techniques, everyone benefited.

But Zeke had a way of pissing her off. She couldn't stand the idea that he'd made an improvement she hadn't thought of.

Of course, all this presumed he'd been the one to reenter the data all night. And where was he now? She had half a mind to go hunt him down. Knock on his door. Drag him out of bed. But that would be a bitchy move on her part since he was probably asleep, and he deserved to stay in bed late considering all the work she knew in her gut he'd done.

Why did the infuriating man have to be so damn good-looking? She struggled every day to ignore him. There were dozens of people working in this bunker. None of the others drew her attention. In fact, no other man from any walk of life had captivated her attention.

Until Zeke awoke, she'd gone about her business every day without so much as thinking about entering into a relationship. She didn't have time for such a thing right now, nor did she have options since she never left the bunker.

She had no idea why she cared. It wasn't as though he was the only good-looking man in the bunker and she needed to impress

25

him. She didn't need a man at all. She had devoted her life to education and then research. Medicine was her passion.

The few men she had dated in her early twenties before she buckled down and swore off all men had left an impression. They weren't worth it. She could easily take care of her own sexual needs with a vibrator and a set of batteries. In fact, she did so far better than any man she'd slept with, which made it easy to put relationships on the back burner and concentrate on her job.

Nope. She did not need men in her life. They did nothing for her.

Except Zeke. The man who reentered her data all night even though he rarely did more than growl at her.

A noise behind her grabbed her attention, and she spun around in her chair to find the very man who wouldn't stay out of her thoughts striding into the lab. He didn't even look tired. Damn him. "You're up early," he said as he headed for his desk.

She swallowed, staring at his back. "Did you even bother to sleep at all?" she responded.

He shrugged, still not facing her. Yeah, he'd done this. For her. No need to ask. Her heart beat faster. It made no sense. The infuriating man didn't even like her. He made that perfectly clear every day. She couldn't imagine why he would go out of his way to do something so kind and thoughtful. He easily could have gone to bed and left the entire mess for her to deal with today. It hadn't even been his fault.

"Thank you," she managed in a voice that barely traveled across the room.

He glanced over his shoulder. "For what? Just helping out the team. It's my job."

It was way more than his job, above and beyond. No one even knew he'd done it. She hadn't had a chance to tell Ryan yet about the disappearing data.

"Well, thank you anyway. You didn't have to do it." She turned back around to face her computer, but she didn't see the screen.

All she could see in her mind was a conjured vision of a different Zeke, one whose brows weren't drawn together in aggravation. Surely, today of all days he wasn't scowling. She had no way of knowing, but she imagined his face relaxed. Perhaps not smiling, but at least less angry. He'd done her a solid, and she hoped it softened him a bit.

CHAPTER 4

Two weeks later...

Thank God Zeke had spent every possible moment for the last six weeks working out in the small gym at the bunker because tonight he was putting his endurance to the test. The last hour had been a whirlwind of insanity he still couldn't wrap his mind around. Until he could pull himself together and manage to paste on his best poker face, he needed to remain outside the bunker, where he was currently pacing in the moonlight.

He spun around for the millionth time and faced Ryan. He had so many questions he wasn't sure where to begin.

Ryan Anand was the head of the latest team of doctors and scientists who moved into the bunker two years ago to find a cure for AP12 while simultaneously figuring out how to reanimate the previous team. Ryan had been dedicated to this project like no other human. After all, both his parents had been preserved in the bunker.

Ryan was a rock. He was the glue that held both the old and

the new team together and forged ahead to ensure every last one of the original team members was successfully reanimated.

The only problem was that Dade's prognosis had not been good. And tonight in a whirlwind of information, Zeke had learned that Dade would not live, only to find out five minutes later that it was a lie and Dade would indeed grow old and gray.

"So, let me get this straight. The experimental stem cell replacement you gave Dade totally worked, and yet we're going to keep this information to ourselves, and not a single soul besides you and I know about this?"

"Correct." Ryan was patiently waiting for Zeke to absorb the information. He was also pacing in the darkness where the two of them had wandered about fifty yards from the bunker to have this private conversation.

"I can't decide if I'm elated you decided to include me in this ruse or if I want to punch you in the face."

Ryan nodded. "I understand. And honestly, if you hadn't been in the room when Temple came in to hear the bad news, I'm not sure I would have included you. But it suddenly seemed like too big a burden to carry alone, so I let you see the slides for yourself."

"Great." Zeke threw up his hands and tipped his head back. "Drop the burden on me, why don't you?"

"Like I said, several things came to mind. I hated for you to think your best friend was dying, and it seems prudent for someone besides myself to be aware of the situation, just in case something ever happens to me. Besides, I know you obviously can't be the person leaking information about the bunker since you were still preserved when shit started attracting my attention."

Zeke ran a hand through his hair and tipped his head back to face the sky again. It was no secret there was a mole inside the bunker. Someone was leaking information about the reanimation of the various team members as they were revived. Information that reached the press, religious zealots from all over the country, and anyone else willing to pay a buck to find out who was revived and when.

The leaked information was the reason Dade had left the bunker with Blair weeks ago to hide out in a remote cabin. He was also the first person to successfully do so without being tracked down—impressive since every one of them had a tracking device imbedded in their forearms, which evidently the mole was taking advantage of.

The information about the GPS trackers was kept to a select few people also, but eventually word would get out since every member of his team was now privy to the fact as they awakened, particularly because it seemed the trackers were being used against them.

After a wild race against the clock to save Emily when she was abducted by a madman, none of the team were left in the dark about the tracking devices. If Emily had known she was fitted with one, she wouldn't have spent several hours worrying about how anyone would find her.

"Where is Dade planning to go?" Zeke asked. "And how can he possibly remain hidden anywhere as long as he has that tracker in his arm? Someone will figure it out eventually. I don't understand how no one found him at the cabin in the first place."

"No one found him because I deactivated it before he left the bunker. But, I've been watching those devices in everyone like a hawk for weeks now. Someone broke into the system in attempt to find him. They even managed to reactivate the chip. At this point I wasn't even surprised, and I hope they had a field day chasing their tail to the hotel in western Colorado where Dade left the tracker weeks ago. I cut it out of his arm before he and Blair left town."

Zeke actually smiled. It was rare for him, but it was warranted. "Maybe you should have been a detective instead of a doctor."

Ryan laughed. "If I had taken that route, you wouldn't be standing here today."

That was sobering. "Right." He did owe this man his life, a guy who was just a young kid in the middle of college when he last saw him ten years ago. Thank God Ryan had never given up hope. He and Dr. Damon Bardsley were responsible for everything that had happened in the last few years. Ryan had worked furiously on curing AP12. Damon had worked just as intently on how to revive the preserved team.

Female voices caught Zeke's attention at the same moment Ryan turned in their direction also.

Emily and Michelle stepped into their line of sight.

"Ryan?" Emily asked. "What are you guys doing out here?"

"Just getting some air. It's been a long day."

Zeke watched Emily step in front of Ryan, set her hands on his arms, and tip her head back. In the moonlight, he could see the shimmer of tears as they trailed down her face. "We just spoke to Temple. She told us about Dade."

Zeke swallowed, emotions bubbling up inside him, one of which was jealousy that Ryan would spend the night in the arms of a woman he loved, being comforted for the loss of a friend—no matter how fake the story was. He wondered if Ryan would tell Emily at some point. It seemed strange to keep such an emotional secret from his own girlfriend.

A glance at Michelle made Zeke soften to the woman he spent most of his time avoiding or grumbling at. She wiped a tear from her own eye, though she tried to hide it.

If Zeke were capable of normal emotional reactions, he would give her a hug or at least pat her on the shoulder. But he wasn't normal. He was Zeke. He had a shield around him that no one could penetrate, and he liked it that way. No way in hell was he going to touch any part of Michelle Houston. If he ever touched her skin, he feared he might break the spell that kept him distant from her.

She was both soft and firm at the same time. Considering she was military, she was fit and strong. Meanwhile, he saw glimpses of her vulnerability all the time. Things that made her far more human and set her further apart from his damn ex-wife every day.

At first she had reminded him of Meredith far too much to swallow, but over time, he came to realize they were nothing alike. Eventually he wondered how he ever thought the two of them were even physically similar.

While Ryan pulled Emily into his embrace and kissed the top of her head, Zeke stood an awkward distance from Michelle, dragging his toe in the dirt.

"How long do you think he has?" Michelle asked in a weak voice.

Shit. Zeke hadn't thought to ask Ryan how far the lie extended and what the details were.

Ryan set his chin on Emily's head and met Michelle's gaze. "It's hard to say. Maybe a few weeks or even months if he's lucky. I can't predict how fast the disease will attack his blood cells."

Emily tipped her head back, still gripping Ryan around the waist, but setting her chin on his chest. "You're sure? There's no way?" She was grasping at straws in desperation. Zeke had known her for years. She was as educated as any other member of their team. If she had seen the test results as he described them, she wouldn't be asking Ryan for a ray of hope.

Blood cells didn't lie. They were either multiplying or they were diminishing. Ryan would now begin convincing everyone they knew that Dade's blood cells were not reproducing.

The bombshell that had landed on Zeke an hour ago now took on new meaning. He not only had the privilege of knowing with immense happiness in his heart that his best friend would live, but he also had to put on a show for everyone around that would not be easy to maintain day after day.

On the other hand, he knew he'd been a bit of a jackass for the last few weeks. Once he'd established himself as someone who didn't quite respect Michelle, he had easily slid into a rut, grumbling at everyone around him and maintaining his stupid façade as some form of self-preservation. Pride. Even the small connection they'd shared after she thanked him for reentering her data was doused moments later by his instinctive surliness.

It shouldn't be too much of a stretch now to add grief and frustration and even anger to his repertoire. He shifted his gaze to Michelle to find her swiping away a tear. A lump formed in his throat as she stood there with her arms crossed over her chest, looking shell-shocked and so very sad.

He wanted to reach out for her, as a human being if nothing else. But he couldn't bring himself to move a single inch.

The reality about his feelings for Michelle was far different from the game he played. He didn't simply respect her as a colleague; he was downright awed by her. She was brilliant. Her IQ was surely higher than his. She retained information like a sponge, even weeks after it was presented to her.

She had ten years of additional research experience on him that made her far superior in a field where they could have been equals if he hadn't taken an unintentional decade-long hiatus.

On top of all that, she was sexy in a way that most men probably wouldn't notice or appreciate. The reality was, he found her intelligence attractive, which meant every time she moved around a room, he got tongue-tied. And yet, he continued the farce.

"This is all so unfair," Emily cried.

"I know, babe. I know." Ryan smoothed his hand up and down Emily's back, consoling her. Lying to her.

What a mess.

Another glance at Michelle—which probably hadn't been wise —showed her lips pursed in an obvious attempt to avoid full-on crying.

Yep, Zeke was officially a world-class asshole. The stab to his heart was new, however. It had been a long time since he felt any sort of emotion toward a woman, including shared sorrow.

After Meredith, he'd sworn off all women and buried himself

in his work. He had never quite figured out if he'd been a fool to fall for her or if she'd been a two-faced bitch who gave him the bait and switch. Either way, he was the loser, and he had no intention of ever making a mistake like that again.

The plan had wreaked havoc on his sex life, since he also hadn't slept with a woman in the last few years—the ten-year gap not included in his mental calculations. The only sex Zeke had been a part of in the four years since Meredith left had involved his fist and usually his shower. But they did the job amazingly—as long as he didn't mind having no human contact.

The truth was, he was exhausted from the ruse. Day after day of pretending he was sour and didn't give a fuck about anything or anyone but himself. He'd been in this same funk even before he was preserved, and it hadn't improved with vitrification.

If anything, his heart was even more frozen than before.

The sudden distinctive sound of a gunshot rang out loud through the night air. Ryan immediately tossed Emily to the ground, his body covering hers completely.

Michelle looked too stunned to move, and without thinking, Zeke took two long strides closer to her and dove for her, tackling her to the ground. He covered her head with his hand and then tipped his ear to the sky to listen.

Michelle yelped as she hit the ground, and now she was panting while struggling to free herself. "Jesus, Zeke. Get off me. I'm perfectly capable of taking care of myself. You're smashing me. I can't breathe. Though it's also possible you collapsed one my lungs in your unnecessary macho attempt to save the day."

"Shh." He set a hand over her mouth to stop her rambling. It wasn't that he didn't enjoy her voice. He did. It was deep and rich, the sound vibrating through her body and into his, plastered on top of her. But he needed to listen.

She shoved at him repeatedly while he held a hand over her mouth and waited. For what? Anything. Another gunshot.

Moments ago, the light from the moon had seemed

impressive. Now, with the threat of gunfire, the night seemed darker. Zeke glanced at Ryan who was inching toward him with Emily practically smothered under him.

Michelle grabbed Zeke's hand and wrenched it off her mouth. She shot him a glare as she wiggled out from under him. Her words were aimed at Ryan. "What direction do you think the shots came from?" she whispered.

Ryan nodded over his shoulder. "Front entrance." He rolled onto one hip and pulled his phone from his pocket. After tapping the screen, he spoke. "What the fuck is going on, Dad?"

Zeke could hear Tushar's voice clearly. "Some crazy man is waving a gun around, firing at random outside the front gate. Where are you?"

"Outside." Ryan pushed to sitting.

Zeke did the same, as did Michelle and Emily. The front gate was far enough away they should be safe from stray bullets.

"Has anyone been shot?" Ryan asked.

"Not yet. He's aiming at the sky."

"What does he want?"

"Based on the report coming from the entrance, he's holding a Bible in the other hand and rambling about God's will."

Zeke rolled his eyes. "Great," he muttered. Just what they needed. A religious zealot gone nuts.

Another shot rang out.

Even though the four of them were a relatively safe distance from the entrance, they all ducked. "Let's get out of here," Zeke proposed. "We're too close." He rose to a crouched position and pointed toward the line of small homes that had been erected to house employees. There were about a dozen lined up in a row that hadn't been there ten years ago. They were closer than the bunker itself.

Another shot filled the air as Zeke scrambled in a hunched position toward the homes. He could sense the others behind him. "What's wrong with people?" Stray bullets were extremely unsafe. Didn't this asshole realize what goes up must come down?

He rounded the first home and reached out instinctively to grab Michelle and pull her behind him. At least they could stand from this new position. The barrier made him relax.

Zeke realized Ryan was still on the phone with his dad when he spoke again. "We're safe."

"Good. Stay there until they can get this guy tackled," Tushar ordered.

Michelle set a hand on Zeke's arm, surprising him. Her gaze was serious. "You're bleeding." She grabbed the front of his scrubs and lifted the hem to dab at his forehead.

Zeke had no idea he'd been injured. From what?

Emily peered around and rose onto her tiptoes. "Probably from diving over Michelle." She smiled. "I didn't know you were so calm under pressure," she teased. "Or so quick."

"Who says I'm calm?" he shot back. He felt anything but calm as he swatted Michelle's hand away and touched his forehead with his fingers. He winced at the sting. He hoped the bleeding had stopped because the last thing he needed or could endure would be Michelle's gentle touch on his skin.

Emily's face lit up and she slapped her forehead before digging in her pocket and pulling out a set of keys. She dangled them in front of them as if she held the secret to the universe.

"Babe?" Ryan asked.

"I have Blair's house keys. Hers is the third one over."

Ryan smiled. "Excellent." He grabbed her hand and half jogged behind the row of homes to the third one.

Zeke followed behind Michelle.

When they reached the back door, Ryan took the keys and opened it. "Why do you have Blair's keys?"

"She wanted someone to have them to check on things while she was gone." Emily's face fell as she sighed. "I had hoped her departure wouldn't be forever."

Ryan pulled her close to his side as they all stepped into the kitchen. "I'm sorry."

"Do you think she'll return?" Emily asked. "After..."

Ryan shook his head. "Honestly, no. I think she's going to give notice to Temple soon."

Emily pursed her lips as she nodded. "I figured that would be the case, and I can't blame her. I hope one day you can arrange for me to be able to speak to her."

"I will. As soon as I can," Ryan responded.

Zeke's throat was too closed to comment. Even though no one had mentioned Dade's name, the reason for Blair's departure and her resignation was because she had left the bunker to protect Dade. How many stories would have to be concocted to explain why she never returned? Ryan was making shit up.

Zeke was both happy that Dade had found a woman he loved, while at the same time depressed to know it might be a long time before Zeke was able to speak to his friend again. Possibly forever.

Michelle's hand landed on Zeke's arm again. "Come on. Let me look at your forehead in the bathroom. I'm sure Blair has a first aid kit."

Zeke followed her around the corner and down a short hall, even though the last thing he wanted was for her to fawn over his stupid cut or any other part of him. Arguing would only make matters worse.

It had been one thing to keep his distance from her before he'd touched her. Now, he was slightly fucked. Landing on her, touching her face, her hand on his forehead, his arm. Her face so close to his...

When they entered the small hall bathroom, she shut the door, flipped on the lights, and pointed at the toilet seat. "Sit. Let me see."

He stared at the door for a moment, wondering why she'd felt the need to close them inside before realizing she was one step ahead of him. It would be best for no one to suspect anyone was inside the house if by chance a crazy person happened to breach the gates.

The idea was preposterous. There were always half a dozen guards at the entrance and six others around the perimeter. An idiot waving a gun and a Bible didn't stand a chance. Nevertheless, there was no reason to risk anyone finding them in Blair's home.

Michelle ran a washcloth under the water and then pressed it to Zeke's temple. "You scraped it good." She stepped closer, straddling his thigh, one hand on the back of his head, the other dabbing the wound.

Zeke held his breath. Her damn vanilla shampoo wafted toward his nose. Her chest was inches from his face. Her legs were parted. He bit his tongue to keep from making an embarrassing noise.

He'd never stood this close to her. He'd avoided her as if she were diseased for weeks. And now all his efforts to keep his distance were running out the window with one stupid scratch on his forehead. His reaction to her was bordering on ridiculous. How hard had he hit his head?

"Can you tolerate a little pain? I should try to get the dirt washed off." Her brown eyes were soft and concerned. Normally she reserved that caring look for everyone else in the bunker except him. For him, she reserved cold frustration.

He could tolerate any amount of pain. What he couldn't tolerate was her standing so close, touching him so intimately, exhaling against his skin. "I'm sure it's fine." He sat still anyway, afraid if he moved an inch, it would either be to swat her away and hurt her feelings or haul her closer and kiss her senseless.

Her braid had come loose at some point, the rubber band missing. The thick mass of wavy hair fell across her shoulders as it worked its way free.

Zeke fisted his hands on his lap to avoid the instinct to run them through her hair. He'd give anything to see if it was as soft as it looked. Hell, he wanted to bury his face in it and inhale her scent.

At some point in the last six weeks he'd lost his mind entirely. Zeke Holleran had taken a leave of absence and left an unknown imposter in his wake.

"Sit still," she whispered. The sound of her sweet voice so filled with concern burrowed under his skin.

He had no idea he had been moving at all. He winced again when whatever she did next hurt. "What the hell are you doing? Put some damn ointment on it, so we can get out of here." *This room is too damn small.*

She leaned back and glared at him. "You want your forehead to heal with dirt in it?"

"Good grief." He twisted his body around to glance in the mirror and realized she was right. He'd obviously slammed his head into the dirt. "Let me lean over the sink. Flush it out with water." At least there were no more sounds of gunfire. Hopefully the fool at the gate had been taken down.

Zeke stood between the toilet and the sink and leaned forward.

Michelle turned on the faucet, tested the temperature with her hand, and then used a cup to pour the warm water over his temple. After three tries, she seemed satisfied. "There. Much better. Sit back down."

He held his breath as she resumed her perusal, dabbing the cuts dry and then putting ointment on the spot.

Her breast brushed his cheek, and he squeezed his eyes closed in an attempt to ignore it. It was ridiculous to be reacting to her since she was wearing scrubs. She was almost always wearing scrubs. They all were. Everyone who lived in the bunker had a wardrobe of scrubs in every color.

Tonight, Michelle's were a soft blue.

When her knee hit his thigh, he grabbed her waist and shoved her backward. "That's enough."

She gasped. "I didn't put a bandage on it yet."

"You're not going to. It's fine." He held her at arm's length, praying she would back off. He didn't even lift his gaze to look her in the eye.

She jerked herself free and turned toward the sink to wash her hands. "Zeke, you are the singular most difficult person I have ever met. I get that you're an introvert or whatever, but you don't have to be an ass when someone's trying to help you."

He flinched, still sitting on the toilet. *Fuck.*

She dried her hands and planted herself in front of him, palms on her hips. "It's fine if you don't like me. I'm sure there are plenty of people in the world who don't like me. I reconciled with myself that not everyone in the world was going to like me a long time ago. But we're stuck working together for the foreseeable future, so it would be nice if you didn't treat me like pond scum."

She twisted around, taking a step toward the door.

He would probably hate himself later for his next move, but he couldn't stop himself. He reached out, grabbed her wrist, and tugged her backward so that she nearly fell into his lap.

When she struggled, he threw his other hand around her waist, pulled her between his legs, and held her sideways against him.

"Jesus, Zeke. Let me go." She twisted her hand, but he held her tighter.

He'd held on to this stupid game with her for so long that it had gotten harder and harder to climb out of the hole he'd dug. He'd considered apologizing many times, but stopped himself every time. It was easier to continue to grunt at her and ignore her as if she had the plague and wasn't worthy of a cure than to admit he was a dick.

Digging up every ounce of willpower he ever had, he lifted his gaze and waited until she looked him in the eye. "You're right. I've been an ass. I'm sorry."

The fight went out of her immediately. She softened. At least her body did. She stopped struggling. Her eyes narrowed, however, and she stared at him with her head tipped to one side. She didn't trust him. "Did I do something to piss you off? I know you don't have something against female coworkers in general, because you don't treat anyone else with the same level of disdain as you do me."

He swallowed, hating himself. And then he shook his head. His heart was racing. There was no way he could let her walk out of this bathroom thinking he hated her. Maybe he should, but he couldn't do it.

He also didn't want her to know he was attracted to her. It would be disastrous if she had that kind of power over him. He couldn't let a woman get him to that place again where he would end up gutted and feeling as if he'd lost everything. Vulnerable. Meredith had done a number on him. He knew that, but he also knew he wouldn't give anyone the power hurt him like that again.

Add to that, there was no way in hell should he be fraternizing with another staff member, especially not one he worked so closely with. It wasn't exactly a written policy in the bunker, but it was his own policy. A policy that had allowed him to steer clear of women ever since his wife left him. *Yeah, keep telling herself that. Maybe you'll believe it eventually.*

He needed to say something. No way was he going to use some lame excuse about not dating coworkers. Nor did he want to reveal how he really felt. But he wouldn't lie either. "You look a little like my ex-wife. She was a raving bitch."

Michelle's eyes went wide. "I look like her? So, you've been punishing me for something I can't even control?"

He winced. "Basically, yes." It was true. Not entirely true, but sort of true.

"Well, get over yourself because I can't change how I look. And I'm not her." With those words, Michelle jerked herself free, turned off the lights, and opened the door.

Before he could react, she was in the hallway, walking away.

She most definitely was not Meredith. Meredith didn't have an

41

ounce of the strength Michelle had. If she had been the one he'd slammed to the ground at the sound of gunfire, she would still be lying outside, sobbing and worrying about her hair or her nails. She would never have noticed he'd been injured. And she sure wouldn't have dragged him into the bathroom to clean the wound.

Nope. Michelle was not Meredith. But Zeke knew that. It had become increasingly clear over the past three weeks.

Now he just needed to figure out how the hell not to be attracted to the woman.

CHAPTER 5

Michelle was washing a beaker in the lab sink early the next morning when she sensed Zeke step into the room and come up behind her. She could never escape the man. He seemed to follow her everywhere she went. He even showed up earlier than anyone else to work.

He was a daily test to her willpower. In fact, she tried to ignore him and focus on the damn beaker.

He leaned his hip against the counter next to her, too close. "You sleep okay?" he asked.

She nodded. "Yep," she lied. As soon as the threat had been eliminated at the front gate, the four of them had returned to the bunker. Emily and Ryan had headed for their suite in the newly renovated section of the bunker that housed the medical team. Zeke had silently headed for his own suite. Michelle had headed in search of Temple to get more details about the gunman.

Zeke chuckled, a sound Michelle had rarely heard coming from him. "You look tired, and I know you're as badass as they come, but we did run from gunfire. Any sane person would have an adrenaline rush after that. It took me a few hours to relax."

She shot him a glance. "I'm hardly a sane person." Why did he have to look so good? Calm. Cool. Arms crossed. Thick dark hair ruffled as if he'd showered but hadn't combed it since it dried. She jerked her gaze back to the sink, wishing she had something else to wash.

He was standing way too close. The scent of his soap wafted to her nose. Even his minty breath from toothpaste was alluring. Why would she be attracted to a man who spent weeks treating her like shit only to finally admit she looked like his fucking ex-wife? She didn't need that kind of drama.

"I wanted to apologize again before anyone else showed up in the lab."

"Fine." She shot him a quick forced smile and turned away to dry her hands and put some distance between them. "Accepted. I have an early meeting with Temple this morning. I'll catch you later." She didn't look back as she left him standing there. Her hands were shaking and her throat was dry.

She was also extremely aggravated that she let him get to her. It was ridiculous that she was still obsessed about getting him to like her. She shouldn't care. But, she couldn't stand the idea of someone not liking her, so she'd gone out of her way for weeks doing anything she could to force him to stop scowling at her.

She had failed, of course.

And now this new revelation.

His ex-wife. She couldn't compete with that.

Or maybe she could. The most ridiculous idea had been rolling around in her head since she got out of bed that morning and looked in the mirror. She shouldn't give a shit about his ex-wife, but it got under her skin that he compared her to the woman Emily had said was a gold digger.

Michelle was extremely relieved when she rounded the open doorway of Temple's office to find her boss behind her desk. "You have a minute?"

"Sure. Come on in." She gestured toward the chair across from her and set her elbows on the desk. She had an air of power that floated around her no matter where she went. Her gray hair was pulled back in a tight bun at the base of her neck, and Michelle wondered how long it was. She'd never seen it down.

Michelle shut the door behind her and took a seat across from Temple.

Temple didn't comment on the privacy. "You okay after last night? Emily said it was stressful."

"I'm fine. We were never in any real danger."

"True, but you didn't know that at the time. What were you four doing outside so late anyway?"

Michelle sighed. "I think Ryan and Zeke went out there to blow off steam after the bad news about Dade. Emily and I went to find them. We never got to discuss it, though. Gunfire interrupted our frustrated pacing." She forced a smile in an effort to make light of the situation.

Temple's shoulders fell and she glanced away. "I still can't believe it. What a loss. Makes me question the presence of a higher being when shit like this happens."

"Yeah. Though, as a scientist, I have to admit, I've always questioned the existence of a higher being." Michelle had never been to church in her life. Her parents had been of two different faiths, so rather than introduce her to one religion or the other or even both, they'd chosen to let her decide when she got older.

She'd decided on atheism.

"I was raised Catholic," Temple stated. "It's hard to shake, no matter how many years go by."

"Well, if there is a God," Michelle added, "I hope He's not vindictive enough to intentionally let Dade die after everything he's been through. I refuse to believe some God is the reason he's not going to make it."

"Agreed." Temple leaned forward. "How's progress on finding a cure for Myasthenia Gravis?"

"Slow. Until recently, it was rare enough that there weren't many studies."

Temple nodded. "Talk about God. I wonder if He has a hand in the constant changes in diseases. It seems like we're always one step behind. I sometimes feel like God is a puppet master who is enjoying this little game where He lets us solve one problem only to toss another one at us that's bigger and more dangerous before we've even had a chance to gloat."

"That's depressing." Michelle slouched in her chair.

"How's Zeke doing? Is he catching up? I know he's stubborn."

Michelle laughed. "Ya think?"

Temple smiled. "Okay, more than stubborn. Sorry, I didn't warn you ahead of time. When he came in here half-cocked and wanting to get back to work, I tossed him at you and ran from the room. Not my finest hour."

Michelle shrugged. "I can handle him." No way in hell was she going to admit defeat to Temple. She *would* handle him. Somehow. Her next plan was to trip him up so that he stopped seeing her as his ex. If she managed that, perhaps they could move forward civilly. Her plan was ridiculous, but it was in her mind now anyway.

"I can assure you he's brilliant in his field and probably frustrated to find himself ten years behind on the research. I can talk to him if you want. I've been thinking about moving some of the team to other facilities. Maybe he would take me up on the offer."

Why the hell did that make Michelle's chest seize? "You're going to move some of us?"

Temple shrugged. "Eventually. Between the twelve of you and the twenty-one members of the first team, we're going to be on top of each other soon. That's a lot of brilliance in one place," she joked. "I might develop a complex."

Michelle could feel her face heating irrationally. She should be overjoyed with the prospect of Zeke being transferred. Instead, her hands were sweating. "I'm not sure anyone's going to be super-thrilled at the idea just yet. As we bring more of the preserved back to life, they need each other to lean on."

That part was true. Every one of them had a pile of issues to deal with. They were like a giant growing support group. They had to deal with things no other humans on earth faced. Families who had aged and were shocked to find them alive. Old friends who couldn't wrap their heads around their reanimations. The media hounding them. Religious zealots calling them abominations. The list was long. They needed each other.

Temple nodded. "Just an idea I've been pondering."

"If you move people, it will just put a bigger strain on the government to protect them. After what happened last night, I'm sure the administration doesn't want to provide added security in multiple places. Seems like it would be more cost-effective to bring on more security and add temporary housing."

Temple nodded again. "You may be right. Good points. Speaking of which, we *are* adding some security outside the gate."

"Already? I was speaking more hypothetically for the future. I mean, no one would be able to actually get in, would they?"

Temple shrugged. "Let's hope not, but I want to know how rumors are spreading through the crowd. It's like someone stands out there roaming among the people, telling internal secrets. Far too many people have inside information before it's released."

"How is added security going to help? No one's going to walk up to one of our own and offer to sell information."

Temple smiled. "They are if we plant someone undercover."

"Ah. Good idea."

"Already lined up a woman. She's a detective out of Denver." Temple glanced down at the file in front of her and tapped her finger to the page. "Nicole Salway. Twenty-eight years old. She's been with the force for six years. She starts tomorrow. She'll blend right in with the picketers and see what she can find out."

"Perfect. I hope we can catch someone in the act."

BECCA JAMESON

Temple sighed. "Not sure what good it will do. We've already arrested more than one person in the last eight months. Whoever's hiring them to spread information covers their tracks well. I'm not sure Salway will be able to solve the mystery, but at least she can give us a heads-up if it seems like something's about to go down. I hate surprises."

"What a mess."

Temple waved a hand through the air. "Sorry I shared so much. Not your job. You cure the world's diseases. I'll keep you safe doing it."

Michelle set her hands on the arms of the chair and pushed to standing. "On that note, I should get back to work." She rounded the chair, heading for the door.

"Wait. You never told me what you came in here for in the first place."

Michelle smiled over her shoulder. "I was hiding. Thanks for the reprieve." She winked and left the office.

Zeke sat in Ryan's small office, running a hand over his face and then leaning back with a sigh. "What's the plan here?" Zeke still couldn't wrap his mind around the fact that Dade was not only going to survive, but no one but Dade, Blair, Zeke, and Ryan knew it. Mind-boggling.

Ryan tapped his pen on the desk and leaned forward, glancing at the door. It was closed, but he still kept his voice low. "I can't answer that yet. All I know is that my gut told me to keep Dade's survival a secret and see what he might be able to do for the team from the outside."

"That's an enormous task. He's going to need resources."

"He has money. His cash flow won't be a problem. Right now we're taking things one day at a time while he digs around. He wants to get to the bottom of things as much as any of us. The last thing Dade wants is for anyone on your team or mine to get hurt."

"What in the hell do you think the end goal is in trying to compromise us?"

Ryan shook his head. "I still can't figure that out. It feels like someone is trying to get us to disband, scatter, end our research."

"Why would anyone want that? Our job is and always has been to cure disease. Who the hell is opposed to discovering the cure for diseases?"

Ryan shrugged. "Religious zealots for one. People who think we're playing God, messing with natural selection. Those same people view us as an abomination for existing."

Zeke took a deep breath. "I get that, but I can't imagine someone having the power to destroy Project DEEP, and I certainly can't wrap my head around it being an inside job."

"But you see how it could be helpful to have someone totally on our side secretly working from the outside, nosing around to find out information."

"Yes. Though it makes me cringe to keep such a thing from Temple. She's wrecked over Dade's impending death." Temple had been their superior from the beginning. Never once had she done a single thing Zeke would have considered suspicious.

He understood the need to keep everyone, including her, in the dark, but he also suspected they were going to get fired when they got caught. And getting caught snooping around behind the scenes of a government project was not only going to cost them their jobs, but probably get them thrown in jail. "I hope to God you're right."

"You and me both." Ryan nodded slowly. "I know this is a lot to take in. You've only been awake for six weeks. But trust me when I say there's no doubt in my mind something we can't even begin to imagine is happening right under our noses. We just don't know where to look or what to look for. There's no other explanation."

Zeke closed his eyes for a moment, tipping his head back. Ryan was right of course, but like a foul-tasting liquid antibiotic needed to save a life, it still didn't go down easily.

Ryan cleared his throat. "What's going on between you and Michelle?"

Zeke jerked his head forward. "What are you *talking* about?"

Ryan tilted his head to one side, his eyes narrow in an expression that insinuated he was not born yesterday. "Don't deny it. You two tiptoe around each other in the lab as if you're both contaminated with one of the infectious diseases we're studying. You also fight as if there's prize money for whoever can cure said disease first."

Zeke shrugged as casually as possible. "We don't get along well. That's all. It's no big deal. I didn't realize it was affecting other people." Zeke was actually relieved to find out Ryan assumed Zeke and Michelle didn't like each other. That was the plan.

Ryan rolled his eyes now. "You expect me to buy that line of bullshit?" he asked before smiling with raised brows.

Zeke felt a flush crawl up his face. Okay, so maybe he'd miscalculated. Perhaps Ryan was more intuitive than Zeke gave him credit for. "I don't care what you buy. I wasn't selling anything. You're the one who asked." He did his best to sound offended and snarky. He needed to get out of this small office before he suffocated on his own words.

Ryan chuckled. "So defensive."

"I don't know what you're talking about." Zeke had no idea why he felt the need to keep up this farce with Ryan. The truth was, he could use a friend. He didn't exactly have a long list of them at the moment. His best friend was out working undercover like he was a member of VICE, and most of the rest of the people Zeke had once been close to were still vitrified one story below him.

Ryan was his best option. Besides, the two of them already shared an enormous secret. After the information Ryan had trusted Zeke with, the least Zeke could do would be to trust Ryan to keep his own secrets.

Zeke slouched back in the chair.

"Do I sense a love-hate thing?" Ryan asked, mirth in his voice.

"Probably." There. He'd admitted it.

"Why? What could Michelle possibly have done to piss you off in the few weeks you've known her? I've always found her to be courteous and professional with everyone she encounters. She's a people pleaser."

"Well, at first I thought she looked like my ex-wife," Zeke said.

Ryan flinched. "Really? No one has mentioned that."

"Or maybe I just latched onto that idea as a means of self-preservation and then told myself they look alike over and over as a way to justify how I was treating her."

"Why would you do that?"

Zeke rubbed the back of his neck. "It's easier than letting her get to me. However, she's managed to do so anyway, even though I've treated her as though she were spawned by the devil."

A few moments of silence passed before Ryan's lips parted, and he spoke again. "So, you've been trying to ensure Michelle doesn't like you because you're afraid to take a chance on another woman? Your ex must have really done a number on you."

"Trust me. She did."

"Okay, but Michelle is one of the nicest people I know, and even though I noticed you two bumping heads for the last three weeks, I also saw the way you leaped through the air last night to protect her."

"Yeah. Instinct. She's pretty pissed at me today too. I wasn't very eloquent while she was trying to clean my forehead in the bathroom last night, and I might have botched our conversation earlier this morning too." Zeke's shoulders dropped lower on his already slouched body.

He'd been walking a fine line with Michelle for weeks, trying to keep some distance between them day in and day out, but he didn't like her thinking he was a total dick. It rubbed him wrong. So, he'd stepped over the line last night to try to fix things.

Ryan lifted another brow. "Did you apologize?"

"Of course." *Poorly.* It was suddenly hot in Ryan's office. Zeke reached for his collar to pull it away from his neck.

A slow smile spread on Ryan's face. "I'm thinking you might need to try again. I saw her stomp down the hall a while ago. She didn't look like a woman who'd accepted your apology."

She certainly hadn't. Zeke was well aware.

"I'm going to go out on a limb here and suggest that she probably wouldn't be quite so flustered by you if she wasn't also experiencing some level of attraction."

Zeke suspected Ryan was right, but that only made matters worse. He didn't want Michelle to be attracted to him. He didn't want anyone to be. Women were complications he didn't need. Especially sexy ones with amazing eyes, great hair, and an IQ he only barely could compete with.

Zeke closed his eyes and let his head dip. This was bad.

"Talk to her."

"Seems like I've said enough," he murmured toward the floor.

"Talk to her, man. Do it today. It's eating you alive."

"I already apologized. Twice. I wouldn't even know what else to say."

"How about instead of skirting around the obvious, you confront it head on and admit you have feelings for her? I guarantee that method will get you a lot further than growling at her and shooting daggers across the room from your eyes like you're on a grade school playground."

Zeke took a deep breath. Ryan was right. He knew it. Besides, Ryan obviously had some knowledge about how to talk to woman. After all, Emily adored him. He had to be doing something right. Zeke had known Emily for years. Any man who managed to grab her heart had to be made of gold.

"All right," Zeke conceded. "I'll find her later tonight. But if this goes badly, I'm blaming you tomorrow." He forced a smile as he stood. He was so done with this conversation.

Ryan laughed. "Good luck."

∽

"You sure you want to do this?" Emily asked. She was sitting on the beige Formica counter in the suite she shared with Ryan. All the suites were the same. They reminded Michelle of hotel suites. Small living room with attached kitchenettes, a bedroom, and a bathroom. All of them had the same light wood furniture and cabinets and beige carpet and walls. The only differences were the variety of color schemes for the bedding.

Her friend Kate was holding a bowl of solution over the sink, stirring it. She wore a pair of protective gloves, and she was grinning. "Don't encourage her to chicken out, Em. I haven't had the opportunity to dye anyone's hair in years. This is fun. Girl time. Pour us another glass of wine."

Emily swung her legs, a full glass of zinfandel in her hand. She glanced at it. "We haven't finished the first glass yet." Her gaze shifted to Michelle. "But about your hair, have you ever highlighted it before?"

"No." Michelle was sitting on a chair in the middle of the bathroom with a strange purple cap covering her head and thin sections of hair pulled through tiny holes all over the tight rubber cap to make her look possessed. "But it's about time I did something different."

"Why the sudden urge today?" Kate asked as she lifted the little brush and applied the dye solution.

"I thought it was time for a change. That's all."

"Really?" Emily let that word drag out for a long time. "This doesn't have anything to do with impressing a certain sour coworker does it?"

Michelle flinched. "What are you talking about?" She glanced at Emily to find her grinning too wide. *Shit.*

"The way you two argue with each other makes everyone in the bunker suspicious." Emily took a dainty sip of her wine.

"Argue with who?" Was it really necessary for Michelle to dig her heels in further on this issue? It would help if she had some girlfriends to talk to. She hadn't been able to be authentic with any of the girls she'd known growing up, and when she'd been in college, it has been so competitive that she'd never opened herself up to vulnerability. But Emily and Kate were friends. Coworkers. Reanimated recently. No one was competing for anything here. She felt safer with them. And maybe it helped that they knew Zeke.

Kate giggled as she continued to apply the highlighting solution. "Why is it such a secret? If you like the guy, go for it."

Michelle tipped her head back. "You too? Is this a conspiracy?" She still wasn't sure they were talking about the same thing.

Emily shook her head. "No one has had the guts to say anything. We figured you would come around on your own time. But these highlights... And the cut... I assume you and Zeke had some sort of moment last night while you were tending to his scrapes."

Michelle sighed. "He said I look like his ex-wife."

"What?" both women shouted at the same time.

"Meredith?" Kate continued. "You don't look anything like Meredith. That woman was bitter and angry and frivolous and needy and greedy and...I could go on."

Michelle met Kate's gaze. "Did she have long brown hair and brown eyes?"

Kate cringed. "Yeah. I guess. But she always looked like she stepped out of a salon with her makeup perfect and her expensive styles and her heels and dresses. How the hell could Zeke say you resemble her at all?" She took a breath and continued applying the color.

Emily picked up where Kate left off. "I'm not seeing it. It never occurred to me. His ex was a bitch. You are not. Maybe that's not his problem. Maybe he's afraid to fall for someone else, and he's using your hair color as an excuse. Because even your eyes aren't the same shade. You're taller. More slender. Less flashy. Her boobs were enormous. Probably fake."

Michelle shot her a look. "Thanks. That helps. So, what you're saying is that the woman was far sexier than me with large tits, a curvy body, better makeup, and stylish clothes?"

Emily scrunched up her face. "You make yourself sound like a withered hag when you put it like that. Trust me. Meredith has nothing on you. She didn't have enough brain cells to compete."

"Maybe Zeke prefers women who don't challenge him intellectually."

Kate shook her head. "Admittedly, none of us knew Meredith well. She hated hanging out with the rest of us. She looked bored. And she probably was since she wasn't a scientist or a doctor. Zeke always seemed uncomfortable around her, probably because he couldn't please her no matter what he did."

"This is a horrible idea," Michelle said, glancing at her weird head in the mirror. "Why the hell did I think it might help if I changed my appearance?"

Kate set the bowl in the sink and leaned against the beige Formica counter. "It never hurts to put forth some effort to get a man to pay attention to you. No matter what he says or does when I'm finished with you, you'll feel fantastic about yourself."

Michelle bit her lip, still looking in the mirror. "I'm not sure he would notice even if I stepped in front of him with the purple cap and the medusa hair." She glanced at Kate. "I've never had highlights, but I've never seen this weird cap when it's on TV."

Kate shrugged. "Yeah, they have this new-fangled foil thing nowadays, but I've never used that method."

Emily laughed. "Don't worry, Kate is a great stylist. She's the only MD I know who learned to cut hair while she was still in high school in between chemistry class and biology." Emily pointed at the funny hair arrangement and laughed. "However, I agree. I'm pretty sure they don't still color hair using this method."

Kate shrugged as she picked up her glass of wine and took a drink. "Hey, some people babysat for extra spending money. I cut hair. This is how my mom taught me when I was in high school, so this is what you get."

CHAPTER 6

It was late when Michelle left Emily's suite to head toward her own. Her two new friends weren't wrong about how the cut and color made her feel. She hadn't looked this hot since high school. The three of them had even played around in Emily's closet with her limited wardrobe, trying on skirts and tight shirts until Emily insisted Michelle borrow a few things.

On their second bottle of wine, the three of them had moved to the bathroom to put on makeup. Kate and Emily had given Michelle some pointers that made her look like a new woman.

Michelle had no idea when she would ever have the opportunity to wear anything except scrubs since she never left the bunker and rarely even left the lab. There was also no reason to get up early each morning to apply makeup for the job of curing diseases. However, tonight had been the first time in months she'd taken several hours to enjoy herself. She felt free. Happy. She was smiling.

It had also been the first time in a long time she'd had anything to drink. She was calmer, relaxed, even confident as she headed back to her own suite. Barefoot, wearing the tight jean skirt and white tank top, she swung the bag of scrubs at her side. Her hair was styled so well that she didn't look like herself. The eyeliner and mascara had made her eyes pop out.

When she rounded the corner, pulling her keycard out of her pocket, she stopped dead.

Zeke was leaning against her door. He glanced up and then back at the floor.

She didn't move. Frozen several feet away from him. What was he doing there?

After a few seconds, he slowly lifted his gaze again. "Michelle?"

She almost laughed when she realized he hadn't recognized her. Which was absurd. Instead of going with her first reaction—comedic relief, she schooled her face. "Seriously?" She continued forward, shoving him out of the way with her hip so she could open her door.

This had been a horrible idea. Changing her hair had been one thing, but now the entire package made her feel self-conscious, especially since he'd had to do a double take.

Wasn't that the goal?

Suddenly, she hated the entire notion. So what if he found her attractive? Fuck him. If he didn't like the old Michelle, why would she want him to fall for her just because she had on makeup, real clothes, and styled hair?

She was a complete moron.

After managing to get the door unlocked with shaky hands, she pushed it open and tried to hurry inside, leaving him standing in the hallway. She still had no idea why he was outside her door, but she no longer had the confidence she'd exuded moments ago. She didn't want to speak to him at all.

He set a hand on her door before she could close it, pushed it open farther, and stepped into her suite without an invitation.

This was worse. He'd never been in her private space. She didn't want him in her rooms. "What do you want, Zeke? It's late. Can it wait until morning?"

Ironically, he wasn't wearing scrubs tonight either. He was wearing a fantastic pair of jeans and a navy polo. He scanned her body from toe to head and back down again. "Do I have the right room?"

For a second she wanted to scream and slap him, and then she noticed one corner of his mouth was tipped up. If he wasn't careful, someone might mistake his expression for almost a smile. She rolled her eyes, turned around, and headed for the kitchen. "Don't be an asshole."

She dropped her bag on the floor and jerked the fridge open to grab a bottle of water. The perfect buzz she'd been nursing had taken a nosedive. *Thank you, Zeke.*

He sighed loudly behind her. "I'm not sure there's anything I can possibly do or say that won't piss you off, and I deserve it. I just wanted to talk to you. I was hoping we might be able to clear the air and start over."

When she turned around, she found him running a hand through his hair. He looked distressed. Good. "You want to clear the air…"

She rounded the armchair and flopped down in the corner of the couch. If she hadn't been wearing a skirt, she would have pulled her legs under her. But tonight, she'd made this error in judgment, and she was now trapped by the confines of short, tight denim that showed way too much leg and made her self-conscious.

Zeke slowly came closer and lowered himself onto the other end of her couch. "You look amazing, by the way." His gaze roamed up and down her body. She noticed the scratches on his forehead looked clean and he'd put an antibacterial cream on them. "Did you highlight your hair?"

She lifted her brows, meeting his gaze. Shocked he noticed. She didn't respond. She wasn't even sure how to.

"I like it." He licked his lips and then froze. "Wait. Please tell me you didn't do that because I said you look like my ex."

She felt the heat crawl up her face. This was indeed the stupidest thing she'd ever done, and she was reconsidering Temple's idea of transferring people to another bunker. Was it possible Temple could transfer Michelle, say, tomorrow morning?

Zeke groaned, leaning his head against the cushion to stare at the ceiling. "I've been demoted from asshole to total fucking jackass."

She wasn't particularly sorry he felt that way. In fact, she pursed her lips. Somehow she also managed to tuck her legs semi-gracefully under herself. It made her feel slightly less exposed.

After swiping a hand down his face, he met her gaze again. "I lied to you last night."

She flinched. What was he talking about?

"You don't remind me of my ex-wife."

She lifted a brow. What a weird day. Would it please end soon?

He shook his head as if to clear it. "Maybe you did at first when I met you, but it didn't last long. At a glance, you have similarities, but they're superficial. You're nothing like her, and now that I know you better, you don't look like her at all."

She searched his face. She would have fired questions at him if she could have come up with any, but she was struck dumb. She cleared her throat. "Then, why tell me…?"

He glanced down at his hands and wrung his fingers together in his lap. "Because I thought it would be easier. I've been such a dick toward you for weeks and especially the last twenty-four hours. I didn't want to tell you the real reason, but now, it seems only fair that I admit why I really treated you with such animosity."

Her heart beat so fast, and she couldn't seem to inhale deeply enough. She had no idea what he was talking about. Her mind raced to several possibilities while he hesitated: He hated women. He hated her, in particular. He didn't like smart women. He didn't like scientists. She was too tall. Too short. Too skinny. Too…something.

Suddenly, he scooted closer to her and twisted his body so he was fully facing her. He set a hand on the back of the couch, not touching her but so close.

She truly stopped breathing.

He managed to inhale deeply, however. "It's like I woke up a different person, sort of. I don't even know who's inhabiting my body. The things I used to think were the most important aspects of my existence have slid down the list. New thoughts and ideas are occupying the space where the old ones resided until just a few weeks ago."

She didn't move. She wasn't following, but apparently he needed to ramble to get this all out. She just prayed everything would be better between them when he was finished.

"My priorities have been rearranged. I still love science and medicine, but I don't feel the same urgency I felt before I was preserved. It makes no sense because as far as my brain is concerned, I went to sleep one day and woke up the next. If it weren't for the changes to the bunker and the additional people I've never met, I could easily believe it was still 2008. Sometimes it all feels so surreal."

She nodded slowly at his pause and finally managed to say something. "The others have expressed feeling similarly. You're not alone."

"I know. I've spoken to them. In fact, we're practically a support group now. Every one of us is going to need each other to lean on to get through this crazy time."

"What does this have to do with me?"

He searched her face as if still looking for the mysterious answer, even though she knew he came here tonight fully knowing what he wanted to say. He was simply having trouble spitting it out. Which scared her to death.

"I'm attracted to you."

Her breath hitched. That was the last thing she expected him to say.

"I mean, really attracted to you. Not as a friend. Not as a coworker. As a woman. When I'm with you, I want to move closer. When you enter a room, I know it without looking. I want to reach out and touch you all the time. I want to do so right now."

She had never been so confused in her life. He was leaning so close to her that she could feel his breath. The only other time he'd been this close was last night when she'd tended to his forehead.

Suddenly, his proximity was more than she could handle. She unfolded her legs and jumped up from the couch to back away. "So, let me get this straight. You like me, so you've been scowling at me like I have the plague for weeks."

"Yes." He bit his lower lip and then released it. "It was a dick move. I was hoping to keep you at arm's length. I still am." He stood also and started pacing. "Maybe this was a bad idea. I'm botching it. I sound and feel like a twelve-year-old boy."

"I'll give you that much."

"I'm not good at relationships. I'm not good with women. I was born kind of dorky, and I still am. I've always been book smart. I've never been good with conversation or dating or anything related to women."

She had never once thought of him as nearly the dork he seemed to think he was. Sure, he was intelligent and well-read, but that didn't make him a nerd. Or maybe it did and she had no radar to detect that since she too was nerdy. "You were married," she pointed out.

"Yeah, and I chose badly and did a poor job of that too."

"You must have spoken to her at some point. At the very least to ask her to marry you."

He shook his head. "It was a train wreck from the start. I didn't see the signs. I was working on my PhD when I met her. She pursued me relentlessly until I agreed to go out with her. She made all our plans and directed every aspect of our relationship. I was enamored that a woman like her was interested in me, so I let her walk all over me."

Michelle cringed. She felt sorry for him for the first time since she'd met him. Somehow his surly attitude took on new meaning. "What do you mean by 'a woman like her'?"

He shrugged, still pacing. "Cute. Funny. Outgoing. Sexy. That kind of thing. Attractive."

"Why wouldn't someone like that fall for you?" *Has he not looked in the mirror?* If he wasn't frowning all the time, he would turn heads.

He rolled his eyes. "Come on. I just told you. I'm not good with people."

"Okay, I'll give you that much. But what about high school and college? Surely you dated."

His scrunched up his face. "Not really. I went to a private all-boys school and spent most of my time studying so I could get into the Naval Academy. It was all I ever wanted to do from the time I was a small boy. When I was chosen to follow this path, working for the government, I thought I had died and gone to heaven. I doubled my efforts. I wanted to prove to the government I was worthy. I got the highest grades, even at Harvard."

She decided to lighten the mood and maybe ease his stress a little. "Well, it was just Harvard. It's not like your PhD is from Emory or anything."

He flinched, his gaze meeting hers before slowly seeming to catch on that she was kidding. "Says the woman who went to West Point. Did the Naval Academy turn you down?"

She laughed. She had no idea he was capable of making a joke, let alone one so well-executed.

For several long seconds, they stared at each other, sobering. Finally, she spoke again, softer. "So you never dated at all?" Even *she* had dated in high school and college, and she'd been voted *most likely to cure cancer* by her high school classmates.

"Nope. Just Meredith. She slammed into my life like a whirlwind. It seemed so amazing. I thought I'd struck gold. I should have seen the writing on the wall. But I was so enamored by the idea that someone might love me, I ignored the signs."

"What happened?" Michelle had heard stories from the others, but she wanted him to tell her.

"In hindsight, she was only after me because she wanted to marry a doctor. She didn't realize I wasn't what she would call a 'real' doctor. She thought I would be rich since I was so smart. She pictured a glamourous life.

"When I told her we were moving to Falling Rock, she hesitated, but she pretended it would all be good. At least in front of my face. Behind my back, she was cheating on me every chance she got."

Michelle winced. *What a bitch.*

"When I was studying late at night, she went out with friends. I didn't realize she was out with other men. I was so naïve. Blinded."

"Were you living together?"

He shook his head. "Not until we got married. She moved into my apartment at the university with great reluctance. Every day she complained about it. She had no understanding that even though my education was paid for, I didn't have extra spending money. Lucky for me, I also didn't have a very high limit on my credit cards because she maxed them out quickly, and then shit really went downhill."

Jesus. The woman was a piece of work. "Why did she even come to Falling Rock with you?"

"I think she still had hope I was about to make a ton of money and provide her with a life of luxury. She was spoiled rotten and did nothing but bitch and complain from the moment we got to town. You should have seen her face when we walked into the apartment I'd already rented." He smirked. Almost a smile, but not quite.

"I would love to see video of that day," Michelle teased.

He shuddered. "Not me. It's burned into my mind. She lasted about two months before she finally left me one day. She didn't even have the courtesy to tell me to my face. She left divorce papers on the kitchen table and disappeared."

Shit.

Zeke was still pacing, but slower. He kept running a hand through his hair, not meeting her gaze.

"Not all women are so cruel and insensitive, Zeke."

He stopped walking to face her. "I didn't tell you all that so you'd feel sorry for me. I'm a grown man. I'm well aware I made mistakes. There are a lot of things I should have done differently. I take full responsibility."

"Why *did* you tell me, then?"

He tucked his fingertips into the pockets of his jeans and rocked forward uncomfortably. "I thought it might help you understand why I'm so awkward."

"I've never thought of you as awkward, Zeke. Rude, maybe. Frustrating. Aggravating. Angry. But not awkward." Maybe she was being too blunt, but as long as they were airing their feelings…

He nodded. "Yeah. I can see that, but I think I just outwardly portray all those characteristics in order to keep people at arm's length. In order to keep *you* at arm's length."

She took a step back, grabbing the edge of the couch where she'd been sitting earlier. "Why?"

"You're intimidating."

"Me?" She pointed at herself. "How the hell am I intimidating? After all, I went to the lowly schools of West Point and Emory. A man with such a superior education as yourself wouldn't be intimidated by a skinny plain woman who wears very little makeup and tucks her hair into a half-hearted braid every day." She tried to push the sarcasm, but it dwindled at the end.

He might have smiled when she made the joke about the

schools, but he sobered entirely, his brows knit together when she moved on to describe herself. "Now who's got low self-esteem?"

She rolled her eyes. "I don't have low self-esteem. I'm just realistic and dedicated to things that are far more important than flirting with men."

He glanced up and down her body a few times until she shivered under the scrutiny. "Is that why you spent the evening getting your hair done, putting on makeup, and selecting an outfit that would make any man drool?"

She was too stunned to respond. Is that how he saw her tonight?

Isn't that what you wanted?

"Don't get me wrong. You look amazing every day, even in scrubs and a ponytail. But tonight, you're knockout gorgeous. So, yes. You intimidate me. I'm not good with women. I don't even *want* to be good with women. I've been burned badly. I never want to set myself up for that kind of rejection again.

"So, I mostly ignore women. But you... You've got a grip on me that makes me glance twice every time I see you. It's frustrating and infuriating. It's not like me. I'm possessed or something." He took a step backward. And then another.

For a moment, she thought he might actually leave her suite, and she wasn't sure her legs would be able to respond to commands from her mind to stop him.

But he didn't turn around and open the door. Not yet anyway. He leaned against it as if he needed it to remain standing. "I went to sleep one day never expecting to wake up again, and when I did, I found this amazing strong woman always in my space, captivating me with her looks, her brain, her smile, and her wit."

"You're unbelievably articulate for a man who says he's tongue-tied around women." A flush rushed up Michelle's face at his description of her.

"I'm forcing myself to spill everything because I've treated you poorly, and I don't want you of all people to think so badly of me for another minute. It keeps me up at night."

"Thank you. For coming here. For telling me all that."

He nodded. "I don't mean for it to change anything. I'm not that presumptuous. I just...wanted you to know. It's not like I would ever act on my feelings. I'm not sure I'm ready for something like that, and I just woke up after ten years. Plus, we're coworkers. We live in tight quarters. We have to see each other every day. I would never risk our precarious professional relationship by attempting to turn it into something else."

What the hell? Now he was just making shit up.

"I just want you to know I'll try not to be a jerk anymore. I'll do my best to treat you with more respect. You might have gone to Emory of all places, but you do have ten years of research on me that I'm going to be scrambling to catch up with. I need you. I need to be able to pick your brain to learn everything I've missed. I want to climb back to the top of my profession. I can taste it. And I won't jeopardize it by getting all mixed up in feelings I have little experience handling.

"I just...I just wanted you to know." He wrapped his fingers around the door handle.

In a split second, Michelle made a decision she hoped she would not regret. He may have come to her suite to bare his soul, but he wasn't the only one with an agenda. "If you open that door, I swear to God, Zeke, I will never forgive you."

He froze. "What?"

"Get your hand off the knob before I lose my shit."

He released the handle, but his face was tipped to one side, confusion evident in his eyes and the way his mouth hung open. "Why?"

"I'm going to count slowly to ten, and if you're not standing in front of me with your mouth on mine, I will flatten you to that door and set a tone for this relationship that will give new meaning to your vision of how I can dominate a room."

Several seconds ticked by.

Michelle pleaded with him in her mind to make the next move. She wasn't kidding. She would leap over the coffee table and claim him herself if he didn't act fast, but she really wanted this to go differently. She wanted him to find a way to bury the insecurity he didn't deserve and have the guts to take control. She wanted him to believe in himself. All that bullshit about them being coworkers was just that. Bullshit. Excuses he used to avoid the fact that he liked her. She was counting on it.

"Michelle..."

"Five seconds."

He swallowed, shuffling from one foot to the other. And then he shoved off the door and rushed forward.

She turned sideways, gripping the arm of the couch at her side with both hands to keep from swaying or falling over.

When he reached her, he stopped inches away, cupping her face and scanning her eyes. "Jesus, woman. You're killing me."

She lifted her brows. *She* was killing *him*?

And then his lips were on hers. Soft. Gentle. He held her gaze while he slowly explored her mouth.

She melted, her body feeling so heavy she thought she might collapse. Thank goodness for the arm of the couch. She didn't dare let go and reach out to touch him yet. She wasn't sure she could control herself if she did.

She was convinced she needed to let him set the pace. If she pushed him, she might make him feel less of the man she knew was hiding under the nervous exterior. Given the opportunity with the right woman, he would be amazing in bed. But she could easily blow that by tackling him too soon.

It wasn't as if she were so experienced herself. She'd dated few men and none in the last several years since coming to the bunker. She had never considered herself to be a great prize, but she didn't lack self-esteem either. She was average with the potential to be more if she put forth the effort. Maybe she was too slender, but no man had ever insinuated he found her narrow frame unattractive.

She might have dabbled in a few relationships in her younger years, but she'd never felt the sense of urgency she felt right now with Zeke. She wanted him with a power she'd never experienced before. Perhaps it was a bad idea, but she had no control over it. It took over her common sense.

He slid one hand into her hair and tipped her head to the side, deepening the kiss. When his tongue teased the seam of her lips, she parted for him, stifling a moan. Her eyes fluttered shut. She wanted to savor this moment for the rest of her life.

There were no guarantees for the future, but she would never forget this first kiss with a man she'd been lusting after for weeks, day in and day out.

His other hand smoothed down her back, pulling her closer until their bodies lined up and their chests touched.

Her breasts swelled, her nipples pressing against her bra, tingling with the need to be touched. When she couldn't resist another second, she wrenched her hands from the arm of the couch and slid them around his waist.

He was solid beneath her fingers. He'd worked out every day since he'd been reanimated, and she could tell.

Just when she thought she might not live without breathing soon, he dragged his mouth from her lips to her neck, devouring her, hauling her closer. He kissed a path to the V of her tight tank top, teasing her skin with every stroke of his lips until goose bumps rose across her chest, and she had to bite her tongue to keep from moaning.

"Where the hell did you get this shirt?" he asked as his hands slid around to her waist, resting just beneath her breasts.

"Emily," she whispered, as if the question required an answer.

His thumbs grazed the undersides of her breasts, his grip on her unrelenting. She was trapped. And not the least bit sorry. She had guessed correctly. Unleashed, Zeke would be a man on a mission.

Perhaps it was slutty of her, but she wanted nothing more than for him to strip her naked and fuck her right here in the living room. Consequences be damned.

He licked the edge of the shirt, his tongue trailing along the top swell of her breasts. "Don't wear this again unless you want people to see you getting mauled in the lab." One hand slid down to cup her ass and then lower to toy with the hem of her denim skirt. His fingertips grazed the back of her thigh, stealing her last brain cell and forcing a deep moan from her lips.

Frustrating her to no end, he slid that hand back up to her lower back, kissing a line toward her ear and then nibbling on the lobe. His warm breath combined with words she had to struggle to listen to. "You're safer in scrubs. You're safer without so much makeup. You're safer in a braid." He threaded a hand in the back of her hair and tugged.

She tipped her head back, her mouth falling open.

He trailed kisses around her neck and then found her mouth again. This time, his kiss was more urgent, insistent, deep. He groaned several times while he devoured her.

And then he broke free, gasping for air. His eyes were glazed over when he met her gaze. "You think you can keep from leaping over the coffee table to tackle me if I leave now?"

Her eyes went wide. "What? Why would you do that?"

He smiled. The first full smile she'd ever seen from him. And it was directed at her. His lazy bedroom eyes were a darker green than usual, and his damn fingers were caressing her back maddeningly. "I'm going to leave," he repeated.

She shook her head, gripping his waist. "No. Bad idea. Why?" Her sex was pulsing with need. Her breasts were heavy and demanding attention. She might actually die if he left her like this.

He grinned wider. "We said a lot of stuff. I didn't come here to maul you. I came to apologize. I'm not taking advantage of you tonight."

She shook her head again, growing dizzy from the action. "You're not taking advantage of me. If anything, I'm taking advantage of *you*. I didn't give you much of a choice."

This new infectious smile of his took her breath away. "I hate to point this out, but I outweigh you significantly. If I'd wanted to leave, you couldn't have stopped me."

"True, but I'm not sure I ever would have forgiven you."

"And this is why I'm standing here right now. I'm not stupid."

CHAPTER 7

Zeke didn't sleep long that night, and he went to the gym in the lower section of the bunker early, hoping not to encounter anyone else. A workout would clear his mind and help him focus. He hoped.

Two hours later, he was caffeinated and shaking. The tremors had nothing to do with the caffeine and everything to do with his nerves. He had absolutely no idea how to face Michelle this morning.

Flashes of holding her in his arms raced through his mind every few seconds, driving him to distraction. Their parting had been slightly awkward, so he wasn't sure how she might feel in the daylight.

When he entered the lab, wiping his hands on his thighs, he was shocked to find far more people there than usual and a lot of commotion.

"'Bout time you showed up," Ryan joked as he passed Zeke in the doorway.

"What's going on?" Zeke followed Ryan, his gaze searching for Michelle. He found her across the room in the far corner, her back to the door. When Ryan stopped walking, Zeke slammed into him.

Ryan turned sideways, his brows drawn together. "You okay?"

"Yeah, sorry. I wasn't looking. Catch me up." Something was going on.

"Computer glitch." He waved a hand through the air encompassing the entire room. "It's like the damn things wake up alone at night and plot our demise." His words were slightly humorous, but there was no humor in his voice.

"What happened?"

He shrugged. "Who knows? Everyone's files are scrambled. The data is a mess. It's going to take half the day to retrieve the backup files and get back on track."

"Sounds like something that shouldn't happen these days. Your systems are so much more efficient than ten years ago."

"It shouldn't happen. There's no explanation." He swiped a hand over his eyes and cleared his throat. "I think we have a hacker."

"Seriously? You think someone is hacking into highly secure government computers? That would almost have to be an inside job, right?" No wonder everyone was rushing around. In truth, Zeke had also considered the possibility there was a hacker ever since Michelle's data disappeared. He'd gotten the feeling it hadn't happened in the lab or directly at her computer.

"Could be an outside job. These days security is about trying to outsmart hackers. Hell, the Russians probably have the capability to turn off the power supply to our entire country with a few keystrokes. Staying one step ahead of security breaches is a full-time job for every business."

"Shit." Zeke hadn't heard about anything that nefarious yet.

"And, as if we don't have enough going on around here, General Custodio's wife is waiting in the conference room."

Zeke cringed. "Yikes." He knew the general was in the next group of people being reanimated, but he hadn't had a chance to think much about it. Every time someone was revived, there were a pile of new issues to consider. Most of them had families to get reacquainted with—parents and siblings who had no idea their reanimation would ever be a possibility.

Winston Custodio had been the first person in the bunker with AP12. He'd been stationed in Africa when he contracted the virus that caused what was a new rare form of anemia at the time. He'd been transferred to the bunker in Falling Rock, but when the team realized they couldn't find a cure before he would succumb to the virus, he became the first person to be cryonically preserved before his official legal death.

The first of many, because eventually every member of the team would be preserved from exposure to the same form of anemia. And all of them had been secretly vitrified before they could fully succumb to the disease. Many of them had come to the bunker after General Custodio had already been preserved. They never even met him.

It had been fifteen years since Custodio's arrival. He'd been fifty at the time. He would still be fifty of course. His wife could be in her mid-sixties if she was the same age as him when they met.

"Why is his wife here?"

"She wanted to be with him when he awoke." Ryan grabbed the mouse next to the closest computer and cursed under his breath about whatever he was looking at.

"Did she...wait for him?"

"Apparently. Or not so much 'wait' as simply didn't move on."

Zeke shuddered. With the exception of Tushar and Trish, who were married to each other, Zeke had been the only one of the original team to have ever been married. He'd been wondering what Meredith looked like now and where she might be, but not enough to search her out.

Ryan sighed and rubbed his forehead. "Someone has to talk to her. Everyone's busy. My parents were supposed to meet with her, but they're down the hall dealing with this computer mess now."

"You want me to do it?" It was the last thing he wanted to do. But he needed to find a way to be helpful. It was hard to be useful most days since he was so far behind on research.

Speaking to other people was outside of his comfort zone. That's why he'd gotten his PhD in immunology to begin with. He knew he would never be the sort of person to face patients. Not living ones at least. He was too introverted to interact with most people.

You did a fine job last night.

He still couldn't believe how far out on a limb he'd gone to spill so much information to Michelle. It shocked him while it was happening, and it continued to shock him up to this moment. He owed most of his courage to Ryan urging him to confront her. For better or for worse, at least she no longer would believe he hated her.

"Would you?" Ryan was staring at Zeke. "That would be great. Maybe if she meets someone else who's been reanimated, she'll feel reassured about the general."

"I'll do it. Conference room, you say?"

"Yes. Thank you."

Damon rushed past them, looking fit to kill.

Zeke jerked his gaze back to Ryan. "Are the cryostats or chambers in danger?"

Ryan shook his head. "No. The cryostats are always safe. And the chambers have sufficient backup generators for any eventuality, but Damon still doesn't like any glitch. It drives him crazy. He worries about data as much as the rest of us." Ryan was already backing up. "Thanks again for stalling Mrs. Custodio."

Ryan nodded, his gaze returning the spot where Damon had fled. Reanimating everyone was Damon's life's work. If anything were put in jeopardy…

Zeke let his gaze roam toward Michelle again as he left the lab.

She must have sensed him because she turned her head and gave him a small apologetic smile.

He returned the smile, even though it felt unnatural after scowling at her and everyone else for the last six weeks. He had no idea what was going to happen next between the two of them. They hadn't discussed it at all.

She would undoubtedly prefer no one know about them. Frankly, he would agree. He was still uneasy about the idea of pursuing her at all. He had no confidence he could be relationship material for her. He didn't relish the idea of taking a risk like that again. Let alone the dubious ethics of sleeping with a coworker.

Sure, Tushar and Trish had been married for many years and their son, Ryan, had moved Emily into his suite months ago. It didn't really matter that it wasn't a strict government policy inside the bunker. The concept made Zeke uneasy. What if something went wrong and they broke up and created workplace tension?

Zeke was certain something would inevitably go wrong. It always did. He wasn't exactly boyfriend material.

Ironically, the thought of meeting with Custodio's wife in the conference room was almost refreshing compared to awkwardly interacting with Michelle in the lab.

When he rounded the corner, he found Winston's wife sitting at the long oval table. He couldn't see her face yet, but she was wringing her hands together.

As Zeke entered, he forced a smile. "Mrs. Custodio, so nice to meet you." He held out a hand. "Zeke Holleran. It's crazy around here today. I thought I'd stop by and say hello."

Her eyes were wide, and she looked nervous. When she took his hand, he realized something he hadn't known before. This woman was not sixty-five years old. She must have been younger than Winston when he was preserved. Possibly even significantly younger.

He surmised she was Hispanic and she looked nothing like the gray-haired grandmotherly woman he'd expected. She had dark hair cut and styled at her shoulders. Dark eyes that stared at him with hope and sorrow. Her skin was tanned. Either she aged well, or she was young.

"Elena," she said in a soft voice. "I was expecting Tushar Anand."

Zeke took a seat across from her. "Yes. He's trying to break away. He'll meet with you as soon as he can."

"I don't know anyone else here except General Levenson."

Zeke nodded. "Temple is around here somewhere too. We've had a computer glitch this morning. Everyone is scrambling."

"I understand."

"I was also one of the preserved. I awoke six weeks ago. I thought I might be able to answer any questions you might have."

She glanced up and down his body. "Are you...healthy? I mean, is this really feasible? I haven't let myself believe it might be true yet."

Zeke nodded. He knew his expression was serious. It was the only one he had. Hopefully he could ease her mind a bit. "It's true. Assuming there are no complications, Winston should be awake and talking in two weeks."

She slowly shook her head and covered her mouth. "Seriously?"

"Yes. We can't let you into the room yet, but you can see him through the glass if you'd like. He looks exactly the same."

"Why isn't he awake now?"

"Each of us has to spend four weeks in the reanimation chamber and then four weeks in an induced coma. He's halfway through that second stage now. It gives the organs time to awaken and start functioning properly."

Shock was apparent on her face. "I can see him?"

Zeke nodded. "I don't see why not. The environment is sterile, so you can't go inside, but you can see a lot through the window," he repeated. It was surprising that she was struggling to believe him.

"And he will look...the same?"

Zeke nodded. "I hadn't aged a minute."

She cringed. "I have."

He smiled again and managed to find uncomfortable words. "You must have been a teenager when you married." Did he sound like an idiot?

She rolled her eyes. "I get that a lot. I'm ten years younger than Winston. Or I was. I'm fifty-five now." She winced. "Older than him, I guess."

"I don't think he's going to mind." Again, Zeke worried he'd said the wrong thing. He was making this shit up on the fly. This was so far outside of his comfort zone he didn't recognize himself. Hell, he had no idea what the state of Winston and Elena's marriage had been fifteen years ago, and he certainly couldn't be sure Elena hadn't moved on.

"I've never been so nervous in my life. I know I wasn't supposed to come for another two weeks, but I couldn't stand waiting any longer. I needed to know for sure, I guess. It didn't seem real while I was still at home."

"Where is home?"

"Virginia. I still own the same home."

"And you never remarried?" Yeah, he was crossing boundaries, letting his inquisitive mind run his mouth.

She shook her head. "Everyone tried to set me up with a variety of men over the years, but I couldn't seem to move on. Maybe a part of me held out hope a day like this would come."

He couldn't imagine holding on to hope like that. He'd been in touch with his own parents nearly daily since waking up, using video conferencing so they could see each other. At no point in the past ten years had they expected to see him again, and they talked non-stop about planning a trip to Colorado to see him as soon as Temple gave him the all-clear.

Maybe it would have been different if he'd left a wife he loved, but he hadn't even left a wife he didn't love. He and Meredith had been divorced for four years when he got sick.

The door opened behind Zeke, and he turned around to find Temple entering. Thank God. Her face was lit up, and Elena jumped to her feet to give the general a hug.

Zeke excused himself and quietly stepped out of the room. After rounding the corner, he paused and leaned against the wall. He was emotionally drained from last night and this morning. Making small talk with General Custodio's wife had been a giant leap for him.

"Zeke? You okay?"

He lifted his head to find Michelle striding toward him from several yards away. "Yeah. I'll live. I just needed a minute."

When she reached his side, she set her hand on his arm. "Ryan told me you were talking to Custodio's wife. I'm still trying to visualize how you filled the silent gaps with words." Her eyes were twinkling with mirth.

He smirked. "It wasn't easy. I managed."

"It was a kind gesture."

He shook himself out of his funk and stood taller. "Did you get the computers working?"

"They're working fine, but the data in them is still scrambled. It's going to take time to reenter most of what we've done in the last few weeks from the backups."

"How is it even possible for you to have such an enormous breach in this decade?"

"It's usually not." She glanced around and lowered her voice. "Someone had to have sabotaged it."

"I got that vibe from Ryan too. But what the fuck? Again? How is this happening over and over?"

She shrugged. "I'm super-tired of it."

"I can imagine."

She gave his arm a tug and then released it, nodding behind her.

He followed, realizing she wanted to talk to him somewhere besides the hallway.

After stepping into a small office that Ryan used most of the time, she shut the door behind them. She fidgeted nervously and ran a hand through her hair, not meeting his gaze. Her hair was down. It was gorgeous, but did she wear it down to impress him? Was she also wearing more makeup than usual?

She paced back and forth in the small office while Zeke leaned against the door watching her. She stopped abruptly and met his gaze. "I can't even think today, and especially not in this small room with you standing two feet away."

He smiled. Thank God he wasn't the only one. He reached out a hand, snagged her sleeve, and gave a tug. "Come here."

She shuffled forward, swallowing.

When she was closer, he grabbed her hips, drew her toward him the last few inches, and kissed her. God, he loved kissing her. He'd loved every second of it last night, and he loved it just as much today.

He loved it even more when she leaned into him, melting against him. Her hands smoothed up his biceps and around the back of his neck. She returned the kiss as if she might die soon without recharging, but she was also the one who finally eased back. Her face was flushed, and she had a shy smile. "Thank you."

He chuckled. How did she seem to bring out that odd side of him? "You going to thank me every time we kiss?"

She shrugged, turning a darker shade of red. "I just mean, I needed that. I wasn't sure where we stood."

"I don't know where we stand either. We'll have to figure it out together, but I can tell you that I've done nothing but think about holding you again from the moment I left your suite."

She cocked her head to one side. "Surely you weren't thinking about me while you were sleeping."

He lifted a brow. "You think I could sleep? Every time I closed my eyes, I pictured you."

If it was possible, she grew two more shades darker red.

This banter was so out of his element, but it felt natural with her for some reason. He didn't feel nervous when he was holding her. He reached up to tuck a lock of hair behind her ear. "Where's the braid today?"

She shrugged, glancing away.

He kissed her gently again. "If you're wearing your hair down to impress me, I want you to know something."

"What's that?"

"You're sexy as hell with it down, but you're just as sexy with it pulled back. You look studious or something when it's braided. Serious. Intelligent. Like your game face is on. It's a different look, but still makes me take notice from across a crowded room. And those glasses…"

Apparently she could turn even redder. "You quote that from a romance novel?"

"Do I look like a guy who reads romance novels?"

She shook her head, grinning.

He pressed her away from him and released her. He couldn't think while touching her. "Tell me more about the strange things happening around here."

She took a breath, seeming to calm down from before he'd kissed her. "Ryan has a list you can look at. He's keeping track now. But most of the incidences are freaky things that wouldn't ordinarily happen."

"Like what?"

"First there was a beaker explosion that practically made Emily catatonic."

"A beaker? Are you serious?" He stiffened. "A bizarre broken beaker is what caused us to all get sick in the first place."

Michelle nodded. "I know. That's why Emily lost it."

"Can't blame her. I would have too. What else?" He didn't like any part of this story.

"There have been at least three instances with strange data entries that ruined a study."

"Someone on your team transposing numbers?" He hoped.

She shook her head. "Not a chance. Somehow the numbers are changing after they're entered."

"That's insane." Computers weren't that unreliable even ten years ago.

"Yes. It's very stressful. Computers around here are also known to shut down at inconvenient times. We've had several experts look at them and find nothing. On top of that, we sometimes lose electricity at random in parts of the building which can ruin samples in the fridge or otherwise destroy whatever we're working on."

"But today's craziness is a new thing?"

"Yes."

He shoved off the door. "Okay, then I guess we need to get to work. Tell me what you want me to do first, and I'll handle it."

She scrunched her eyes, an unusual smile on her lips. "You want me to tell you what to do..."

"Yes... What?"

"Is this new Zeke a permanent member of the team? Or is he just hanging around temporarily because he likes kissing me?"

He straightened, tugging on the hem of his shirt. She had him. "I have no idea what you're talking about."

She threw her head back and laughed before lurching forward and flattening her body against his. "I like this agreeable Zeke who smiles instead of frowns and doesn't argue with me every moment of the day. Can I keep him?" She smoothed a hand up his chest and then cupped his cheek.

"I think he got struck by lightning, so it's hard to say how his personality might waffle once he clears his head."

"Fair enough, but give a girl warning, yeah?" Without hesitation, she reached for the door and opened it. "It's going to be a long day. You up for it, Mr. Insomniac?"

He grabbed both her biceps from behind before she had a chance to step into the hall. Holding her close to his chest, he set his lips on her ear. "I'm up for anything you throw at me, but I'm not ready for everyone to know I've tasted you, so can we table whatever is happening between us for the day?"

"Absolutely."

He breathed a sigh of relief as he followed her back to the lab. At least she agreed and didn't appear angry. He was still struggling with how ready he was to get involved with a woman again at all, let alone one he worked with. He was not ready for anyone else to be suspicious of them, so he would avoid her for the rest of the day and make a point of scowling as often as possible.

It was a weird reputation he had, but if he broke the mold now, people would notice.

Everyone in the bunker worked frantically throughout the day and into the evening. There would be more days like this one to follow. People were on edge. Frustrated. Scared even. From every angle, it appeared to Zeke they had been compromised.

When Zeke could no longer see straight, he stood, stretched his arms in every direction, and glanced around, looking for Michelle. She wasn't in the lab.

She'd been in and out all day. They hadn't spoken much, which was understandable since the last thing he'd told her was that he wasn't ready for people to know about them.

He still wasn't. It felt too weird. Awkward. He didn't have enough experience with women and didn't trust himself not to screw things up. He didn't have the foggiest notion how to behave around a woman he liked who liked him back, let alone one he was going to see every day at work.

Zeke busied himself shutting down his computer and shuffling papers around on his desk, waiting for Michelle, hoping to speak to her. But she didn't return, and it was late. She'd probably eaten dinner at her desk. Hell, she'd probably been exhausted and gone to bed.

Carrying the unfamiliar sensation of regret, he headed to his own suite, showered, and dropped into bed. It wasn't how he'd pictured the evening ending, but it was probably for the best. After all, he couldn't very well corner her several times a day and kiss her like a starving man when he didn't know where he wanted to take things next.

Surprisingly, he fell asleep quickly without tossing around all night, worrying about where his improbable relationship with Michelle was headed next.

Two days went by before Michelle found herself alone with Zeke again. She'd been busy. Everyone had. She might have also avoided him a few times to keep her head clear and to keep from outing herself in front of the whole bunker. She noticed him constantly. Every time she entered a room, she would see him first as if he were taller or glowed brighter or something ridiculous like that.

At the same time, she forced herself to glance away when he turned her direction. He didn't approach her, nor did he scowl at her like he used to. The few times she'd glimpsed his expression, she'd found his brow furrowed.

She knew she was probably confusing him. Sending him mixed signals. But she couldn't help it. His last words to her in Ryan's office the other day kept ringing in her head. He'd wanted to keep them a secret. She wasn't sure how she felt about that.

On the one hand, she agreed. It would be so much easier if no one knew they'd crossed a line and kissed. On the other hand, it stung a bit. He'd seemed so into her the other night. Granted, she'd nearly forced him to kiss her, right? Maybe he'd had second thoughts.

That didn't make sense either since he'd been the one to draw her into his arms in Ryan's office and initiate their second round of kissing.

She was overanalyzing and dragging her feet. She needed to stop hiding and confront him. See if the sparks were still there. Though she already knew the answer to that. The sparks were ever-present even in a crowded room with a dozen other coworkers. It was a wonder no one else experienced the zing of anticipation she felt at all times.

When the day finally wound down enough for her to feel like she could separate from her work for an entire evening, she shoved from her desk and went in search of him. She vowed she would either find him in the cafeteria or find the courage to knock on his door.

As she stepped from the lab, she ran right into him. In fact, she had to plant her hands on his chest to steady herself. "Hey," she said, feeling like a teenager.

"Hey, yourself. I was looking for you."

"You were?" She stood taller, biting her lower lip. That was promising.

He nodded. "Yes. I was hoping we could spend the evening together. I know we've both been crazy busy for a few days, but things are coming back together in the lab. You think you could take a few hours to relax?"

She smiled, flattening her palms on his chest and smoothing them over his firm pecs before she yanked them away and glanced around. Fondling him in the hallway was not conducive to keeping their strange relationship a secret.

He returned her smile, however, and reached to set a hand on her shoulder. "Your fancy beige suite or mine?"

"Mine." She was shaking like a teenage girl as she turned around and led him to her rooms. She was a grown woman. He

85

was a grown man. It was absurd for her to feel so nervous around him.

After they reached her suite and shut the door, she started to cross the room, but he grabbed her hand and pulled her backward. He leaned casually against the door, cupped her face, and gently kissed her.

She sighed deeply as he released her lips and settled his forehead against hers. "Can I get you a drink?" she whispered.

"Water would be great. It always seems like I don't stop to hydrate enough during the day." He slid his hands down her arms and then released her.

She was both calmer and more confused as she walked away from him. At least he'd broken the ice. But what did it mean?

When she returned, she handed him a bottle of water, kicked off her shoes, and settled into the corner of the couch with her legs tucked under her. She tugged the rubber band out of her hair and ran her fingers through the strands, untangling it.

Zeke sat next to her, turning his body to face her and setting his elbow on the back of the couch. His gaze was on her hair as she played with it. "I do love the color," he stated as he reached for a strand and held it.

"Thank you. Apparently Kate was a hairdresser in high school."

He didn't comment, but his gaze slid to her face. "I missed you."

"I was right here." She smiled. Her chest fluttered at his admission.

"Not close enough, though."

"Well, you said you didn't want people to know about us," she pointed out.

"I did. It just feels messy. I don't mean for us to remain a secret forever, but maybe for a while?"

"Seems reasonable. We aren't really an *us* exactly, so there's no sense spreading around unnecessary gossip prematurely."

"Exactly."

God, he seemed almost relieved. Were they on the same page? She wasn't sure. "So, what *are* we doing exactly?" she asked, hearing the hesitation in her voice. She stared at his mouth. They hadn't said much, but she really wanted him to kiss her again. That might clear things up. At the very least, it would take her mind off the rest of her pitiful life. In fact, she wasn't opposed to sleeping with him.

He was attractive and kind of funny when he opened up. He had a brilliant mind. His work ethic was out of this world. Plus, he could kiss, and he lit a fire in her every time he did so. Would it hurt anything if they had sex? Even if their *relationship* never fully took off, who cared? They could enjoy each other's company for a while.

This was uncharted territory. She'd never in her life considered sleeping with a man for no reason other than sexual gratification. But it suddenly seemed like a fantastic idea.

His gaze alone was hot and penetrating.

Finally, he answered her question. "We're two people who have switched from arguing all the time to not speaking to each other at all, as if that would somehow keep anyone from realizing we're attracted to each other and we'd rather be somewhere else... alone together." He smiled.

She liked it when he smiled. It was much better than his frown. "That sounds right. Do you think we're fooling anyone? People are probably wondering why we stopped clawing at each other." She grinned.

He shook his head. "We aren't fooling Ryan. He confronted me."

"Of course he did." She wasn't surprised. That also meant other people had noticed their odd behavior.

"Let them think whatever they want. We can play it cool in the lab while we figure ourselves out, and wait until we're alone to explore it further."

She swallowed. "We're alone now."

He slowly smiled broader. "Indeed." And then he closed the distance and claimed her lips again, his hand sliding into her hair.

She loved the feel of his lips on hers. Gentle. Soft. Caring. She didn't remember ever experiencing a kiss like his before. The guys she'd been with had been sloppy and really not interested in kissing so much as getting naked and finishing the deed.

Michelle leaned into him, setting her hand on his chest as she tipped her head to one side and licked the seam of his lips.

He opened his mouth and met her tongue with his own, the grip he had on the back of her head tightening.

As they continued to kiss, the longest lip lock of her life, the rest of her body responded. She wanted more. Crazy. Until the other night, she'd never been in a position where she craved more.

They made out like teenagers for long minutes, Zeke sliding closer until their chests met. He still held the back of her neck, but his other hand was at her waist. Finally, he broke free, still nibbling a path of smaller kisses across her cheek toward her ear. He whispered, "I should go."

She stiffened. "Why?" What was up with him wanting to leave again like he had the other night?

"Because if I don't, I won't want to stop soon," he murmured into her ear, making her shudder.

She set her hand on his when it slid to her shoulder. "Who said you needed to stop?" She was so bold with him, but dammit, he seemed to need the encouragement. Again.

"My conscience. The part of me that insists I should spend far more time with a woman than I've spent with you before stripping her clothes off."

She leaned back and met his gaze. "We've spent a lot of time together," she argued.

That slow smile returned. "You make it very difficult to say *no*."

"I'm not asking you to say *no*."

"I'm still not going to have sex with you tonight. We've only spent a few minutes alone. And most of that time we've done nothing but kiss."

"That's not true. Last time we argued first."

He chuckled. "Maybe we should try having a few normal conversations without arguing before I get you naked."

Emboldened, she grasped at one more straw. "If you leave, I'm still going to have sex tonight," she taunted.

His eyes widened and then narrowed suspiciously.

"I'd rather have sex with you," she continued, "but I'm not opposed to using a vibrator to get off. There's no way in hell I'm going to bed like this. I've never been so aroused in my life."

That slow smile graced her yet again. Damn him. He'd gone from nervous to cocky and confident far too quickly. "You're good for my bruised ego."

"You think I'm kidding?"

He moaned, leaning closer. "No. And now I'm going to toss around all night, picturing you with that damn vibrator."

"It could be you instead. Your choice." Who the hell was this woman occupying her body tonight?

He kissed her again briefly. "You've tempted me enough. I would never forgive myself if I rushed you into the bedroom. I'd rather give this weird one-eighty of ours some time. I want you to be sure. I want to be sure I can give you what you need. I'm still trying to wrap my head around the possibility of us. And, we work together. I know it's old fashioned, but even kissing you goes against every moral bone in my body. We both need to take a step back and breathe."

Damn, he was unflappable.

She gave him a sultry fake pout, though she still had no idea what woman had possessed her body and taken over her every movement and thought until she didn't recognize herself.

After one last kiss to her forehead, Zeke released her and stood.

She wouldn't chase him. He was right. They needed to back up a few paces and regroup. She didn't like it. It wouldn't have been her first choice. But he was right. He was also a stronger person than her. Besides, if he had doubts, jumping into bed with him would be a horrible idea. She wanted him to have confidence in himself and the possibility of them before they took that next step.

When he reached the door and grasped the handle, he turned around. "What color is it?"

"What color is what?"

"Your vibrator. I want to picture it fully while I stroke myself."

She gave him a slow smile. "I haven't decided on the pink one or the purple one yet. I'll let you know tomorrow."

Yep. He groaned loudly as he turned around and left her suite.

For a long time, she stared at the door, half of her thinking she'd imagined the entire last hour. She glanced around to see if there was any evidence that would prove he had been there at all. Nothing.

Nothing except the pounding of her heart, the stiffness of her nipples, and the wetness in her panties. He'd definitely been there. And he'd taken a piece of her with him when he left.

Now she just had to pray he didn't trample on that piece and leave her sorry they'd had this experience at all.

Finally, she found the muscle memory to head for her bedroom. She stripped out of scrubs, and then she dropped her bra and panties on the floor.

She wasn't the sort of person who'd ever slept in the nude, but she craved the feel of the sheets against her skin. Her hands were shaking as she retrieved her favorite pink vibrator from the nightstand and climbed onto the bed. Legs shaking and spread wide, she turned the vibrator onto the lowest setting and touched it to her clit.

Her moan was loud at the intensity of the contact. She let her head roll back and her eyes slide closed. Picturing Zeke's mouth nibbling around her ear, she held the vibrator against her clit. It took about fifteen seconds for her to come, and she came harder than she'd ever orgasmed before.

She barely managed to turn off the dial on the vibrator before she fell asleep, exhausted, sated, happy.

Naked.

~

Zeke stood under the spray of his shower, hands planted on the tile wall, forehead also leaning against the wall, eyes closed, heart pounding, dick hard. He took deep breaths that did nothing to control his erection.

Michelle's words rang in his ears. *If you leave, I'm still going to have sex tonight...*

For a split second, she'd startled him, and then he'd realized there was no way she'd meant that the way it came out.

I'm not opposed to using a vibrator to get off...

There's no way in hell I'm going to bed like this...

I've never been so aroused in my life...

Jesus. How he'd managed to walk out of her suite was a miracle. How he'd managed to walk at all was a miracle.

I haven't decided on the pink one or the purple one yet...

He shuddered as he slid his hand down the wall and grasped his erection. Visions of her masturbating filled his mind. Her eyes were closed. Her mouth hanging open. Her legs were spread wide.

Oh God... His knees nearly buckled as he stroked himself harder. Faster. This wasn't going to take long.

And then he pictured her fingers wrapped around a slender pink vibrator, the buzzing of it clear in his mind. She dug her heels into the mattress and lifted her hips off the bed. Would she cry out when she came?

Zeke had never been graced with any greater fantasy than the one Michelle had planted in his mind. Half of him wished he hadn't been the sort of man who was strong enough to leave her.

He could be in her bed right now, his dick inside her instead of her damn vibrator.

Was he an idiot?

He gritted his teeth as he visualized Michelle's body shuddering as she peaked, a soft moan escaping her lips. He tipped over the edge with his imaginary woman, his come shooting against the shower wall, long drawn-out pulses that had amassed from days of frustration.

Or perhaps years. Years spent alone with nothing but his hand because he didn't have the balls to even glance at another woman.

Coward.

He'd feared rejection. He'd feared having his heart trampled on again. He hadn't trusted his instincts when it came to women because his intuition had failed him so miserably the first time.

Michelle was not Meredith. She didn't have any of the same greedy, selfish qualities. She had never been fake with him. She was pure and real and sweet and kind and full of life.

He needed to man up soon and take a chance on life.

Soon.

CHAPTER 8

One week later…

Temple popped her head into the lab. "Zeke, can I speak to you in my office?"

He flinched, glancing around. His first thought was that she somehow knew he'd had unprofessional contact with Michelle and wanted to squash it. A heartbeat later, he shook the idea from his mind. He couldn't imagine Temple commenting on any relationship between two coworkers. She hadn't minded about Tushar and Trish, and she obviously wasn't concerned with Ryan and Emily.

Besides, even though he and Michelle had spent another evening together in her room two nights ago, rounding second base like two teenagers at a drive-in movie, he still hadn't sealed the deal. It was getting increasingly harder to deny her, though. She was persistent.

"Sure." He stood, reaching for his mouse to save his work and then following her from the room. As soon as he shut her office door behind him, he spoke. "Is something wrong?"

She pointed at the chair opposite her desk and sighed as she sat. "Yes. I hate to burden you with this, but you have a little problem."

He eased onto the chair, wondering if it might have been better to remain standing. "*I* have a problem?" He had about ten of them. Which one was she referring to?

"Yeah. I just spoke to your parents."

"My parents called you?" He sat up straighter, his spine rigid. He was a grown man. What the hell reason would his parents have for calling his boss?

"They didn't have a choice. You weren't answering your phone, and they wanted to warn you."

He palmed his phone in his pocket and pulled it out. Sure enough, he hadn't remembered to take it off do-not-disturb mode when he woke up. Or had it been silent even longer than that? "Warn me about what?"

"Your ex-wife." She winced.

"My ex-wife?" How the hell did that damn woman continue to feature in half his conversations? He hadn't thought about her in years, and now the ghost of their relationship seemed to be this unwelcome presence keeping him from everything he wanted and Michelle deserved.

"Apparently, she called your parents, wanting to get information about you. When they told her you'd been reanimated, she got all excited and said she was heading here."

"What?" he shouted, jumping up from the chair. "Here? As in *here* here? The bunker?"

Temple nodded. She winced. She had been his boss from the moment he'd arrived at the bunker to work, and she knew nearly all the gory details about Meredith. Everyone did. They were a close-knit group. Not to mention his drama had topped everyone's at the time, making for ongoing dinner conversation since most of the original team hadn't had significant others or any excitement to speak of. "Your mom said she was acting strange and talked too fast. She seemed way too excited to hear you had been reanimated."

"When did this happen?"

"Late last night. I wasn't in my office. Your mom left a message. I just now had a chance to return her call."

"Well, Meredith is wasting her time coming here. She can't get onto the grounds."

"She can if we let her."

Zeke groaned as he lowered himself back onto the chair. "Why would we do that?"

Temple shrugged. "In order to find out what her angle is. I'm skeptical about her sudden interest in you, and I don't want any media blowback from a half-cocked ex-wife looking to sell her story."

He lifted a brow. "You and me both. It's crazy."

"That's why I think you should go ahead and meet with her. Here. In the conference room. That way you can feel her out on our turf, figure out if she's got an agenda, and get rid of her."

Zeke couldn't imagine why the woman would want to see him. As far as he was concerned, they had divorced four years ago. For her, it had been fourteen.

He shook his head. "You don't know Meredith. She's manipulative and *always* has an agenda. She isn't coming here for her health."

"So find out what it is. See what she has to say and put an end to it."

Zeke groaned. His brain was overloaded today. He had yet to fully process whatever what happening between him and Michelle. He was functioning on little sleep. And the entire bunker was in upheaval over ongoing computer issues. This situation with his ex-wife was more than he could stomach. "Fine. Jesus. Fuck. How about next week? Let's put her off."

Temple sighed. "Well, your mom said Meredith was on her

way, so she may show up within the next few hours, not next week. Just get it over with so we can all get back to work."

Adrenaline pumped through his system. This day was about to become the day from hell. Zeke stood and began to pace. "This is crazy. In her world, I haven't seen her in fourteen years."

Temple nodded. "I know. I have an undercover officer working out front now. She's been informed. Nicole will text me when Meredith shows up and give us a heads-up."

Zeke sighed. "I have nothing to say to Meredith. Not a single word. I never did. That crazy bitch cheated on me and left me. What the hell would she need to see me now?"

Temple stood. "No idea. But face her, deal with it, move on. I'm suspicious of everyone these days. We don't need someone with an axe to grind. I remember how she left you without a word. She could be unhinged. It's best if we know what she's after so we can get ahead of it. We don't need her talking to the press."

Zeke blew out a long breath. He considered telling Temple fuck no and then heading to his suite to hide from the world. But his boss was right. He needed to pull his shit together and face the crazy woman he never should have gotten involved with in the first place.

He was also reminded why he'd sworn off women. Obviously, he had horrible bitch radar. He'd been too naïve when he fell for her charm and let her into his life. He wasn't at all sure he wasn't still that naïve. There was a reason he never dated after she left. Not just because he was married to his job, but also out of self-preservation.

What about Michelle? She was nothing like Meredith. He knew in his soul she would not intentionally fuck him over. He also knew she couldn't do so if he didn't let her. Walls that had slowly crumbled around him over the past several weeks slammed back up.

He needed to get rid of Meredith and then reevaluate any thought he'd had about starting up something with Michelle. He'd only been reanimated for six weeks. It was way too soon to get involved with someone. His life was in an upheaval; his priority needed to be catching up in the field of immunology and all the new technology that had been invented in the last decade.

What he didn't need was to allow himself to be led by his dick just because a pretty woman crossed his path and showed an interest.

"Fine."

Temple nodded. "I'll have her escorted to the conference room when she gets here."

Without a word, Zeke turned around and stomped from the room. He needed to regroup before he faced his ex. Instead of returning to the lab, he headed for his suite. He had no desire to face anyone else right now, especially not Michelle, who would read his mood and ask him questions he wasn't prepared to answer.

Sure enough, Temple was right when she suspected Meredith would be there that very day. Not two hours later, she showed up. Zeke was a little surprised when he first entered the conference room. Meredith hadn't changed much in fourteen years. Her physique was nearly the same. Either she worked out hard or she hadn't had children. Or both. Her hair was shorter—just below her shoulders—and styled differently, but it was the same shade of brown. There might have been a few more wrinkles on her face, but other than that, she looked good.

She would be forty now.

Her eyes widened when she saw him, and her mouth fell open. "Wow. You haven't aged a bit."

He sighed. "That's what happens when you're cryonically preserved for a decade. What are you doing here, Meredith?"

She gasped, putting a hand over her heart dramatically as if he'd insulted her. What had he ever seen in his woman? "When I heard the news, I had to see you. I mean, seriously, Zeke, of course I would come as fast as I could. We used to be married. We have a connection. It means something to me."

He searched her lying, cheating eyes and dropped into a chair. This was insane. What was her agenda? "I repeat, what are you doing here?"

She lowered herself elegantly onto a chair across from him. She was wearing a pencil skirt and a pale pink blouse that did nothing to hide the lace of her bra. Were her boobs bigger? He almost laughed. If anyone was vain enough to get a boob job, it would be Meredith. He wondered who was funding her expensive habits.

She pasted on a fake pout, complete with a comically protruding bottom lip. "Zeke," she crooned in a voice he might have once considered seductive, "don't be so stoic. People care about you. I'm one of them." She sat straighter and switched from a pout to a smile. "You look great, by the way. How do you feel?"

"I feel like I want you to say what you have to say and get out of here so I can work. I have things to do."

She glanced through the window that faced the hallway. Every few seconds, people hurried by. He felt guilty sitting here while the rest of the bunker was working hard. He also ignored everyone who walked by, wishing he wouldn't have to explain himself later.

There was no hope for that, however. He was certain everyone in the bunker already had the memo, and word of his damn ex-wife would be circulating fast. And that would include Michelle hearing about it.

Meredith stared out the window again. "Seems really hectic around here. What's everyone in such a hurry for?"

Zeke leaned forward, putting his elbows on the table and narrowing his gaze at her. "Nothing has changed in fourteen years, Meredith. This is still a government bunker. Anything that occurs in this facility is classified."

She nodded. "Right. Of course. I just didn't expect so many people and so much rushing."

He said nothing.

She sighed and trailed her pointer over the top of the table, tilting her head to one side. "Are they taking care of you? I mean, please tell me the government is paying all of you a huge settlement for what you've been through."

He lost every ounce of control at that statement, throwing his head back and laughing so hard his stomach muscles hurt. He even had to wipe his eyes by the time he'd finished.

Meredith's cheeks were red and her face was pinched. "What's so funny? Honestly, Zeke, I do not understand you sometimes."

Sobering, he responded. "You never understood me for a single moment. You never even tried. You didn't care. All you saw were dollar signs when you expected a PhD student at Harvard to be rich enough to support your lavish lifestyle. It must have really stung when you found out you were wrong.

"Surely, with your looks and ability to fool anyone with a dick, you managed to snag someone else to support you? What happened to him? Or were there several men who fell for your stunts before wising up and leaving after you wiped out their bank accounts?

"How much plastic surgery have you had? You must be conveniently between men and hoping to score with your first husband again if you were willing to go to all this trouble to see me."

"Zeke!" she said in her placating voice.

He rose, set his hands on the table, and leaned closer. "You guessed wrong about the settlement. Let me save you the trouble. There was no windfall of money. I'm still just as poor as I was the day you left me when I couldn't afford your manicures and hundreds of pairs of shoes anymore. So, you've wasted your time.

Get out of here. Look elsewhere. I pity the next man who falls victim to your schemes, but I have important work to do."

He spun around, opened the door, and waved a hand toward the hallway. "Let's go," he continued when she didn't jump up fast enough.

With a loud *hmph*, she finally rose, held her head high, and paused in the entrance to address him again. "You would think a man who came so close to death would have softened and become less of an asshole from the experience. Obviously, I was wrong."

"Obviously," he confirmed.

She threw her hands in the air and then stomped down the hallway.

He stayed on her heels until they reached the front desk where he told the guard to escort her off the property and inform the security team at the front gate not to admit her again for any reason.

Luckily, Meredith didn't bother to speak again.

Michelle's hands were shaking so badly that she had to excuse herself from the lab. She hurried down the hallway and slid undetected into her suite at the other end of the bunker, exhaling long and slow when she was finally alone.

The entire morning had been a shit storm, and the afternoon had not been better. But nothing had prepared her for the rumor that circulated around that Zeke's ex-wife was in the building meeting with him in the conference room.

She could kick herself for giving a single shit and heading that direction. A small piece of her had been pissed that he hadn't told her Meredith was coming, but she gave him the benefit of the doubt and assumed he might be in need of moral support. Plus, she badly wanted to see the woman he had originally thought looked like Michelle.

What she had not been prepared for was rounding the corner to the conference room and finding him inside with his head tipped back laughing as though the woman had just told him the most fascinating joke on the planet.

She blinked several times while he continued to laugh, glancing only briefly at Meredith across from him to find her expression oddly weary. She indeed had brown hair, though it was shorter than Michelle's.

She also didn't look old enough to have been married to him fourteen years ago. Seated at the table, it was difficult to tell how tall she was, but it was true she was slender. Her breasts however were huge.

Michelle shoved off the door and headed for the fridge. She grabbed a bottle of water when what she really wanted was several shots of tequila or something hard like that. She didn't have any hard alcohol in her suite, however.

Plus, she needed to find a way to pull herself back together and get back to work. Everybody in the bunker was needed, including the recently revived. They'd had a small break-through with Myasthenia Gravis. Not a cure yet, but a possible inoculation vaccine. Everyone was buzzing.

Only the last four who had been brought out of their comas two weeks ago and were still gaining enough strength to stand and walk were excluded from the hustle and bustle of the lab. Zeke's entire group of four from six weeks ago were all hard at work in whatever capacity they could manage.

Oh, wait. Zeke wasn't working with the others. *Noooo.* He was currently having a laugh-fest with his ex-wife.

Michelle took long swigs of water, set the bottle on the counter, and then tipped her head from side to side to work out the kinks. After several deep breaths and a short pep talk about what idiots men were and how she didn't need one now or ever, she headed for the door.

She would have to claim temporary insanity for having

jumped Zeke so thoroughly on several occasions now. Thank God she hadn't slept with him. A few kisses and some groping wasn't that big of deal. Right?

Apparently, kissing and groping hadn't meant a damn thing to him if he didn't think it was necessary to inform her he was meeting with his ex-wife, and then somehow found the woman to be so hilarious that he smiled and laughed harder than Michelle imagined he'd ever done in his life.

He sure hadn't done anything like that in front of her or anyone else in the bunker. His sour expression initially put everyone on edge. Sure, she'd made some sort of headway with him the past few weeks, helped bring out the occasional smile, but laughter?

Fuck him.

No longer feeling sorry for herself, Michelle made her way back to the lab where she summarily ignored Zeke and proceeded to get an update from two of her coworkers working on the vaccine.

She didn't permit herself to glance at Zeke a single time for the rest of the day. She didn't even go to the cafeteria to eat dinner, instead asking Emily to please make her a plate when she went herself.

Michelle returned to her suite late that evening, but she barely kicked off her shoes before someone knocked on the door. Half-expecting to find Zeke outside, she groaned as she looked through the peephole.

Emily. Thank God.

She opened the door to let her friend in, not realizing until then that she had Kate with her.

Michelle held the door open politely even though she was exhausted and would prefer to take a long bath, drink a half a bottle of wine, and drown herself in her self-inflicted sorrows.

"What's up?" she asked as they filed in.

Kate held up a bottle of wine, though she had one in each hand. "We need an update."

"Update on what?" she asked, feigning innocence.

Emily narrowed her gaze. "Something happened after Kate colored your hair last week. And I bet it's happened more than once. So spill." She flopped down on Michelle's sofa and held out her glass toward Kate. "Get that wine open. We're going to need it."

"I don't know what you're talking about," Michelle lied.

Kate moved to the kitchenette to find a cork screw and spoke when she held it up in victory. "Yeah, that's not going to work with us. We know you better than that."

Michelle lowered herself into the armchair, tipped her head back, and closed her eyes. "What are you guys, psychic?"

Emily responded, "It would be far more interesting if we pretended we were, but the truth is much less interesting. Ryan told me Meredith was here earlier. He also told me you and Zeke used his office one day last week."

Michelle jerked her head up. "Shit."

Emily giggled. "He isn't mad. No big deal. He doesn't care. He just turned around and went the other way to give you guys privacy, which apparently you needed. And, rumor has it you two stopped fighting in the lab all the time."

Michelle groaned. The last thing she wanted was for people to know she'd had any interaction with Zeke at this point. Too late.

Kate handed Michelle a glass of wine and sat next to Emily on the sofa. "So, what led up to whatever has been going on with Zeke? I mean, surely the man didn't walk into the lab, see your gorgeous new highlights, and yank you into a closet to make out." She laughed. "Or is that exactly what happened?" She faked a swoon, tossing the back of her hand across her forehead and leaning to one side.

"Good grief," Michelle said, "your imagination is out of

control. Besides, it doesn't matter what's been happening between me and Zeke. It's over now."

"So something *did* happen." Emily leaned forward. "Why is it over?"

"Something happened all right. I took leave of my senses and let the man get under my skin. More than once. But today my mind is clearer. Obviously he's not over his ex-wife. I'm not stupid. I don't want anything to do with that."

Emily jerked. "What the hell makes you say that? He hates her."

"Didn't look like it from where I stood when I walked by the conference room this afternoon. He was laughing so hard at whatever cute thing she said that his face was about to split open."

Kate frowned. "That doesn't sound like Zeke. Laughing?"

Michelle smirked. "Yep. The kind of laughter that leaves you wiping your tears away." She shuddered. "I can't believe I fell for his story about how quickly he was over her and how long it had been since he'd even thought about her. He must have been trying to convince himself instead of me. I should have seen the signs on the wall when it seemed his ex was still impacting how he interacted with other women."

"Wait," Emily interrupted, "when did you have such a long conversation with him? When you left my suite last week? Or in Ryan's office? Because before that, you hadn't exchanged more than a few civil words with him in the past six weeks. But, wait, you didn't duck into Ryan's office for long enough to have discussed Meredith. Which means..."

Michelle groaned. "I saw him after I left your room that night."

Kate's eyes bugged out. "After you left us?"

"Yes. He was waiting at my door."

Emily grinned from ear to ear. "Did he like your hair?" She clapped her hands. "You were wearing that skirt and that tight tank, and you had on makeup. Perfect."

"Not perfect. I wish it hadn't happened now."

"Because of Meredith?" Kate asked.

"Among other things, but yes."

Kate shook her head. "I don't know what you saw this afternoon, but I can assure you Zeke is not into that bitch. He never even mentioned her again after they divorced. He might be leery about dating again, but he can't possibly have feelings for Meredith."

Michelle shrugged. "I don't know what to tell you. I nearly threw myself at him that night. I've seen him a few other times too. I'm so embarrassed I want to fall through a crack in the floor. I can't believe I was so stupid. I even teased him about my inability to pull more than a few smiles out of him. So, yes, it pisses me off that he could laugh that hard with his damn ex. She can have him."

Emily shook her head. "I agree with Kate. Something's off. He was livid when Meredith left earlier. Ryan thought he was going to punch a hole in the wall. He even told the front desk to never let her back on the property again."

Michelle frowned, confused. "Well, whatever, it was a bad idea anyway. The man isn't ready for a real relationship."

"Did he say that?" Emily asked.

"Several times. His self-esteem was trampled on by Meredith. Or so he implies. Even when we're alone together, he keeps an emotional distance between us. I've tried to break down his barriers, but he shoots me down every time, rambling about it not being fair to me for him to take things further between us. I should have read the signs. The man's obviously not that into me."

Emily's gaze was incredulous as if she didn't believe what Michelle was telling her.

"So you didn't sleep with him yet?" Kate asked.

Michelle shook her head. "No, but shit. I feel so stupid. I would have. He apparently has more willpower than me."

"He turned you down?" Emily took another drink of wine and then grabbed the bottle from the coffee table.

"Yep."

"Ouch." Kate took the bottle from Emily.

"Clearly, he's still hung up on his ex-wife. I should have realized. No wonder he doesn't want to have sex with me."

Kate was shaking her head. "I don't believe that for a second. Something else is going on with him."

"Whatever. It doesn't matter now. Ugh." Michelle rubbed her temples.

Emily leaned back. "We might need more wine."

Michelle forced a smile. "I need sleep. It's been a long day. I'm exhausted. I'm over it. Tomorrow, I'll return to working with him and not mention a thing. I can be professional."

"Sure." Kate nodded.

"For the record," Emily added, "Ryan and I went through a similar phase when we hooked up. We were super-worried about what would happen if we broke up, and we took things slow at first. But I've never been this happy, and I wouldn't trade what we have for the world. It's so nice having someone to climb into bed with at the end of the day when working under such stressful conditions for months at a time."

"I'm so happy for you two, but Zeke has made it clear he isn't going to take that risk because he doesn't think he's cut out for relationships. I don't know why I haven't gotten that through my thick head sooner. I feel like an idiot for how many times I've put myself out there. I'm done. Lesson learned."

Kate blew out a breath and looked away.

Michelle caught her wiping a tear from her cheek. "Kate?" She realized they were both being insensitive. Emily had a permanent man, and Michelle at least had a few evenings of excitement. How long had it been since Kate had a relationship? Michelle had never asked.

Emily grabbed Kate's hand and squeezed it. "Kate's story is complicated. I'm sorry, hon. I wasn't thinking."

Kate shook her head and pursed her lips, wiping more tears

from her cheeks. "Don't be sorry. I'm being silly. I'm happy for you."

Michelle didn't want to pry, so she said nothing. But the emotions on Kate's face made her heart squeeze.

After a few moments of silence, Kate took a deep breath and faced Michelle. "I'm in love with a man who's still preserved." She let out a sharp chuckle. "Huh. I've never said that out loud."

Emily smiled and squeezed her hand again. "But I knew. I could tell ten years ago."

"I figured you knew."

Michelle smiled too. "What's his name?"

"Graham Wentz."

"I've seen his name on the records."

"Well, keep it to yourself. He doesn't know I exist."

Michelle laughed. "He must know you exist. You worked together for years before you were preserved."

She rolled her eyes. "He might know my name. That's about it."

Emily perked up. "Well, you'll just have to change that when he wakes up."

"Sure," Kate responded sarcastically. "I'm pretty sure I could slide onto his lap naked, and he wouldn't notice."

Michelle laughed again. "Can't be that bad. Although, maybe you have a point. These scientists are pretty nerdy. I came close to stripping for Zeke in an effort to get him horny enough to want to sleep with me, and I failed miserably." She shuddered. "Thank God for small favors."

Emily set her empty glass on the coffee table. "We should go and let you sleep, but don't give up on Zeke so fast. He's been through a lot. He'll come around. Give him time."

Michelle didn't respond. She had made up her mind. Everything that happened today helped her see reason. Getting involved with a man who didn't trust women had been a horrible idea, and it was even worse that she still had to work with him. Whatever. Time to move on.

CHAPTER 9

One week later...

Zeke hugged his jacket around his body against the wind. It was May, but the days in Falling Rock were still chilly. He looked at Ryan, who had his arm wrapped around Emily. "Did you speak to Dade?" He still felt a little nervous about Emily knowing about Dade, but keeping it from her had put pressure on Ryan.

Ryan nodded. "Yes. He and Blair are in Montana looking for clues about what might have tipped someone off about my parents."

"Right. That's where your parents were hiding when someone found them and hunted them down."

"Yes. On a ranch. Should have been secure."

"But it wasn't." Zeke sighed. "So we know someone isn't super-pleased with our reawakening, but we have no idea who."

Ryan nodded. "Exactly. I'd bet anything it's an inside job, but there's no telling where it's coming from. That's why I don't want anyone to have a clue that Dade lived. It not only makes him a target, but it also thwarts his efforts to work behind the scenes.

Having someone outside the bunker digging around is a godsend."

"You don't believe someone inside the bunker would be sabotaging our efforts, do you?"

Ryan shook his head. "Not really. But someone somewhere is. The question is, why? Obviously Temple has to report to people higher up the food chain. Who knows who among them might tell other people about our progress and the reanimation of your team. It's classified, but we all know how useful that label is at times."

"It's the damn government, though. Why the hell would they be trying to injure, kill, or kidnap their own people? People who gave up their lives to work hard to cure diseases and paid for their efforts with a decade in preservation?"

"I seriously don't get it. Neither does Dade. He has only encountered dead ends so far."

"How's he feeling?"

"Amazing. He sounds fantastic."

Emily smiled. "That might have something to do with Blair. They're attached at the hip. Neither of them cares a bit that they gave up their entire lives and everyone they know to snoop and hide together."

Zeke felt a tug on his heart thinking about anyone enjoying that sort of relationship. Ryan and Emily obviously did also. In fact, Ryan kissed her forehead as she spoke. Nope. It definitely wouldn't have been reasonable for Ryan to leave his own significant other in the dark.

Zeke didn't imagine he would ever enjoy whatever bond other people seemed to find together. He had failed miserably the first time, and he hadn't exactly done a bang-up job with the only other women he'd ever had feelings for.

Emily glanced at Ryan and then looked at Zeke again. "What happened between you and Michelle?"

Zeke flinched. "What do you mean? Nothing happened."

She rolled her eyes. "Come on. I know the two of you got together that night after Kate and I highlighted her hair. I also know you met up a few other times after that. I just don't understand why you're both being so stubborn about it."

Ryan looked about as uncomfortable as Zeke felt. Women sometimes had this uncanny need to poke people to death about their private lives. But Zeke was a little shocked to find out Michelle had mentioned their time together to anyone. "She told you about us?"

"Not really. Kate and I more or less yanked it out of her."

"Kate knows too?" His voice rose and then he groaned. "Jesus." Ryan cringed.

Emily continued. "Good grief. We're girls. We talk. We knew she was into you. That's why she wanted us to do her hair."

Zeke swiped a hand down his face. This was getting worse by the second.

"She said she was into me?"

She frowned. "Well, of course."

Then why the hell is she no longer talking to me? He realized he had played a key role in the fact that they had drifted apart. He hadn't done a thing to encourage her. And she'd made it easy when she seemed to withdraw from him, giving him an excuse to go back into his shell. His insecurities had slammed right back into place when she stopped meeting his gaze or finding excuses to run into him.

His encounter with Meredith had drained him, forcing him to remember what a bad choice he'd made fourteen years ago. He didn't need that kind of headache again.

Michelle's obvious disinterest helped confirm what he already knew—that he wasn't relationship material. Thank God she'd figured it out before they'd taken things further because his heart would be stomped on now if they'd slept together.

"I think the two of you had a misunderstanding, and you're both too stubborn to admit it and talk about it."

"I'm pretty sure we both agree that it's a bad idea to start a relationship with someone you work with." He winced. "No offense. I'm glad it worked out for the two of you, but not everyone is that lucky."

"I think you're making excuses because you're scared."

He took a step back, frustrated.

She pressed on. "Did you ever speak to her after your ex-wife visited?"

"Of course. I speak to her every day. We work together."

"Yeah, but I mean about your laughing."

"My what?" Damn, this woman was twisting him in knots.

"She walked by the conference room while you were with Meredith and caught you laughing. It kind of threw her for a loop because we all thought...well, that you hated Meredith."

Zeke was too stunned to respond. His mouth hung open while he tried to recall what Michelle would have witnessed. And then it hit him, and he slapped his forehead. "Shit."

"Brings tears to your eyes, doesn't it?"

Michelle turned her head to the side to find Temple standing next to her, her eyes watering.

"Yes." She had just left General Custodio's room when she encountered Temple in the hallway.

Temple, who was rarely emotional, put a hand over her heart and sighed. "I've never been married myself, so I can't imagine that kind of love."

"Me neither." It was amazing seeing Elena reunited with her husband after fifteen years. He'd only been awake two days, but his wife had never left his side. She had stars in her eyes and held his hand as if they were in high school.

"How are things in the lab?" Temple asked, wiping her eyes.

"A full week without an incident. It's a blessing. I keep waiting for the other shoe to drop. I think we're all on pins and needles."

Temple nodded. "Hopefully everything that has happened has been a series of bizarre accidents, and it's over now. I'm sure that's wishful thinking, though, so we're still looking for the source of the leaks."

"Any new incidents out front? Has your undercover cop heard any rumblings?"

"Nothing too troublesome. Nicole checks in with me a few times a day to report anything suspicious, but so far nothing serious has caught her attention. The usual picketers and media."

"That's good, I guess."

Emily rushed past the two of them in the hallway. She smiled awkwardly and gave a quick wave. "Hey." And then she was gone.

Michelle watched her back, her blood pressure rising. Emily's face had been flushed from the outdoors. Not unusual lately. In the past week, Michelle had hardly spent any time with her friends. She kept telling herself everyone was busy. Emily had a life. She had Ryan.

But something was off, and it niggled under Michelle's skin often. Maybe Emily felt awkward about the fact that Michelle had decided not to pursue Zeke, though Michelle didn't understand why the woman would care. It wasn't as if Zeke had attempted any contact with Michelle either. By mutual agreement, they seemed to have stuffed their awkward relationship in a drawer and pretended it never happened.

The question was, why did that have anything to do with Emily?

"You okay?" Temple asked. "You spaced on me."

"Yep. Just thinking. Gotta get back. I'll see you later." She turned around and headed for the lab. It seemed like she practically lived in that damn lab. When she entered, she noticed Ryan taking off his jacket and then arranging it over the back of a chair. Zeke was doing the same thing.

It was as if the three of them had a private little club going that took place fifty yards from the entrance to the bunker most days. If it were 1960 and they were smokers, she wouldn't flinch. But it was not, and they weren't. Instead, Michelle felt a pang as if she were being left out.

It was her own fault. Emily and Zeke had been friends for years. Zeke and Ryan had hit it off and become close also. Michelle was simply the new girl who had a few awkward encounters with a man she later ignored while he did the same. She had known Ryan for a long time, but until Emily came along, they hadn't been close friends.

While she was subconsciously staring at Zeke, he turned around and met her gaze, holding it. He looked chagrined as if he felt bad about something.

She jerked her attention away from him and headed to her workspace to focus on anything that wasn't Zeke. A self-conscious chill climbed up her spine at the irrational feeling that Zeke was not only still staring at her back, but that whatever he'd been outside discussing with Emily and Ryan had to do with her.

She gritted her teeth and fought for composure. Did they somehow have something against her? It made sense considering how distant Emily had been. Maybe they were mad about something she'd done in the office, but if they were gossiping about it, she would really be pissed.

Unable to keep from confronting one of them, she stood and looked around for Ryan. He'd left the room, so she headed for his office. Finding him at his desk, she shut the door as he looked up. "Hey. What's up?"

She sat across from him in the tight space that felt more like a closet and dove right in. "Did I do something to annoy anyone?" What if Zeke was mad at her for blowing him off, and told Ryan?

Ryan's eyes widened in shock. "No, why?"

"You're sure? I get the feeling I'm the topic of a secret side conversation happening behind my back lately."

His face turned red as he lied to her. "Nope."

She took a breath. "Ryan, come on. I've known you for years. I realize we aren't so close that we hang out after hours or anything, but whatever is going on, I wish you would just tell me. I can't fix it if I don't know what I've done."

He groaned and slumped in his seat. "Some days I wish I were a hermit."

"Well, you're not. So spill."

"You should really talk to Zeke instead of me."

She jerked in the chair. "Ah, so this has to do with Zeke. Please tell me it isn't personal. I will kill him."

Ryan winced.

She nearly jumped out of her chair. "Zeke has been talking to the two of you behind my back about our personal business?" Her voice rose with every word.

Ryan shook his head. "No. Never. It's just that Emily got on him to talk to you. And now I'm on you to talk to him. Whatever misunderstanding you two had, please fix it before I lose my mind trying to keep up with the he-said-she-said."

"No one should have *said* anything," she shouted. "There's nothing to say. We had a thing. That's it. No story. It was a horrible idea. I'm sorry I ever spoke to him."

The door opened behind her, and she spun around to find Zeke standing in the doorway. He looked miserable. "I could hear you from the hallway."

She cringed. "Great." Pushing herself to standing, she shoved the chair aside and then took the two steps for the door. With nothing more than a glance at Zeke, she brushed past him and headed the opposite direction down the hallway toward the living suites.

Unfortunately, he followed her. She could feel him at her back.

When she reached her door, she opened it with shaky hands and turned around. "You're not coming in. I don't have anything to say to you."

"I think you have a lot to say to me. I just heard some of it from the hallway."

Voices sounded from around the corner. The last thing Michelle needed was for someone to catch her arguing outside her suite with Zeke, so she stepped back, grabbed his shirt, and jerked him inside.

As soon as the door shut, she lost it. "Look, I don't get why you're pissed at me."

His mouth fell open. "I'm not pissed at you. Clearly you're pissed at *me*."

She stepped back. "Fine. You're right. But I'm not blabbing about it to other people. I haven't said a word to anyone about us. You're the one holding clandestine meetings out in the cold discussing me."

"Oh for heaven's sake. That's pure bullshit. And so is the fact that you haven't spoken about us. Emily knows quite a few details about us. So does Kate."

She flinched. He was right about that. "Fine. Yes, I told my friends we kissed. I thought they were my friends. It didn't seem like a big deal. Now not only is everyone avoiding me, but you're still discussing it behind my back like it's an issue. So what? We kissed. We're adults. We can move on. Why the secret meetings and ducked heads?"

For a moment he said nothing, and then he finally licked his lips and spoke in a softer voice. "We did way more than kiss."

What was he talking about? "Fine, some kissing and groping. It's not like we had sex. I think I would remember that."

"That's not what I mean." He rolled his eyes.

"What the hell do you mean, then?"

"I mean, you speak of us flippantly as if it meant nothing."

She took another step back, more confused than ever. "Apparently it did mean nothing to you."

He shook his head. "That's not true. I admit I got cold feet worrying about what might happen to us if we started dating because I'm a little unsure of myself and I didn't want to screw things up when we have to work together, but what we had meant a lot to me. If we didn't work together and I was a stronger person and I thought I could ever be the kind of man you deserve, I would pursue you in a heartbeat."

She inched backward slowly until her knees hit the edge of the couch and she lowered to sit.

He continued. "Emily said you were hurt because you found me laughing at Meredith."

Michelle swallowed and looked down at her lap, wringing her fingers together. "That's true." She found it hard to admit, but she kept talking in a low voice. "I was jealous. We spoke a lot about how hard it is for you to even smile. You never laugh. And then I found you falling out of your chair laughing with your ex-wife as if she were the funniest person on earth."

He rushed across the room and sat next to her, wrapping one large hand over both of hers. "Meredith is a bitch. You must have walked by at the exact moment I realized she had only come here because she imagined I would get some sort of giant payout from the government for my trouble. She's a gold digger. When I figured out her agenda, I did fall out of my chair laughing. *At* her, not *with* her. I'm sorry."

Michelle lifted her face. "She came after you because she thought you had money?"

He nodded, giving her one of his half smiles. "You missed the part where I sobered and told her to get the hell out of the bunker and never return. I marched her fancy ass to the front of the building and someone escorted her off the premises."

Michelle didn't know what to say. "Why didn't you say anything?"

He sighed. "I'm an ass. Meredith reminded me how terrible I was at relationships so I got it in my head that we shouldn't pursue this thing between us, and then you seemed to think the same thing, so I let it go."

"Then why were you and Emily and Ryan discussing it outside like it's some sort of private club?"

He smiled again, melting her a little. "Emily brought it up. It's not like we've discussed you before. Today was the first time. She started nagging me about clearing the air with you. She's relentless. I was blindsided."

Michelle matched his smile. "Yeah, Emily can be that way. But she's been avoiding me."

"Maybe it's just a coincidence? I don't think she's avoiding you. She spent fifteen minutes reading me the riot act. She wouldn't do that if she didn't care about you."

True. "Did the three of you take up smoking?"

He shot her a strange look. "Nooo. Why?"

"Because you keep sneaking off outside together like smokers."

He gave her a sampling of his laugh. "Nope. Not smoking. It's getting nice out. We like to get fresh air and get out of the lab sometimes. Emily is attached to Ryan, so she usually comes along."

"So, I could join this club of yours?" she tested.

"Of course. Please do. Unless you intend to join Emily and gang up on me as if I'm a complete idiot."

Michelle bit her lip. "So, where does this leave us?"

"I don't know. I'm sorry I gave you the wrong impression. I should have had the balls to face you. I guess I didn't because I knew if I got you alone to try and explain why we shouldn't be together, I would feel like I do right now and end up kissing you instead."

Her smile widened. "How exactly do you feel right now?" If he felt half as many butterflies in his stomach as she did, he wouldn't be talking any longer.

He released her hands, eased his palm up her arm, and cupped the side of her face. A second later, he leaned forward and kissed her. The kiss was soft and sweet for several seconds before he tipped his head to the side and deepened the contact, turning it into something urgent and hard.

Her nipples jumped to attention at the sudden change of events, and she spun her body to face him, grabbing his waist with one hand and flattening the other on his chest.

Like every time he kissed her, she had no idea how much time passed, nor did she care. It felt so good to be touching him again. Goose bumps climbed up her skin. Nothing had changed. She wanted him. Maybe she was desperate from months cooped up in a bunker with so few options, but she didn't think so. Especially since any other doctor or scientist on staff would be a better choice if she was judging them by how they treated her and how often they spoke or smiled.

Maybe she liked the challenge? She was a pleaser, and she'd been aware of herself reverting to her old ways when it came to Zeke. A strong desire to ensure he liked her even while she'd been pissed at him for seemingly enjoying his ex-wife's company a bit too much.

When he released her lips, it was to kiss a path to her ear and breathe into her. "If we don't stop now, we'll never make it back to the lab, and people will start wondering where we went."

Her face heated. "Shit. We've been gone a while," she whispered, wishing the rest of the world and all its problems would disappear for a few hours so she could live a little. She still wasn't sure this was a good idea, but she at least wanted to spend some time with him to see if they were compatible.

He pulled back, holding her arm and her face still. "You have plans for tonight?"

"I was going to hide in my suite and stare at the pages of a book I haven't been able to concentrate on since you blew me off."

He smiled. "Maybe I could join you? I'm reading the same book."

She closed her eyes. "I like that plan."

CHAPTER 10

It was late by the time Michelle got back to her suite. She had grabbed dinner from the cafeteria and returned to the lab to oversee a new experiment some of the staff was conducting. She hadn't seen Zeke in several hours, so she worried he might have given up and gone back to his suite.

But when she rounded the corner, she found him leaning against her door. In addition, he was holding flowers. "Truce?" he asked as she approached.

She stepped close to him, took a whiff of the flowers, and closed her eyes. "Definitely."

After opening the door and letting them both in, she took the flowers and headed for the kitchen. She didn't own a vase, but a glass would work. "How did you manage to get flowers?"

"I had them delivered to the gate. One of the security guards brought them to the bunker."

"That's impressive."

"It was just a phone call."

She realized he had followed her when his voice sounded close to her ear. Seductive. "It was more than that," she murmured as she set the flowers in the glass of water.

"Okay, you might be right. I've never bought flowers before. It took a few minutes."

She glanced up at him. "You've never bought flowers?"

"Nope. I'm not really a flowers kinda guy."

"And yet..."

"And yet." He stepped closer, crowding her against the counter. When he set his hands on either side of her, blocking her in, she inhaled sharply. His expression was intense. He scanned her face. "Have I mentioned how sorry I am?"

"Yes. But you only get half the blame. I'm sorry too."

"Accepted. Can we skip to the part where I kiss you again?"

"Please." She settled her hands on his waist as he leaned in and set his lips on hers. Her entire body relaxed as he claimed her mouth. She hadn't realized how tense she'd been until then. Weeks of frustration and anxiety related to both work and her awkward relationship with Zeke.

She was still wearing the usual scrubs, which were not attractive on anyone but practical for their work. She wished she had showered and dressed in something more appealing, but there hadn't been time.

Zeke had damp hair, jeans, and a navy designer T-shirt on. He looked like a man on a date.

She looked like a woman who'd just come from the lab. She leaned back, breaking the kiss, and met his gaze. "Would you mind if I took a shower? I feel gross, and you smell amazing." She leaned closer and nuzzled his neck, inhaling his scent mixed with whatever soap he'd used.

His hands slid to her waist, and he pulled her closer. "You may if it makes you more comfortable, but don't feel like you have to on my account."

"It would make me feel less self-conscious."

His hands slid to hers. "Go ahead." He permitted her one of his rare smiles.

"You'll wait?"

"Of course."

She blew out a breath. "Thanks." After ducking under his arm, she hurried through to her bedroom and into the bathroom. The hotel setup of the suites meant no one had a large space, but they were new and much better than driving back and forth into town every day.

In the last few months, no one had been permitted to leave the facility without a good reason anyway. It was lucky for them that they had enough housing to accommodate everyone. More trailers were being brought in every few weeks too.

Eventually the bunker would be bursting at the seams. She wondered if Temple was still considering transferring some people.

Michelle shut the bathroom door, turned on the water, and shed her clothes to drop them in the hamper. The second the water was warm enough, she slid inside. Normally she could shower quickly. She wasn't a high maintenance kind of woman. But tonight, she wanted to shave and take a little extra care. Just in case.

Feeling rushed, she worked fast, and got out in short order, only to realize she didn't have any clothes in the bathroom. "Shit," she muttered. Had she shut the bedroom door?

She dried off, combed through her hair, and wrapped the towel around her. If she could quietly slip into the bedroom, maybe he wouldn't notice her tiptoeing to the closet.

Her plan was completely thwarted when she opened the door softly to find him lying on her bed. He was on his side, head propped in his hand, facing her, smiling.

She licked her lips. "I forgot clothes."

"Do you really need them?"

She inched closer. "Depends."

"Depends on what?" he asked narrowing his gaze.

"On whether or not you intend to keep yours on."

He smiled. "That's up to you. I'm in favor of the idea, if you are. But, I don't want to be presumptuous."

She was only a few feet away from him when she spoke next. "You're in my bedroom, lying on my bed, looking good enough to eat, and you don't think that's presumptuous?"

He reached out a hand and snagged her wrist, pulling her the rest of the way to the edge of the bed until her thighs hit the mattress. "Will it be presumptuous if I tug that towel off you and lick the last drips of water from your body?"

She gasped. Her nipples were hard points. Her sex was now wetter than she'd been in the shower.

He lifted a finger and traced it along the top edge of her towel. "Am I moving too fast? I'll stop if you want. I couldn't help myself. When you said you were going to take a shower…and I couldn't keep from picturing you naked…and then you came out without clothes…"

"Not too fast," she whispered. She would have had sex with him every time he'd been in her suite if he hadn't been so damn cautious. He somehow managed to chase all common sense from her mind when he was around.

He was also a different man when they were alone together. At work, he was quiet, reserved, serious, stern. As soon as he was alone with her, he changed. He somehow managed to talk and smile and flirt and make her body hum with need.

She gave him a playful shove so he fell onto his back, and then she climbed up next to him and settled against his chest on her side. As she stared down at his face, she knew for certain she wanted to have sex with him.

To hell with reason. She hadn't had sex in many years, and she was strung so high she was going to implode soon. Deciding she should mention that fact, she blurted out, "I'm going to fumble. I haven't been with a man in a long time."

"Well, technically I haven't had sex in fourteen years," he joked. "So I have you beat."

She swatted at his chest. "Ten of those don't count, but I'll still give you the point."

"Are we keeping score?" he teased.

"No. Just warning you that I'm not that experienced and it's been a while. I might embarrass myself."

He chuckled deep and low. And then he flattened her on her back and swapped positions so he hovered over her from his side. "I may have been married, but you should know Meredith was my only sex partner, and it became obvious fairly quickly that she didn't have any interest in sleeping with me, so it didn't happen often. I'm about as nervous as a man can be at the age of thirty."

She slid her hand up his arm. "Don't be. We'll agree that the first one doesn't count, get it awkwardly out of the way, and then start over. Okay?"

He laughed. "Michelle, every second I'm with you counts. Holding you like this while you're wearing a towel counts. Kissing you counts. Looking into your eyes counts. I'm counting the seconds until I can see you naked and run my tongue across your nipples."

A chill raced up her body. He was so damn articulate when it mattered. And apparently it mattered. She stared into his eyes as he held her gaze for a long time.

Slowly, his hand came to her waist, and then he slid it up to the spot where she'd tucked the towel in above her chest. Still holding her gaze, he tugged the towel free and pushed it aside.

The cool air of the room made her shiver, but when he set his hand on her stomach, she absorbed his warmth.

His gaze burned a hole in her until he finally lowered it to her lips and then lower. His actions felt incredibly reverent as he turned his attention to her chest, his hand easing up to cup her breast.

Her nipple jumped to attention, the stiff peak growing incrementally tighter under his perusal.

His fingers danced around her chest, eliciting exactly the

response any woman would have to such contact. Each time he grazed a finger over a nipple, she arched slightly. When he circled the sensitive tip, she bit into her lower lip. If he kept this up, she might come from him worshiping her chest alone.

She was powerless to intervene in any way. Her brain wasn't firing right. She couldn't even convince her arms to lift from her sides. Instead, she only managed to fist her fingers in the towel and sheets beneath her.

Finally, he leaned over and took one nipple in his mouth, suckling it gently. He flicked his tongue over the tip rapidly, making her part her lips on a moan.

Perhaps emboldened by her reaction, he nudged her legs apart with his jean-clad knee and settled it between her thighs.

Somehow she found the will to lift her free hand and grab his waist. She smoothed her fingers under his shirt, finding warm skin that she needed to see more of. "Off. Zeke. Take off...your clothes."

He lifted his face a few inches, smiling. "I'm busy."

"Get un-busy. Please. You're making me self-conscious."

He tugged his shirt over his head, obliging her at least in part, and then he surprised her by sitting up and undoing his jeans. He leaned back to lift his hips, and then the denim disappeared, his underwear with it.

Finally, he was as naked as her, his erection pressing into her thigh as he resumed his position leaning over her. "Happy?"

"Very."

His lips covered her nipple again, sucking harder this time. His hand was at her waist, pressing her into the mattress as if he realized she was about to squirm out of his reach.

When his knee resumed its place between her legs, she moaned. Her fingers found his biceps. Her nails dug into his skin. "Zeke..."

He lifted his face a few inches, letting his fingers take over the exploration of her nipple. "Damn, I like that sound."

"What sound?" she murmured, trying to meet his gaze through the haze of her arousal.

He pressed his thigh against her sex and pinched her nipple.

She moaned.

"That sound."

"Zeke…" He was killing her.

"And that sound too. My name on your lips." He gave her nipple a slight twist, watching her face.

She arched.

"Too much?"

"No. Just right." She had no idea how she was able to communicate, but somehow she managed, knowing he needed her words.

After squeezing her breast in his hand, he flattened his palm on her belly and smoothed it down toward her sex. He was still watching her face, unnerving in his intensity. When his middle finger reached her clit and stroked across it, her mouth fell open and she cried out.

"Oh, yeah. That sound is even better."

She licked her lips, but couldn't speak. Her eyes rolled back, but she could still feel his gaze.

He slid his fingers lower, stroked two of them through her folds, and spread her wetness over her clit.

She squeezed his arm. "I'm gonna come."

"That's the idea."

She rolled her head to one side, slightly embarrassed. She had never felt this raw. Exposed. Mostly because no man had ever made her feel like this before.

When he slid one finger inside her, she pursed her lips against the urge to scream and braced her body to keep from coming.

"Uh-uh. Don't stop it. I want to watch you come undone."

She released her breath while he stroked in and out of her, pressing his palm against her clit. In seconds, she was on the edge and then she fell over.

She wasn't sure what sound she made, but it didn't seem human or hers.

He continued to stroke in and out as the pulsing subsided, leaning in to kiss her lips gently. "Beautiful. I had no idea..."

She tried to focus, licking her dry lips, finding her voice as his hand stilled. "No idea about what?"

"About what a woman looked like when she really let go and enjoyed herself."

"But..."

He shook his head. "Apparently not all women do that, or let themselves, or find me attractive, or whatever."

She cringed. "She's a fool."

"That's been well established."

"I'm not her."

"Also well established."

She slid her hand down to meet his, pressing his palm against her deliciously. "Please, Zeke. Don't make me wait any longer."

"You're sure? I don't want you to feel pressured."

She smiled. "Never been more certain of anything."

He climbed between her legs, his elbow shaking slightly. "This is going to last two seconds."

She ran her hands up and down his waist. "That's okay. In fact, it will make me feel powerful knowing I'm the cause."

He smiled, shaking his head. "You're excellent for my ego."

"That's the plan." She reached between them and wrapped her hand around his length, stroking up and down slowly.

He moaned. "Michelle..."

She gripped his back with her free hand and lined him up with her entrance. "Now."

He pursed his lips and closed his eyes as he slid into her.

It was tight. It had been so long. But she didn't make a sound for fear she would freak him out more than he already was.

When he was fully seated, he blew out a breath and opened his eyes. "Jesus."

"Nope. Still Michelle."

He grinned. "Woman…"

"Now, that's correct." She lifted her hips against him. "Do it again."

He pulled almost out and then thrust back in. The next time, he moaned. "Oh, God." His words were low and breathy. After two more strokes, he groaned loudly and held himself deep inside her.

His entire body quivered with his orgasm as he set his forehead on the bed next to her. She swore she could feel every pulse coming from him until he finally settled part of his weight over her, still gasping for air. "Thank you," he whispered into her ear.

She giggled. "Okay, you don't have to thank me for having sex with you. It's my pleasure."

He lifted his face. "I'm thanking you for taking a chance on me. For caring enough to pursue me. For pushing me. For being who you are."

She swallowed the emotion that bubbled up inside her, unable to respond.

He slid out of her, settled at her side, and stroked his fingers up and down her arm and then across her chest. When he found her hand and brought her fingers to his lips to kiss them reverently, she felt a tear slide out. She left it, hoping he wouldn't notice her silly emotional reaction.

Suddenly, he jerked his head up, concern etched across his face. "I didn't use a condom."

She patted his arm. "I'm on the pill."

He exhaled. "Jesus, I'm sorry. That was stupid of me."

"Not a problem. I assume after fourteen years, you're clean. And I am too."

"Of course, but I still should have been more thoughtful."

She slid her hand up to his cheek. "You're far more thoughtful than you give yourself credit for. Stop being so hard on yourself.

No one else is."

He held her gaze. "You continue to amaze me."

"I could say the same."

"Give me five minutes and I'll do it again, better this time."

"Three minutes, and you have a deal," she said as she squirmed against him. Already her body was craving more.

He chuckled, the sound vibrating through her body. It was the best feeling in the world.

She prayed to God he didn't get cold feet again and back out because of his self-doubts.

CHAPTER 11

When Michelle woke up, she was alone. A glance at the clock told her it was early. The sun wasn't up. The bed was warm next to her. Zeke must have left recently.

She rolled over to find a note on the pillow.

I went to the gym. Tried not to wake you. See you in a few hours.

He added a smiley face. She laughed. A smiley face. From Zeke.

Michelle dragged herself out of bed, knowing sleep would not return. Besides, she had slept fantastically for the approximately six hours since they had turned out the lights. Considering she had never slept with anyone before, she was surprised at how well she rested. She had even snuggled into his side for a while until she got too hot.

She felt lighter and more relaxed as she showered and dressed. A half hour later, she was in the cafeteria grabbing a bagel. Kate and Emily were sitting together across the room, and she joined them. As she slid into the seat next to Kate, she said, "You two can stop dancing around me. Zeke and I worked things out."

Emily's face lit up across from her. "You did?"

Michelle nodded.

Kate gave a strained smile. "So happy for you."

Michelle remembered yesterday had been the day Graham Wentz had been moved from the reanimation chamber to a room. He would spend the next four weeks in an induced coma with the other three people in his group. But Kate might be preoccupied over the transfer. "Did everything go okay yesterday?" she asked.

Kate nodded. "Yes. All four of the latest patients were successfully moved. The last two people on our team started the process earlier this morning."

There were four chambers now. Twenty of the twenty-two preserved people had been through that stage. Only two remaining souls needed to be revived. It would relieve a lot of stress when this process was over.

Michelle grabbed her hand and gave a brief squeeze. "He'll be fine."

Kate chuckled lightly. "I'm not sure why it matters. I'm being ridiculous. He didn't know who I was before we were preserved. Why would he now?"

Emily set down her fork. "He knew who you were. He's just shy or something. And we were busy. And then we were all dying."

"True."

Michelle shuddered. "Some days I feel like I've slipped into another dimension. Half the people I live and work with were technically dead for the last decade. I'm starting to forget which ones are which." Not really, but it *was* getting confusing.

"Ladies." Ryan slid into the chair next to Emily with a tray of food. Damon took the seat next to him.

Emily leaned around Ryan to speak to Damon. "Everything okay with the last two patients?"

"Yes. We moved them into the reanimation chambers earlier. It's a relief in a way."

"It's also probably a letdown," Ryan pointed out.

Michelle had to imagine he was right. Reviving the twenty-two souls had been Damon's entire reason for existing for years. Now his work was almost done. "What will you do next? After these last two are reanimated, I mean." she asked him. She had personally worked with him for over two years.

Damon sighed. "I've already been reassigned."

Everyone stiffened. Obviously it was news to them all.

"Where?" Ryan asked.

"Another bunker," he stated, giving them almost no information.

"Holy shit. I knew there was talk of transferring some of us, but I didn't visualize it happening so fast." Emily's eyes were wide.

Michelle took a breath. "I'm not surprised. There are a number of government bunkers all over the country. We've all known for a while there were other locations under the Project DEEP group. We just haven't been connected. I've often wondered what the heck they're working on. Sometimes I suspect they could be working on the same things as us in order to see if more than one location comes up with the same solutions to problems."

Emily shuddered across from her. "That gives me the chills."

Ryan nodded. "Yeah, but it explains how Temple has other locations to send us to."

Damon didn't look thrilled. Understandable. This was his team.

"You have details yet?" Ryan asked him.

He shook his head. "No, but if I did, I'm sure I wouldn't be at liberty to tell you. I suspect they won't tell me where I'm going until I'm there."

Michelle swallowed. She didn't want to see Damon transferred. She didn't want to see any of them transferred, and yet it seemed like their days were numbered. It was inevitable. Clearly Temple didn't realize the importance of them staying connected, or she felt that splitting them up would be more beneficial.

Michelle was still grappling with this news when Zeke slid into the chair next to her, across from Damon. "Everyone okay? You all look like you just heard bad news." He set his hand on Michelle's thigh under the table and gave a quick squeeze before removing it to set his elbows on the table. His gaze met hers, brows drawn together in concern.

"The last two people went into the reanimations chambers today. Damon is getting transferred soon," Michelle informed him.

Kate and Emily were moving food around on their plates with their forks.

Zeke turned to face Damon across from him and groaned.

After spending a fantastic night with Zeke, this morning was taking a serious nosedive. Michelle wanted to escape reality, return to her room, and crawl back into her bed with Zeke by her side. For the first time in her life, she had relaxed and let her guard down with a man. It had been amazing.

She knew the future held no guarantees. Their lives were up in the air. If Damon could get transferred, any of them could. In a heartbeat. There was unrest. Now was a terrible time to start a relationship.

Nevertheless, Michelle wanted to feel every ounce of what she'd felt with Zeke again tonight. She wanted a repeat performance. As many of them as she could get before the floor fell out from under them. No way was she going to allow another wasted day to go by without seizing her opportunities. They might still have differences, but these early days of a new relationship were invigorating. They breathed life into her.

She glanced at Zeke and swore she could read the same thing she felt on his face.

Good.

"Guess we better get to work," she said, shoving from the table and grabbing her tray. The sooner she got her day job done, the sooner she could find her way back into Zeke's arms.

Ten hours later Zeke leaned over Michelle's shoulder, knowing his proximity would get her attention. "Your fancy beige suite or mine?"

She smiled at the same question he'd posed to her a few weeks ago. "Yours," she responded.

"Meet you there in ten?" She hadn't been to his room yet, but then again, it didn't make any difference. The suites were identical with the exception of whatever people had added to make them more personal. Zeke hadn't added anything. He'd only been awake two months. He hadn't left the bunker.

Ten minutes later, he found himself smiling as he opened the door to Michelle. He wasn't even the same man he'd been two months ago, or fourteen years ago for that matter. A weight had been lifted from his shoulders at the prospect of something normal in the midst of all the chaos around them.

Granted, there were no guarantees. But there never were in life. He and Michelle hadn't spoken about many important topics. So far, all they'd basically done was trade growling for fucking. And he was okay with that. For now.

Based on the way she grabbed his waist and backed him up until he found himself in the bedroom, he had to believe she was on the same page of the same book.

"Guess we're going to skip the chit chat." He chuckled as she reached for the hem of his scrubs and pulled the shirt over his head.

"We're going to skip the foreplay too." Her hand landed on his erection next, her fingers wrapping around it through the thin material of his scrubs.

He moaned, and then he wrenched free of her grasp by jerking to one side and grabbing her wrist. He spun her around and shoved her onto the mattress.

She fell with a light bounce, giggling. Without him saying another word, she pulled her shirt over her head and then wiggled out of her pants. Her bra and panties went next, and then she was naked. On his bed. In his suite.

She was so damn gorgeous.

He was afraid to blink in case this was a figment of his imagination. He kicked off his shoes and stepped out of his pants, and then he climbed onto the bed, hovering over her.

Last night it had taken him two rounds before he could make love to her properly without coming prematurely. He wasn't sure tonight was going to be any different. Already his length was reaching for her.

When he had his hands planted at her sides, his knees between her legs, she reached for him. Her small palm stroked up and down his length, so lightly he had to grit his teeth.

His erection strained into her touch.

"I want to taste you," she whispered.

He jerked his gaze from where her hand held him to her face. If she wrapped her lips around him, he would come way way way too fast. "Someday," he promised.

She shook her head. "Today." She released him and shoved onto her elbows. "Roll onto your back."

He stopped breathing. He'd gone his entire life without experiencing a blow job. His ex had never even suggested such a thing, and he had never been the sort of guy who would pressure a woman to suck him off.

But Michelle was pushing on his shoulders now, squirming out from under him.

His arms were shaking as he flipped onto his back. He cupped her face. "You don't have to do this."

She tipped her head so that her lips found his palm and gently kissed him before flicking her tongue there. "I know. I want to."

She leaned forward to kiss his lips and then nibbled a path down his chin, neck, and chest. As she teased his skin with her mouth, she crawled down his body.

His erection bobbed in anticipation. He threaded his fingers in her hair. "Michelle, I'm going to come too fast for this."

She lifted her face, and both brows rose. "It'll be good for my ego. I've never done this before."

He swallowed. "Well, I've never had this done to me before either."

She smiled. "Perfect. Then neither of us will know if we do it wrong."

"Baby, there can't possibly be a *wrong* as long as your teeth don't get involved."

She giggled against his length as she flattened her body along his legs and wrapped her hand around the base. When her tongue darted out to lick the tip, he nearly shot off the bed. He had to plant his hands at his sides and fist the comforter to ground himself.

When she slid her tongue down his entire length, he held his breath. He had seriously been missing out. She didn't even need to take him into her mouth for him to come. He was certain of it. Precome leaked from the tip already. His erection was pulsing.

Nevertheless, Michelle wrapped her lips around the head and gently sucked him into her mouth.

He moaned. *Holy shit.* Last night had been the best night of his life. Tonight was looking to top it already.

As she lifted back off until just the tip was in her mouth, she swirled her tongue around and around it, driving him mad with the desire for her to suck him back into her warmth.

He lifted his head to watch her, his neck straining at the sight of her breasts bouncing on his thigh, her small hand wrapped around the base of his length, and her lips swollen and eager on the head.

His neck couldn't support him any longer when every ounce

of his blood seemed to flow to his erection. He dropped his head back and stared at the ceiling.

Michelle sucked him into her mouth again, deeper this time. And then she bobbed up and down several times, increasing the pressure.

His fingers strained to fist the comforter, but he couldn't manage to send any messages to any parts of his body.

Heaven enveloped him. Sheer bliss.

A moment later, she added her hand to the actions of her mouth, drawing her palm up and down his length simultaneously.

That was the last straw. He opened his mouth to warn her, but no sound came out. As the first juts of his come hit the back of her throat, she lowered her mouth and sucked him harder.

Pulse after pulse of his orgasm was forced out of him while Michelle swallowed. Finally, he was spent, and she let his still semi-erect length slide from her lips.

She climbed up his body, straddling him, her warm sex lining up with him, rubbing against him as she set her hands on his chest. When he managed to focus on her face and reach for her biceps, she was flushed. "Did I do it right?" she teased.

"How would I know?"

She lifted a hand and swatted playfully at his shoulder.

For several moments, he stared at her, taking in her beauty. He loved the way her breasts bounced in front of him. Her pink cheeks. Her swollen lips. The glaze covering her eyes. Finally, he had the energy to grab her waist, and he did so, flipping her onto her back in a fluid motion that put him on top and left her gasping.

Her eyes widened and she squirmed beneath him as he shoved her knees apart with his and situated himself between them. "My turn."

"We weren't taking turns," she pointed out. "I had the urge to do that, so I did it. Reciprocity wasn't expected."

He shot her a grin. "Even better." His gaze roamed down her

body next, taking in her stiff nipples and the goose bumps that rose on her breasts making her shudder. She might not have anticipated him going down on her, but she was excited by the prospect.

He was too. Another first. His ex had never shown any interest in anything but quick, missionary-style sex. In retrospect, she had only done even that much out of some sense of obligation to a man she barely tolerated and only married for money.

The woman beneath him now made his blood pump. He'd never imagined anything like this happening for him. Michelle was so into him. Really and truly into him. She was not faking, which as the only sex he'd ever known. He'd never wanted anything more in his life. He bent forward to suck her stiff nipple between his lips first. She arched her chest on a moan, her hands going to his forearms.

When he switched to her other breast, she squirmed again. "Zeke..."

He suckled the tip for a minute and then kissed a path down to her belly, situating himself between her legs. When he inhaled her arousal, he closed his eyes, memorizing her enticing scent.

She wiggled some more, so he grabbed her thighs and held them wider, pressing them against the mattress. "Talk to me while I taste you, baby," he said, lifting his gaze to hers. "I won't know what you like if you don't speak."

She was panting as she repeated his words. "I'm so aroused, it's like you said. As long as you don't use your teeth, I'm going to come really fast." She licked her lips. "Actually, you can probably even use your teeth, but don't draw blood."

He held his breath at those words, unable to think of anything hotter than grazing his teeth along her clit. Last night she had come from minimal attention to that swollen little bundle of nerves. He had every confidence he could do the same only better tonight with his mouth.

Without warning, he lowered his lips to her clit and flicked his tongue over the pink nub.

She moaned, trying to squirm away from the contact.

He held her tightly, though, and closed the distance so he could suck her clit and the surrounding area into his mouth.

"Jesus." Her hands landed on his shoulders, her nails digging into his skin.

He didn't care. In fact, he loved her reaction. Emboldened, he lowered his mouth to thrust his tongue into her tight heat. Arousal coated her entire sex. Intoxicating. The reaction to the invasion of his tongue hadn't been as violent as what he'd done to her clit, so he kissed his way back to the bundle of nerves and proceeded to suck, flick, and tease her.

She writhed beneath him, panting heavily, pushing or pulling on his shoulders. He had no idea which. She probably didn't know either.

"Zeke..."

He loved the way she moaned around his name. Already he recognized the tone of her voice that indicated she was close. When he flattened his tongue against her clit and lathed it slowly with as much pressure as he could apply, she cried out.

He felt her orgasm against his lips and tongue, the pulsing of her sex as she came. Her legs shook, and when the pulses subsided, she shivered.

He kissed her sex one last time and climbed up her body to hover over her. "Sexiest thing I've ever seen. Thank you."

Her eyes were closed, but she giggled in a deep voice. "Feel free to do it any time, if it pleases you that much."

He wiped her arousal from his lips with the back of his hand and then nuzzled her neck as he slid to one side to line his body up with hers. "I guess I did okay?" he teased.

"How would I know?" she responded, that giggle vibrating through them both again.

It warmed his heart that they shared so many firsts together.

He seriously doubted most people managed to enjoy sex as much as the two of them did with so little experience between them. He'd expected them to fumble around until they got it right, but that was not what was happening. Every single touch was right. Perfect. Beyond expectation.

She ran her hand up and down his arm. "Do you wonder if our entire relationship is based on sex?" she whispered.

He lifted his head to meet her gaze, frowning. "I hope not."

She shrugged, glancing away. "I'm just pondering."

"I can understand that, but I look at it this way, any two people can have sex and get off, but I would think a deeper connection has to exist to enjoy it as much as we have with each other."

God, he hoped he was right. If this was an anomaly simply because they were under a great deal of stress and living in tight quarters with very few options, he would be extremely disappointed.

He'd never had a connection like this with a woman in his life. It was beyond his dreams. But she had a point. Perhaps they were both desperate enough for human contact that they couldn't see things through normal eyes.

CHAPTER 12

Two days later when Michelle slid onto a chair in the cafeteria with her breakfast tray, she was exhausted. Spending her nights wrapped around Zeke was amazing, but the lack of sleep was taking its toll on her. Him too.

He took the seat next to her with the usual gang of friends and coworkers, but his shoulders were drooping, and he didn't move to pick up his fork for several moments, finally doing so with a deep breath.

Yeah, they needed to slow down. They also hadn't exchanged much in the way of conversation. They were living on borrowed time, never certain if one of them would get transferred. It was as if they'd silently chosen to seize the day when it came to their incredible sexual chemistry, and put off worrying about tomorrow.

Half of her simply didn't care if their relationship was based on sex. It felt good. They were in agreement on that. It made the days go by faster and the nights more bearable. She hadn't realized she'd been so lonely until she started sharing a bed with Zeke.

When she lifted her face, she found Emily smirking at her. "Some people aren't getting enough sleep."

The same look was pasted on everyone's face, making Michelle flush. Even though this small group of close friends knew that Michelle and Zeke had hooked up, for lack of a better term, Michelle didn't think most of the bunker was privy to the change in relationship status.

Neither of them flaunted their attraction in front of anyone else. They didn't touch each other during the day beyond the casual bump of hands or thighs. They were too busy. Everyone was busy. The days were filled with everyone rushing around trying to tie up loose ends as a sense of urgency took over in the lab. It was clear that Temple was going to split them up soon, though the only mentions of it were in hushed whispers.

Suddenly, an ominous air filled the space when Temple stepped up to the end of the table and leaned forward, setting her hands on the surface. "I need all of you in the conference room in five." She shoved off the table and hurried away without waiting for a response. Two other tables were occupied and she stopped at them also.

Michelle didn't like the vibe at all.

Zeke's hand landed on her thigh again, another gentle squeeze. Reassuring her or himself. It didn't matter.

She'd lost her appetite and rose with everyone else to dump her tray and head for the conference room.

It was crowded when they got there. Tushar was standing at the far end of the room, Trish next to him. Temple had joined them, but she was leaning against the back wall. It seemed that Tushar would be conducting this meeting.

Michelle squeezed in along the far wall with Zeke at her side, the rest of their friends also finding places to stand. The bunker wasn't constructed with the thought of ever having giant meetings. The only room that could have accommodated this group was the cafeteria, and Michelle wondered why they hadn't used the larger room.

Zeke set a hand on her lower back and leaned in to whisper in her ear, "I have a bad feeling about this."

"You and me both."

When Tushar cleared his throat, the uneasy whispering came to a halt. Someone also shut the door. "Sorry about the disruption, but we have a problem." He took a deep breath and continued. "It came to our attention this morning that a bunch of classified information is spreading around outside."

Several people gasped.

Zeke grabbed Michelle's hand and held it. They hadn't discussed how they wanted to handle their relationship in public yet, or even how to define it, but she was glad he lent her his strength, and there was no way anyone would notice the gesture in the crowded room.

She wondered how many of the people working in the bunker were privy to the fact that a woman was undercover outside.

Tushar continued, "There's almost assuredly a mole inside this bunker. Perhaps this room. We called all of you in first because you're all members of either the first or the second team of scientists and doctors. We'll address the rest of the staff next. I can't possibly express how serious this issue is.

"Lives are at stake. Our own. Our families. Our friends. I'm saddened to have to call this meeting. I had hoped the source of the leak might have come from someone outside, but that doesn't seem likely anymore." He glanced around the room, sadness filling his eyes.

Michelle licked her dry lips and held on tight to Zeke's hand. At least she knew he couldn't be the leak. He hadn't been reanimated when things started going haywire. Besides, why would a member of his own team try to sabotage the project?

Temple stepped toward Tushar. "I'll be calling all of you into my office today, a few at a time. Until we get to the bottom of this, please be diligent about keeping confidential information to yourselves. Anything that doesn't apply to someone else, doesn't need to be said out loud."

Everyone nodded.

"Thank you." Temple left the room, and everyone else slowly filed out after her.

It was almost lunchtime when Zeke felt a hand on his shoulder and turned to find Michelle looking down at him. "Temple wants to see you and me." She looked tired. Nervous. Stressed.

He set his hand on top of hers and then released her as he stood to follow her. He didn't say a word as they made their way down the hallway toward Temple's office, but everyone in the lab and any other room along the way lifted their gaze. The tension in the bunker was palpable.

It's like they were each getting called into the principal's office and would continue until one of them ratted out the kid who narced.

"Shut the door," Temple stated as they came inside.

Zeke did as she asked and took a seat next to Michelle, across from Temple.

Temple sighed, leaning back in her chair. "I'm exhausted, and I don't know a damn thing more than I did at eight this morning."

Zeke nodded.

"I can't imagine either of you being involved, of course, but I had to call you both in to be fair to the entire staff."

Michelle glanced at Zeke. "Well, it can't be Zeke. He wasn't here when things started."

"That's what I keep telling myself, but frankly at this point I don't trust anyone. It's possible more than one person is in on the ruse and any member of the first team could have been recruited."

Michelle gasped. "Lord, that's preposterous."

Temple lifted a brow. "If you run down the list of the new team, can you come up with anyone who would be sabotaging this project?"

Michelle flinched. "Of course not."

"I rest my case. Unless it's a member of the support staff who's digging around finding information, I don't know where to start."

"There are significantly more people helping out in the cafeteria and with the cleaning and at the gate now. But weren't they well vetted before they had clearance?" Zeke asked. It was impossible to imagine anyone inside that bunker who was there for any capacity to be sharing information with the outside. And yet someone was.

"They were. The amount of background checks and paperwork our employees go through is significant." She sighed. "I'm out of ideas."

"Could it be a hacker? Someone from outside?" Michelle asked.

Temple shook her head. "I've thought of that. It's possible, but some of the information being leaked isn't anywhere on our computer system." She inhaled deeply. "And, I need to tell you something else." She glanced at Zeke. "We're going to move quite a few people to other facilities next week. Since you've decided to stay on with Project DEEP, I'm hoping you're caught up enough to transfer. I need an immunologist in another location."

Zeke's breath caught in his throat. He couldn't move. After a few too many seconds, he spoke, his voice wobbly. "Where, exactly, is this other bunker?"

"It's classified."

Michelle's hands were shaking in her lap, and she wiped them on her thighs, her back straightening as he watched her out of the corner of his eye. "Are there people preserved in this other bunker?"

Temple shook her head. "I can't tell you that either. The details at other locations are as classified as the ones here."

Zeke wanted to reach out and set a calming hand on Michelle's shoulder, but he didn't dare. Obviously, Temple had no idea the two of them had developed a personal relationship. It also didn't seem prudent to tell her. It shouldn't be taken into consideration with regard to their jobs for the government anyway.

He did, however, realize it was improbable that many other government employees were preserved elsewhere since their families would have come out of the woodwork demanding answers in recent months.

It hadn't taken long for someone from every family of the preserved to contact the government inquiring about their loved one after word spread that Emily and then Tushar and Trish had been reanimated.

Zeke's own parents had been growing increasingly frustrated lately that he didn't have permission to leave the bunker, nor were ordinary visitors permitted on the premises. Honestly, he might have pushed Temple harder to arrange something if he weren't concerned about bringing danger to his own parents' doorstep.

So, he put them off with half-truths and made do with FaceTime and phone calls. At least with today's technology it was easy to see them and vice versa.

Were there other families scattered around the country wondering about sons and daughters who might be preserved in other bunkers?

It didn't take a rocket scientist to assume that if Damon had already been told he would be transferred, there was likely at least one person preserved elsewhere. Which meant what? Did their families think they were dead instead of preserved?

Temple spoke again. "I can tell you that the two reanimation chambers that are no longer needed at this facility will be moved later today. We don't need them here, and we *do* need the space." She glanced down and tidied up a stack of paper on her desk.

In other words, *yes*, there most certainly were at least two people in need of the chambers somewhere else, most likely the same location where Damon was being sent. Zeke had to wonder if he also was being sent to the same location.

He pinched the bridge of his nose with two fingers.

"Even civilian spouses will no longer be permitted inside this facility. Elena Custodio is going to have to leave," Temple added.

Michelle shook her head. "Come on, that's too much. I don't believe for a minute Elena is a threat to anyone. She's just a woman in love with her husband. She was in love with him before he got sick too."

"It's too risky. And I'm not the one calling the shots. The orders are coming from higher up."

Zeke cringed. He'd spoken to Elena. Not a chance in hell the woman was sharing secrets. She was consumed with her husband. She would never risk reconnecting with him for anything.

"I'm sorry. It's going to be a little chaotic around here while we go through these changes. Everyone is understandably on edge. It would help if both of you try to keep people calm. Don't let hysteria take over. It's not necessary. No one should be sharing information or their own personal orders." She closed her eyes. "Please, both of you, just let me know if anything seems out of the ordinary."

"Of course," Zeke responded, wanting to get out of this office that suddenly seemed to be suffocating him. He set his hands on the arms of his chair. "We'll let you get back to it."

Temple stood. "Thanks for coming in," she said as if nothing earthshaking had just happened.

"Any time," Michelle whispered as she followed Zeke to the door. She stayed on his heels as they walked down the hall, not uttering a word.

He paused at the entrance to the lab, wondering if she might like to go somewhere else and talk, but she walked right by him without meeting his gaze. Her hands were shaking—no, her entire body was shaking. And she lifted her fingers to wipe her brow as if she were also sweating.

He decided the best thing to do would be to let her be, since she didn't seem interested in facing him at the moment. Instead, he went back to his desk and tried to concentrate on the research he was working on. Myasthenia Gravis was a top priority for reasons he couldn't fathom. He'd done some research to find that indeed there had been an escalation in incidences of Myasthenia Gravis in the last decade, but the same could be said of about a dozen other diseases and viruses too.

As he set his hand on his mouse, two more people left the room to head to Temple's office. He wondered which ones she grilled and which ones she assumed were not a risk factor.

A glance over his shoulder told him Michelle was also hard at work. Her back was to him, and she was leaning over a microscope. It was weird not being able to speak freely to her, but most people had no idea the two of them were together.

They hadn't discussed when or if they wanted to out themselves as a couple. Hell, all they'd done was have sex every night. She'd agreed readily enough to keeping them a secret. Maybe she never wanted anyone to know. He wasn't sure he didn't agree.

CHAPTER 13

After several stressful hours in the busy lab, Michelle couldn't take the volume anymore. She hadn't been able to focus on a thing the entire day. She'd even skipped lunch because her stomach felt like it might revolt if she tried to swallow.

She suddenly decided she needed to get away from the chaos, grabbed her laptop, and headed for the door. With no particular destination in mind, she wandered down the hallway until she came to the conference room. No one was using it, so she slid inside, took a seat at the far end of the table, and opened her laptop.

There was still no way she could focus on the words on her screen, but at least she could pretend to be intently studying the computer while she silently freaked out inside.

If someone would have asked her last week if she cared whether Zeke stayed at the bunker or left, she would have said good riddance. But that was before she'd started sleeping with him. She'd seen a side of him she was certain few people—if any—ever saw. Tender. Compassionate. Caring.

He was a generous and considerate lover who'd ensured she was well taken care of several times every night. She'd had more orgasms than she could count. And not the sort of orgasms that left a woman feeling like something was missing either.

He'd rocked her world.

And now he was leaving?

How did he feel about the orders? She'd been afraid to even look at him earlier for fear of finding indifference in his gaze.

Coward.

She must have been in another dimension because she didn't hear the door open or close or notice that someone else was in the room until suddenly Zeke was sliding into the chair next to her.

She jerked her gaze up. "Shit. I didn't hear you come in."

He didn't give her a smile, though she might have liked to see one. Instead, he ignored her comment and searched her face. His brow was furrowed in concern. "You gonna avoid me for a week?"

Her face flushed. "Of course not."

"Might be easier." His tone was sarcastic.

"Probably," she muttered.

"Or you could talk to me."

She closed her eyes, trying to gather up the courage to face him more fully, and finally lifted her face to hold his gaze. "I don't know what to say."

He didn't respond for several long seconds, and then he took a breath as if his next words were going to be difficult. "The way I figure it, you're either hiding from me and yourself out of self-preservation, or you don't really care that much that General Levenson just told me she was moving me God knows where next week."

An uninvited tear escaped one eye and slid down her face. Michelle wiped it away quickly. "You know that isn't true. Don't go there. I'm doing the best I can just to breathe through the next few hours until I can reasonably escape to my suite and throw a few things against the wall. I'm holding on by a thin thread. Please..."

He set a hand on the table, and for a moment she was certain he'd intended to reach for her, but he stopped himself. "Okay." The one word was breathy. "Come to my suite when you can get away. I think we need to talk. At the very least, if you throw things, they'll have a vacant room to do the repairs after I move out."

She shot him a glare, but found him finally giving her a small grin. He was joking. Sort of. She nodded, biting her lower lip.

Thankfully, he rose and left the room without another word. If he had touched her, she would have fallen apart. If he had said much more, she would have started crying. Luckily, he'd realized her state of mind and left her alone.

She concentrated on two things after he left—breathing and pretending to intently stare at the screen. Her mind easily wandered to analyze her predicament. On the one hand, she'd only been sleeping with him for four nights. Not a lifetime.

You're kidding yourself if you dismiss this as nothing.

On the other hand, it was impossible to ignore how he'd made her feel every one of those nights. Surely most people could move on with their lives after such a whirlwind and not look back.

There was no way to guarantee that just because they had enjoyed several rounds between the sheets they were compatible for a lifetime. It was entirely possible they would have figured out in the next few days or weeks that they couldn't stand each other for any number of reasons.

Perhaps the heat between them had more to do with the fact that they had both been through a long drought than anything else. The passion probably wouldn't last. How could it?

It was also impossible to ignore just how damn good they'd been together. The quiet, reserved, stoic, surly man who worked in the lab was not the same man who came to her when they were alone and drew her into his arms.

He hadn't just fucked her and walked away. He'd made love to her. He'd done so multiple times. He'd held her gaze and made her so hot for him she thought she might self-combust.

There was a vulnerability in his eyes, and she was certain they hadn't begun to scratch the surface of the kind of man he could be. She couldn't face the idea of him being taken away from her before they had a chance to figure things out.

Frustrated and completely unsure what she should do, she squeezed the mouse so tight it was a wonder it didn't break. Maybe she shouldn't meet with him tonight. Maybe it would be easier to end things now instead of spending more time with him and risking her heart.

Would she forever wonder what could have been if she broke things off now and severed ties to avoid hurting more later? That thought pushed her in another direction. Maybe it would be better to spend every second with him in an effort to burn out the relationship fast and make it easier to say goodbye.

What were the chances they could make it together in the long run anyway? The percentage couldn't be high. Any relationship under their circumstances couldn't stand much of a chance at long-term survival. They didn't know each other well enough yet.

Hell, they'd already been through more than one round of miscommunication and insecurity. Sure, they'd worked things out, but it had hardly been smooth sailing since their first kiss. What if these last few nights were an indication of all they might have together though?

She pictured herself going to him every night and making the most of every second they had before he got transferred. They could stay up late, experimenting with every position known to man, talking, eating in bed, sharing wine, showering...

Her heart clenched. She wanted those things. She would shrivel inside if she had them and lost them.

Someone cleared their throat, and Michelle jerked her gaze up to find Temple standing two feet away, leaning against the windowsill. She looked concerned and a little pissed. She didn't hesitate either. "Are you in a relationship with Zeke?"

Michelle jerked in her seat, released the mouse, and spun

toward her boss. "Who told you that?" The only people who knew about their relationship were Emily, Kate, and Ryan. No way would any of them talk about her behind her back. Would they?

"Is it true?"

Michelle licked her lips.

Temple groaned and pushed off the window to pace the room. "Shit. Why the hell didn't you say anything this morning?"

"Would it have made a difference?"

"No. But I would have been more sensitive."

Michelle breathed in and out, trying not to freak out. It would have been easier if Temple hadn't found out.

"How many people know?" Temple asked.

"Three. Ryan, Emily, and Kate."

"Fuck." Temple stopped pacing to slam her palm against the table across the room.

"What's the matter?" Michelle would have stood if she could have gotten her legs to move, but they weren't taking orders from her brain. "What happened?"

"You want to know how I found out about your relationship?" she asked in a tone that suggested the answer would be the last thing Michelle ever wanted to hear.

She held her breath.

"Nicole Salway told me."

Her lungs expelled all her air in a whoosh. "The undercover cop outside?"

Temple nodded. "Whatever is going on between you two is now privy to the entire world because the picketers out front are gossiping."

Michelle slowly shook her head. "I don't understand why that fact is even interesting." *Nor do I understand who would have leaked it.* It was too painful to imagine that Kate, Emily, or Ryan would say a word.

Temple gave a sardonic laugh. "The story quickly took on a life of its own. Imagine this picture—the mourning wife shows up to comfort her reanimated husband only to find out he's sleeping with a coworker." She spun around in a full circle, hands on her hips. "Dammit, I told Zeke to get ahead of anything Meredith might try to pull."

All the blood ran out of Michelle's face. She thought she might faint. "They've been divorced for fourteen years." How the hell could Meredith be involved?

Temple shrugged. "The media didn't quite get those facts, or they chose to ignore them. This way the story sounds so much better," she continued sarcastically. "Apparently the reanimated have the tendency to wake up so mentally altered that they can't control their sexual impulses and will fuck anyone who gets in their path. They are clearly a dangerous menace to society and can't be trusted to reenter normal civilization."

Michelle shook her head slowly, unable to fully process the picture Temple was painting. "That's what they're saying?"

"Yep." She ran a hand over the top of her head, somehow managing to not dislodge a single hair from the perfect gray bun she wore every day at the base of her head.

Michelle leaned her forehead on her palm, elbow to the table. She was shaking. She wasn't at all sure she wasn't still close to hyperventilating. "I'm sorry."

"Me too. Mostly because I know you're hurting." Her words were calmer now.

Michelle lifted her gaze. "I never should have let anything get in the way of my job. I've never acted so unprofessionally in my life."

Temple frowned. "I know I'm in a total panic, but I didn't mean to imply it was your fault. I don't care if you're involved with Zeke. It's probably good for both of you. Living in this claustrophobic environment isn't healthy. What you do in your free time is your business."

And yet Temple had implied it would have been helpful if they had told her.

"I'm much more concerned about why and how this leaked to the picketers out front than who you're spending your nights with."

Michelle nodded.

"I'm going to have to call Ryan, Emily, and Kate into my office. I can't believe for a moment any of them is selling or otherwise provided private information to the outside, but maybe one of them inadvertently told someone else."

It was possible. Hard to believe, but nevertheless possible.

There was only one way to find out. "Can I come with you to talk to them?"

"Sure. Let's go." She spun around and headed out of the conference room so fast that Michelle wasn't positive what she'd just agreed to. Deciding she should follow her boss, she slapped her computer shut, grabbed it off the desk, and headed for Temple's office.

Michelle immediately regretted her decision to sit in on the meeting with the three of her friends. As soon as they entered the room, Michelle felt a sense of dread fill her chest. What if they felt like she was accusing them?

"What's going on?" Ryan asked as the three of them stepped inside Temple's small office. It wasn't really large enough for five people, but they didn't need to sit. Michelle didn't think this would take long.

Michelle met Ryan's gaze. She'd known him for years. Emily and Kate had both been on the original team, meaning Michelle's relationship with them had only existed for months. "Someone leaked to the press that Zeke and I are in a relationship." It sounded ridiculous to even utter out loud since she and Zeke had not defined their status at all yet, nor had she had the opportunity to tell him this shit storm had landed at their feet.

Emily gasped. "Who would do that? And why?"

"That's what we're trying to figure out," Temple stated. "Did any of you tell anyone else, perhaps even inadvertently?"

All three shook their heads. Kate spoke. "Zeke is my friend. Emily's too. There's no way I would utter a word about his private life to a soul. Besides, I don't even know the details. Not my business."

"None of us would leak that sort of thing. And why would we? Who could possibly care?" Emily asked. "This escalation of insanity is out of control. I don't believe for a second any member of either team would talk to the media or anyone else about anything happening inside this bunker.

"We've devoted our lives to Project DEEP. Most of us were recruited into the program while we were still in college. Most of us went to a military academy. Unless one of us was planted to sabotage some unknown future government project, it makes no sense. Whoever that would be would have had to be groomed from a very young age to do something years later that didn't even exist yet." She shook her head. "I'm not buying it. There has to be another explanation."

Michelle agreed. It was ludicrous.

Temple was nodding. "You're right. I can't figure out which direction to turn."

Michelle had a thought. "I had an argument with Zeke one day in Ryan's office. I suppose someone could have walked by and heard us." Hell, someone also could have seen them coming and going from their suites too.

Ryan shook his head. "What difference would it make? Even if half the staff stood outside my office door and pressed their ears to the wood to listen in, it doesn't change the fact that none of them would talk to the media. Interoffice gossip maybe, but that's it."

Emily agreed. "Also, Ryan and I have been together for months now. People have never seemed to care much about it, beyond the truly weird zealots who think I'm an inhuman monster. Why focus on Michelle and Zeke? It's no different."

Temple pursed her lips and threw her hands in the air. "I've got nothing."

"I need to go find Zeke," Michelle stated, stepping toward the closed door. As she set her hand on the knob, she turned around to face them again. "The saddest part of this is that even Zeke and I aren't sure about our relationship status. In real-world terms, we've been seeing each other for less than a month. We have not discussed the future. We don't even have flipping dinner plans.

"At this point anything that might have developed between us in the future is moot since he's being transferred to another bunker next week. I can't stand that the entire world now gets to dig around in my laundry when it was all clean and neatly folded just a few hours ago. Makes me sick."

No one said a word as she left the office, but she did hear Kate ask Temple, "Is that true? You're transferring Zeke?"

"Yes. I'm transferring a lot of people."

CHAPTER 14

Zeke was surprised to find Michelle at the door to his suite when he responded to her knock at five o'clock. "I wasn't expecting you this early." He'd given up the pretense of working about an hour before and left the lab, but he'd expected her to continue working for several more hours.

The expression on her face was nothing like the one he'd seen when he left her in the conference room earlier that day. He would have described her as distracted to the point of tears earlier. Now she looked fit to kill.

"Did I miss something?"

A low rumble of sardonic laughter caught him by surprise. "You could say that."

Great. Just what he needed. More drama. How had his life gone from drama-free to full-on crazy train in so little time?

Michelle stomped around his suite, not meeting his gaze. "Get this—someone leaked to the media that we're an item."

"Pardon? You and me?"

"Yep." She kept pacing with giant heavy steps. "Temple came to me a bit furious we hadn't told her ourselves earlier."

"You're saying someone informed the media you and I are together between our meeting with Temple and now?"

"Yep," she repeated.

"Why the hell would that even be newsworthy?" He thought Michelle's reaction was a little over the top. Sure, it pissed him off that someone would share his private business with the world, but it wasn't worth having a meltdown.

She stopped pacing, set her palms on her hips, and finally met his gaze. "According to Temple, it's like a bad tabloid article. Jilted wife comes to see her poor cryonically preserved husband after a decade in stasis only to find out he's sleeping with a coworker."

"What the fuck?" he snarled. He set his hands on the back of the couch to steady himself, suddenly understanding the reason for her abundant frustration.

She nodded. "You heard me."

"We've been divorced fourteen years by her calendar. How could anyone spread that sort of gossip?" He stiffened. "That bitch." He gritted his teeth as he spoke.

Michelle held out a hand. "Though admittedly I'm not fond of your ex-wife from what you've told me, I've never met her, so I can't claim to know what she's capable of. But I don't see how she had anything to do with this."

"Who else could have been involved? She came here looking for money. Since she didn't get it, she probably sold her sob story to someone, or decided to punish me for once again not being the rich bastard she was hoping to score off of."

Michelle shook her head. "I could understand if she complained about you for any multitude of reasons, but how the hell could she possibly know anything about you and me? We weren't even a thing when she came here. I mean, yeah, she's likely taken the opportunity to look like the victim now, but she wouldn't have known to if someone hadn't leaked the information about us."

She had a point.

"Hell, we haven't even discussed what sort of *thing* we are, and at this point it seems completely irrelevant since you're getting transferred next week. So, basically, what this amounts to is a fling that the entire world has somehow found out about."

Zeke's mind was running fast. She was right.

"It's like there was a camera in my bedroom or yours. Like someone has us under surveillance. I won't be shocked if the next thing we see is a broadcast of you and me fucking on national television."

Zeke's entire body jerked.

Michelle sucked in a sharp breath, staring at him as the full impact of her words hit both of them. "Fuck." She rushed toward the door.

He followed on her heels.

Seconds later, they were in her suite, scouring the place for a camera. They systematically searched every possible location in the living room and the bedroom and found nothing. When they were finished, they rushed back to his room and did the same thing, again coming up empty.

Zeke stopped in the middle of the room and closed his eyes, trying to think. He could hear Michelle breathing heavily across the room. "There has to be a bug," he stated. "Somewhere. Maybe not a camera, but a bug."

"That would explain a lot of things," Michelle agreed. "Not just this, but all the other leaked information. But where?"

"We need to go speak to Temple," he stated, heading out of the bedroom.

Michelle beat him to the door, and she had her hand on the knob when he stopped her by setting his palm over her fingers and closing the gap between them. He set his other hand on her hip. "Take a breath."

"This is important."

"I know it is. But I want you to look at me for a second."

She hesitated.

He spun her around, holding her at the waist and flattening her to the door. "Just to be clear, what we have is amazing. I don't take it lightly. I know we haven't discussed the future yet, but that doesn't mean we aren't going to. It means we haven't had a chance."

She nodded subtly. "Okay."

"Deep breath."

She inhaled slowly and let it out.

"I don't mean to put words in your mouth, but I'm going to go out on a limb here and guess that you've talked yourself into believing we had a few nice fucks and it's over."

She swallowed but didn't respond.

He continued, knowing he was right. "You know that isn't true. We didn't meet in a bar last night and have a drunken wild romp without exchanging phone numbers. We've known each other for two months. We've been building up to this relationship for weeks. It means something. And we will be discussing it later after we talk to Temple."

She nodded, a sigh leaving her mouth. Good, because he was doing his damndest to let her see him, even if it still scared the shit out of him to do so.

He smiled, knowing it would make *her* smile. He may have been a bit of a dick for the last four years—by his clock—since his divorce, but now that he'd seen how Michelle reacted when he gave her even the simplest partial grin, he found he liked eliciting that response. Making her happy felt good.

And it had been a long time since he'd felt anything but bitter and angry.

Two hours later—after someone with a device that could detect bugs had been called to the bunker from the gate—they found the source of their leaks stuck under the table in the conference room.

There was also a nice story circulating in all the major news outlets that quoted Temple from that morning verbatim.

Michelle cringed as she read the story, which included:

"Apparently the reanimated have the tendency to wake up so mentally altered that they can't control their sexual impulses and will fuck anyone who gets in their path. They are clearly a dangerous menace to society and can't be trusted to reenter normal civilization."

Temple was still throwing things around the conference room. "Who the hell could have planted a bug in here?" she asked rhetorically. "And how long has it been there?" She turned toward Zeke. "Do you suppose Meredith did it?"

Michelle felt Zeke stiffen beside her. "I wouldn't put it past her."

Tushar sighed. "Could have been her or it could have happened months ago. There's no way to know for sure. Hundreds of people use this room, and since information has been leaking for ten months, we may never figure it out."

The man from front gate security had put the bug in a baggy and said he would have it analyzed to see if he could figure out where it originated from and even perhaps how long it had been there.

Nearly the entire staff was standing in the hallway. Everyone was on edge and no doubt trying to remember anything they might have said in confidence in this room.

Michelle was still trying to control her heart rate. Her hands were shaking at the total violation of privacy. She'd made the man with the detector go over her entire suite too. And Zeke's. Nothing had been found in either of their rooms, but she was still freaked out to think someone could have watched or even listened to her having sex.

Worse than that was the idea that anyone had ever spied on

her at any time in the last several years, visually or audibly. How humiliating.

As everyone calmed down, Zeke set a hand on her back and waited for her to meet his gaze. "Let's go," he whispered. "There's nothing else anyone can do tonight."

She nodded and let him lead her out of the conference room and past all the staff still rubbing their arms with pale expressions. Some people looked more horrified than others. As past discussions held in this room were recalled over the next several days, they would probably all have at least one cringe-worthy memory come to mind.

"Your suite or mine," he asked as they made their way to the living quarters.

She stopped and faced him. "I'm too tired and angry and confused to be good company. Can we not do this tonight?"

He narrowed his gaze at her. "Your suite or mine?" he repeated, his voice lower.

She inhaled. "Fine. Mine." She turned around and hurried down the hallway, but inside, she was fighting the need to climb into bed alone and have a good cry. She didn't want to argue with him in the hallway in front of other people, however.

As soon as the door shut, she headed straight for her bedroom. "Give me ten minutes to shower and change." *And maybe calm down enough to avoid breaking something.* He could wait ten minutes. In fact, she was certain he would.

She didn't look back as she entered the bathroom, already yanking her scrubs over her head and then dropping her shirt in the hamper. She didn't turn on the light.

Even though someone had thoroughly checked and double-checked her room for bugs, she felt violated in the worst possible way, and the only thing she could think to do to cut down on the likelihood that someone would watch her shower was to leave the lights off.

After flipping on the hot water, she finished stripping and

piled her hair on top of her head while trying to control her breathing. What she didn't notice until hands landed on her hips was that Zeke had followed her.

She flinched at his touch.

"You gonna shower in the dark?"

"Yes."

His breath landed on her ear. "Mind if I join you?"

She wanted to say *yes*. She minded. She needed time alone. That was the reason she was taking a shower. Alone time. But she was afraid to say the wrong things or use the wrong tone of voice in her current state of frustration, so instead, she slid out of his light grip and stepped into the glass enclosure.

While she was still standing under the spray of hot water, he joined her. He pressed his front to her back and wrapped his arms around her middle. And then he began to sway slightly back and forth.

She set her hands on top of his around her waist, and for a long time they stood there. Long minutes. Neither of them spoke.

Surprisingly, she calmed. The water was soothing. Anger and frustration eased from her body. Not all of it. Her mind was still racing.

She was thankful for the darkness. It helped keep her from feeling violated. Nevertheless, she shuddered when she considered the possibility of someone watching her shower. Ever. Besides the obvious nudity, she often masturbated in the shower.

She clenched her teeth at the reminder and the visual of what someone could have seen at some point.

"Shh... I've got you," Zeke murmured. He held her tighter.

She tried to chase the errant thought of being watched from her mind as he reached for the soap and—still holding her with one arm—began to wash her.

It felt nice for someone to take care of her. No one had ever done anything like this since she was a little girl. No man had ever taken the time to pamper her or even care enough to ensure she was satisfied in bed. Zeke had done both of those things.

When his hand ran lightly over her nipples, she sighed. Her body came alive. Moisture pooled between her legs. It seemed crazy to have thoughts of sex after the day they'd had, but she couldn't stop her reaction to his touch.

His erection was also nestled against her butt, teasing her. Tempting her. Making her sex clench.

She moaned involuntarily and lifted onto her tiptoes, gripping his forearm when he slid his fingers between her legs and through her folds.

"I love that sound," he whispered. "Do it again." He eased a finger up into her, and she moaned again.

"Yes… You have no idea how hot it is to know I can turn you on like this. The timing may suck, but my ego is getting a huge boost."

His ex-wife was a total bitch. Forget everything else she might have done to him, the fact that she hadn't given him the confidence to take charge in bed made Michelle furious.

She shook thoughts of Meredith from her mind. The woman had no place in this bathroom. In fact, for a moment Michelle actually wished there was videotape of her having sex with Zeke just to make Meredith jealous of what she gave up.

When he withdrew his hand, her breath hitched. "Zeke…" she begged.

"Mmm." He knew exactly what he was doing. He turned her around, leaned her against the shower wall, and proceeded to finish washing her and then himself.

She could only make out the faintest outline of his body in the near darkness. Neither of them had turned on any overhead lights in the suite, so all they had was the faint ray from a small lamp she always left on in the living room.

When he finished, he turned off the water without a word and opened the door. He took her hand and led her to the rug and then ran his fingers along the wall until he found a towel and tugged it free to pat her dry. Still not uttering a syllable, he used the same towel to dry himself.

She enjoyed the silence and the suspense. Her nipples were hard rocks in the cooler air. Her sex pulsed with need.

He took her hand and led her from the bathroom to the dim light of the bedroom. As if he read her mind, he released her to hurry across the room and shut the door, once again plunging them into near darkness. And then he was back, and he led her to the bed.

After pulling back the comforter and sheet, he climbed in and reached for her, completely covering them up to their necks.

Her heart rate had picked up again when they entered the room naked, but she calmed anew when he pulled her back against his front and spooned her. "Deep breaths," he said, stroking her arm and making her realize she was once again hyperventilating. "No one can see you. I promise."

He couldn't promise no one ever had.

She inhaled slowly over and over until it came naturally.

His fingertips on her arm grazed her breast with each pass. Did he realize he was coaxing her back to full arousal with his touch? Probably, since his erection once against grew to nudge her butt.

"I'm not sure I can stay here any longer to be honest."

"I understand." At least he wasn't condescending. "I feel the same eerie chill up my spine that you do. You're not alone. I'm sure nearly everyone in the bunker is stressed about the idea of having been spied on."

She pursed her lips. Why did he have to be so understanding? It would be easier if he thought she was crazy. Easier to send him packing. Easier to turn him away. Easier to deal with him moving to another facility in a week.

After a while, he let his fingertips trail toward her nipple, circling the tight bud in a maddeningly increasing spiral without touching the turgid tip.

She pressed her butt against his erection, hoping he would get the hint and slide into her.

Instead, he ignored her and flicked his thumb over her nipple.

She moaned loudly.

"Yeah…"

It wasn't as if she could control her reaction to his touch, nor would she ever in her life fake anything sexual with a man, but damn, she was glad to empower him like she clearly did. He deserved to feel virile. His wife had done a job on him.

After a few minutes of teasing her nipple, he rolled her onto her back, cupped her face, and touched her lips with his. The kiss was soft and sweet at first, and then it grew more urgent until his tongue was tangling with hers and a low groan escaped his lips.

She squirmed against him, reached across with her free hand to stroke his length.

He grabbed her wrist and removed her fingers from their intended target. "You can't do that yet. I'll come too soon."

"Isn't that the goal?" she breathed, her first words in a long time. At least she had a small piece of her humor back.

He chuckled. "Eventually, but not until I make you come so hard you can't think."

She gasped. More arousal leaked from her at his words.

"Where are these vibrators you have so many of?"

His question made her stop breathing. She stiffened.

"Don't tell me you were teasing. I've had the best daydreams of you using a thick pink dildo for weeks. I'll die if it wasn't true." His words were light.

She swallowed.

He cupped her face and leaned in close. She was glad he couldn't see her eyes. "Michelle? Talk to me."

"The thought of ever touching one of those again makes me

cringe. My mind keeps wandering to the possibility that someone at some point watched me masturbate."

He kissed her gently. "No one watched you. I feel sure of it. There was no evidence. Besides, you're totally covered up now, and I'm with you. Let me use it on you."

She bit her lip. Half of her melted at how sweet and patient he was being. Half of her wanted to fall through a crack of worry. The first half won out. "Nightstand drawer."

He planted another quick kiss on her lips and then reached across her to open the drawer. After fumbling around in the dark for a few seconds, he returned with a triumphant sigh. "I can't see the color, but I like the size of this one."

She was glad he also couldn't see the flush of her cheeks. If he thought she was going to use it with him next to her, he was crazy.

He slid the tip between her breasts, the coolness of the silicone making her nipples pucker without direct contact. "Spread your legs for me."

She opened her thighs slightly, feeling self-conscious.

He nestled a knee between hers and forced them wider. Trailing the head of the phallic vibrator over her belly, she bit into her lower lip again. This was far more intimate than anything else they'd done together. She wasn't at all sure she was ready for him to see her come like this.

However, she was just off-kilter enough not to put up an argument, and besides, he couldn't see her well in the darkness and she was completely covered by the blanket.

When he lightly touched her clit with the tip of the vibrator, she arched her butt off the bed. "Damn, you're responsive. How many times can I make you come with this thing?"

She turned her head away, freaking out a little at his question.

"Michelle? What's the record?"

"Zeke..."

He turned it on to the lowest setting and tapped her clit.

BECCA JAMESON

She moaned. This wasn't how things usually went between her and the toy. First of all, it was weird for someone else to be controlling it. It made every contact a surprise. Second of all, she'd never been this close to the edge this fast while holding the dildo herself.

Zeke circled the swollen nub and then dipped the tip of the device ever so slightly into her channel, drawing out her arousal.

"Michelle?"

She moaned, her head lolling toward him. "Mmm?"

"You didn't answer me."

What was the question? She flinched as she remembered.

"How many times can you come? What's the record?"

He wasn't going to let up until she answered him, and besides, what did she have to hide? It would be weird if her answer would be something like ten. *That* would be embarrassing, but the truth was far less interesting. "One."

He paused, the tip of the vibrator resting at the entrance to her channel. "One?"

"Yes."

He blew out a relieved breath. "Thank God."

"Why?" She was confused, and so aroused she just wanted him to stop talking and make her come. Any embarrassment she'd felt moments ago fled when he touched her with the dildo.

His mouth came to her ear, his words sending a shudder down her body. "That's a record I know I can break."

Under ordinary circumstances, she would be concerned about a challenge like that. But not tonight. She was completely confident he was right.

When the tip pressed against her clit again, her mouth fell open, and she let the first orgasm wash through her immediately. It was hard to believe the odd-sounding moan filling the room came from her, but she knew it did.

"That is so hot," he whispered into her ear as he slid the vibrator lower and then eased it into her tight channel.

She gripped at it, holding it tight.

He held it deep inside her with a few fingers and used his thumb to stroke over her clit again.

Too much sensation. So good.

Her brain scrambled, and her knees shook.

When he pulled the vibrator out a few inches and tipped it so that it pressed against her G-spot, she gasped and didn't take another breath.

He pressed his thumb against her clit and then flicked it over and over. "Come again for me, Michelle."

She held her breath a bit longer until she couldn't stop the wash of her second orgasm as it plowed forward and drove straight off the tracks. On a long moan, legs shaking, hands fisted in the sheet under her, she came again. There was no doubt he could feel the pulsing because she could feel it all the way up her body.

Before the last tremors subsided, he tossed the vibrator to the side, climbed between her legs, and thrust into her.

She screamed. It felt that good. So much better than the toy. So much fuller. So might tighter.

That second orgasm morphed into a third as she grabbed his ass and held on to him.

He slid in and out of her faster and harder, his elbows planted at her sides, his face dipped to one side of her head so that she could hear every difficult breath he took.

Never had she experienced sex like this. Never had she imagined it could even exist outside of romance novels.

She was ruined for all other men.

Totally ruined.

CHAPTER 15

When Zeke could once again command his body to move, he slid out of her and to the side, leaving his leg between hers, his thigh pressed against her warm center.

He eased his free hand up to cup her face and turn her toward him so he could take her lips. The vibrator was still buzzing behind his head somewhere, so he eventually broke free of her lips to reach over and turn it off.

Nothing about the last hour had been in the plan. He'd come to her suite hoping to talk and figure out what steps they wanted to take next in their relationship, if any at all.

He'd feared she might turn him down and send him away out of frustration with him. And he wouldn't have blamed her. Part of him would have been in total agreement a few weeks ago.

Now?

Now, he had a new problem. He knew definitively nothing about this relationship was a fluke. They weren't just two people who had gone through a long dry spell and were desperate to fuck. Nope. She rocked his world in a way he'd never imagined possible.

As he tried to slow his breathing, he worried about several

things. Namely that they still hadn't talked. Outside of work, they had spent several evenings scratching each other's itch only to realize it couldn't be completely sated.

Would she agree with his assessment?

He had to assume she would. But that didn't help matters at all. They had a few huge hurdles in front of them, and he had no idea how they could or should proceed.

Stroking a hand up and down her arm, he was glad when her breathing evened out, leaving her in a calmer place than earlier. There had been no guarantee she wouldn't resume her full-blown freak out when her brain returned to earth.

"We haven't talked," she pointed out finally.

"Yeah. I can't figure out where to start."

She pulled his palm up to her mouth and kissed it, smiling against his skin. "Me neither."

"The way I figure it, our relationship so far has gone from growling at each other to ignoring each other to a collegial respect to hot sex."

She swatted at his chest. "You're were the one growling."

"True. Fair point. Oh, and I left out the media coverage. And the fact that apparently reanimated people wake up with a libido that can't be stopped."

She giggled, the sound making him smile. "I like it when you smile," she whispered.

"How do you know I'm smiling?"

"I can feel it in every muscle of your face against my neck and shoulder."

"Though I thoroughly enjoyed this plunge into total darkness, I do prefer to see your face when you come." He nibbled her neck until she squirmed.

"Stop it. I don't have another orgasm in me. You're making me horny again."

"Did you just challenge me?"

She pushed against his shoulder in a half-assed attempt to shove him away. "Not a chance."

"Oh, I think you did." He grinned again, the expression foreign but growing on him. "How many was that? Three?"

She groaned, a mock sound that she forced out. "The last one didn't count. The challenge was with the vibrator."

He lifted onto his elbow. He had no idea how he was going to find the energy to come again, but somehow he would. Because damn, she was pushing him. "Did you really just say that?"

She shoved at him again. "I need clothes." She tried to wiggle out of his grasp.

"Oh, no. No, you don't. Not a chance." He pinned her down with his leg pressing between her thighs and his hand on the mattress on her other side. "Which vibrator was that one? The pink or the purple?" He had no doubt she could identify it without seeing it. The other one had been more slender with a flat part on the tip. He got hard just imagining the specific intended use for that one.

"Zeke..."

"Tell me. Pink or purple."

She groaned. "Why does it matter?"

"Because I want to know. Either tell me now, or I'm going to flip the light on and look before I grab the other one and give it a try."

"You can't turn on the light. You'll ruin the perfect ambiance we have going here."

He started to reach over her for the lamp on the nightstand, but she stopped him with a grasp on his forearm. "Pink. It was pink."

He detoured to the drawer and grabbed the other one before she could stop him. "So this is the purple one, then."

"Zeke, seriously, you broke the record. You don't have anything else to prove."

"You're the one who said the last orgasm didn't count. You

started this," he teased, palming the new toy in his hand to familiarize himself with where the buttons were located.

Her voice rose. "Still, the total was two, which is more than one. So you already won." She wiggled against him, squeezing her legs together against his thigh.

"Two is a terrible number to break a record. I need to get at least a few more out of you in order to have bragging rights. No one goes around bragging they broke a record of one with two," he joked.

She grabbed his wrist. "If you brag to even one person that you know I even own a vibrator, I will personally kill you." She gasped, her body freezing.

"What? Michelle?"

Her voice dipped. "I can't believe we're discussing this out loud in my bedroom after everything we've been through today. I was already in full freak-out mode worrying about people listening in on my conversations. I don't give a shit that someone came in here and declared the place clean. I don't trust a living soul right now. That tech guy could have planted two more mics and six cameras instead for all I know."

Zeke lowered the vibrator to the side of her head and released it to draw her body closer to him. He kissed her forehead and stroked her face. "I'm sorry. I wasn't thinking."

She was breathing heavily again. "I'm being ridiculous. I know. I just can't get the thought completely out of my mind. It makes me want to vomit to think anyone would ever know about my private sex life. Or lack thereof."

He held her, feeling like an idiot. "I'm so sorry," he repeated. "You're not being ridiculous. It's understandable. And I know you don't trust anyone, but I hope that doesn't include me. I would never talk to anyone about us."

She nodded, but he could feel the tremble in her body. She was on the edge of tears.

He stroked her cheek with his thumb and lowered his face to

her side again. He feared she would never feel safe inside this bunker again. If he could just get her out of this claustrophobic hole in the ground, maybe she could breathe freely.

A knock sounded at the door to the suite, making Zeke jerk to sitting. It was just a knock, but Michelle wasn't the only one on edge.

She let out a short screech. "Jesus." He could feel her heart pounding under the hand he settled on her chest.

The knock sounded again. "Michelle? Zeke?" The voice belonged to Ryan.

Zeke blew out a breath. "It's just Ryan. Hang on. I'll get rid of him." He climbed over her and stood, realizing he wasn't going to be able to locate a stitch of clothing in the dark.

Michelle slid to the floor next to him and rushed naked through the room to lean out the bedroom door. "Just a minute," she said loud enough to keep Ryan from pounding again. She hurried past Zeke again and flipped on the bathroom light.

He squinted as she tossed him his clothes on her way back by. Two seconds later he was in his scrubs and she had on a pair of leggings and a long T-shirt. She was smoothing down her hair as she headed for the bathroom, muttering under her breath. He caught the gist of her words. Something about being mortified beyond belief and it being only seven in the evening.

Zeke headed for the entrance to the suite as Michelle shut herself in the bathroom. When he opened the main door, he found Ryan and Emily in the hallway. They looked chagrined.

"Sorry, man. Really sorry. This is important. Can we come in?" Ryan's face was pale.

A glance at Emily showed she mirrored the same expression.

"Of course. Come in. Michelle is just in the bathroom," he lamely said as an excuse. Not that it wasn't true, but he felt awkward. More for her than himself. But still. He had never once in his life been caught in bed with a woman. Granted, he was a grown single man who could sleep with whomever he wanted, but he still wasn't accustomed to being caught naked.

Michelle emerged from the bedroom while they were still standing in the entrance staring at each other. "Sorry. I was..." She waved a hand behind her. "Whatever. What's up?"

Where Ryan and Emily looked pale, Michelle's cheeks were bright red. She had put her hair back up into the messy bun that had fallen out while he ravaged her, but she looked like she'd been fucked. There was no way to hide it.

He reached for her and was relieved she took his hand and let him lead her to the couch. "Sit. What's going on?" The silence was starting to wear on him.

Ryan pointed at the armchair where Emily lowered herself, and then he grabbed one of the kitchen chairs and spun it around to face the rest of them. He met Zeke's gaze and held it. "Can't be helped. I'm going to have to say this out loud in front of Michelle." He winced and then glanced around. "You're sure this room is secure?"

That was when Zeke realized this visit had something to do with Dade. *Fuck.*

Michelle sat straighter, her head whipping around the room. "What's going on?"

Zeke grabbed her hand again and squeezed it. "We kept a secret from you."

Her eyes widened, and she slowly shook her head. "I swear to God, Zeke, I can't take any more today." She jerked her gaze to Ryan. "Unless someone is dead, I think you should keep your damn secret. I'm fresh out of steam." She was shaking.

Zeke wanted to run the clock back several days and tell her about Dade before now. But he hadn't had permission to do that, and it hadn't come to his mind since he'd started sleeping with her. Besides, it wasn't that huge a secret to keep from Michelle, in particular. There was a chance she had never even met Dade.

Ryan nodded. "I'm so sorry, for a lot of things, but you're not too far off base. Someone is actually *not* dead. Same difference."

"Pardon?" Her spine was so rigid, Zeke feared she would literally get hysterical in a moment.

He turned to face her. "Michelle, look at me."

Her eyes were wild. Her pupils huge. She was shaking her head.

He kept speaking. "He's talking about Dade."

"What about Dade?" Her eyes went wider. "God, did you hear from Blair? Did he pass?"

Zeke paused, mouth hanging open, realizing she had never actually known Dade was dead. She'd only known he *would* die. This was the story everyone believed. Did that make things better?

Zeke shook his head. "No. He didn't die. He's not going to die. He was never going to die."

She frowned. "What do you mean?" Her gaze switched to Ryan and then Emily. "He's going to make it?" She looked relieved, but confused at the same time.

Emily cleared her throat. "The stem cell transplant he received actually worked. The three of us have known this for a while. We just didn't tell anyone."

Michelle blinked. "Why?"

Ryan spoke next. "Because no matter how you slice it, there's still a mole. I didn't want anyone to know. Zeke was in the lab with me late one night when I was looking at the blood sample Dade sent me. Temple walked in as I realized the transplant had worked. He was getting better. I flat-out lied to her and told her he wasn't going to make it."

Michelle jerked her hand free of Zeke and jumped to her feet to step away from all of them. "You lied to Temple?" Her hands hung at her sides, fisted.

Zeke prayed to God they could get her to see reason.

Emily nodded. "Yes. He had to."

"But my God, this is Temple we're talking about. Our boss." She put her hands on her head. "There's no way in hell she's the leak. You can't possibly believe that."

Zeke shook his head. "No one thinks she's the mole, Michelle. But she feeds information to her boss and on up the chain of command. There's no telling who above her might be the real problem. With the exception of our relationship getting out, the three of us have never been convinced the leak and all the other mishaps are internal. It could be coming from a higher up person."

She stared at him, not blinking.

He needed to keep going, convince her. "I mean, think about it: Who the hell do you know who would rat us out like that? We're scientists and doctors. Our life's goal is to preserve and protect life. Cure diseases. Reanimate the preserved. Most of us have been dedicated to research since we were kids."

She still stared.

"Surely you've looked around the lab more than once and wondered who might be feeding detailed information to the media."

Finally, she licked her lips and nodded, lowering her hands. "Yes, but God Almighty, it isn't Temple."

Ryan jumped in. "And none of us believe it is, but we needed her to tell her superiors Dade wouldn't make it so that his life wouldn't be at risk."

She nodded again. "Where is he? Isn't anyone tracking him? What about credit cards and bills and stuff?"

Every one of the revived had a tracking device. She was quick to remember that. Ryan winced. "I cut it out of his arm, and he left it at the first hotel they came to."

Michelle inhaled slowly. "You thought of everything. Even before he left. Even before you knew what the outcome would be."

"Yes. If his blood work proved he wasn't going to make it, I didn't want anyone to hound him in his last weeks. I wanted him to enjoy himself. I gave him and Blair new identities and set up

Dade's inheritance so they could access it. It was substantial. They could live for years off it if they're careful."

"My God," she said again. "But he made it. Now what?"

Ryan smiled. "Now he's digging around behind the scenes, helping us. With Blair's assistance, of course."

"Shit." She was trembling again.

"Come here." Zeke held out a hand.

She stumbled back toward him and nearly fell onto her butt at his side. "How did Zeke find out?" She glanced at him as she asked Ryan the question.

"Like Ryan said, I was in the lab at the time. Coincidence. When Temple left, I looked at the cells in the microscope and then met Ryan's wide eyes as he covered his lips to keep me from saying a word. We went outside. He filled me in. Dade is my best friend. I might have killed Ryan if he'd kept this from me." He forced a wan smile.

"And I couldn't keep something like this from Emily," Ryan said. "She also worked with Dade. She was mourning his loss."

Michelle nodded. "I can imagine. I didn't know him. But I don't like to lose anyone. It was especially hard after all he's been through to find out he wasn't going to make it. I felt horrible for him and for Blair. I've known Blair for years."

He put an arm around her and pulled her to his side.

"Which brings us to tonight," Emily said. "We spoke to Dade right before we came to find you."

Right. Shit. They hadn't even gotten to the reason for the visit. "What did he say?" It must have been important for Emily and Ryan to track him down and also take the risk of letting Michelle in on the secret.

"He and Blair have been trailing Meredith's actions."

Zeke flinched. "Jesus. Can I not get that raving lunatic out of my life?"

Ryan shrugged. "Apparently not. Dade was suspicious of her

When Temple gave a long whistle to get everyone's attention, the room fell into a hush.

Michelle suddenly noticed there were armed guards at the front and back entrances. Several of them. Dressed in fatigues and carrying serious weapons. A few others came and went.

Temple spoke in a loud voice. "As I'm sure you noticed, there was an explosion. It was a car bomb that exploded when a vehicle slammed into the front gates. The gates were not completely breached but they have been compromised. All nonessential personnel will be evacuated from this facility until we can be certain it's safe to return."

Michelle sucked in a breath and held it as Zeke set his hand on her lower back.

Temple continued, "Multiple vehicles will be arriving shortly. Please return to your suites and pack a bag. I can't guarantee how long you might be gone. If I call your name, please stay here to receive further instructions." She listed more than a dozen people, including Zeke and Michelle.

As everyone else filed out of the room, the remaining people came in closer.

Temple began to hand out sheets of paper to everyone in the room. "These are your personal assignments."

"How the hell do you have this ready?" Ryan asked her, frowning.

"It's my job. I have evacuation procedures for any eventuality ready at all times. I update them at least once a week. I did so late last night as a matter of fact." She handed Ryan his paper and turned to the next person.

Michelle took her assignment with shaky hands. She blinked several times as she read the important details. She and Zeke and Kate had been assigned to leave in an ambulance with Graham Wentz.

Zeke pressed a hand to her back. "Let's go."

Right. They needed to pack.

Graham Wentz. She processed this detail as she rushed back to her room. Graham had moved from the reanimation chamber to a temporary state of induced coma just days ago. He needed four weeks in that state. How the hell were they going to move him?

She realized Zeke was talking to her. "Will you be okay?"

She nodded. "Yes. Fine." He needed to go gather his own belongings.

His eyes bore into her.

"I'm okay. Come get me when you're ready."

He stopped at his door. She kept going.

It took her ten minutes to fill a suitcase and a bag. She gathered all her important papers and enough clothes to last a week. As she opened the door to the suite, Zeke was just walking up. His brow was furrowed. "You ready?"

"Yes." She followed him through the halls until they reached the medical wing where Graham was in an induced coma. This entire situation made her nervous. She wasn't a medical doctor. Neither was Zeke. Kate, however, was.

As they entered the room and found Kate pacing, Michelle finally remembered Kate also had a thing for Graham. Shit. No wonder she was stressed. Although any one of them would be at the prospect of moving a patient in his condition anywhere.

Zeke dropped his suitcase and made his way to the machines surrounding Graham's bed. "Jesus. How the hell are we going to transport all this?"

Kate joined him. "We don't need everything. We just need the essentials. We have backup batteries. And extras. We can plug into the ambulance during transport."

"Do we know where we're going yet?"

Kate shook her head. "Temple is working something out."

"Hopefully not from scratch," Zeke murmured.

Temple stepped into the room at that moment. "Holleran, give me some credit. As I said earlier, I have contingencies for everything."

He jerked his gaze around to face her, cringing. "Sorry."

She waved a hand through the air. "No worries." She handed him an envelope. "Here's your destination. An ambulance will be pulling up shortly."

"How did you get enough of them on such short notice?" he asked.

"Only needed four. Those who woke up three days ago are going to get into SUVs."

"And the two in the reanimation chambers?" Michelle asked, causing everyone to turn toward her.

"I'm staying with them. As are a few necessary personnel."

Michelle nodded. "For how long? What if you have to evacuate?"

"We'll manage. Worry about Graham. The four people in a coma are the most crucial."

That was true. It made Michelle very nervous. A man's life was at stake. Four people in fact. She took a deep breath and faced Temple again. "How bad do you think this is?"

"Impossible to say. Depends on if the driver was acting alone or has backup waiting to break into the facility. It will be completely locked down as soon as everyone is out. Well-guarded. No one will get in or out."

"Okay."

Zeke had opened the envelope with their instructions and was scanning the information. "How do we know we can trust this woman?" he asked, shaking the page slightly.

Temple shot him another pointed glare. She was losing her patience. "I've known Marcie for a long time. She's well vetted. Trust me. She won't breathe a word of your existence to anyone."

Zeke nodded slowly. "Okay then."

Temple turned back to Michelle. "I'll be in touch as soon as I can. You and the other three teams with critical patients are my top priority."

They all spun around as someone stepped into the room. A

guard. "General Levenson," he said to Temple, "the ambulances are here."

In a whirlwind of activity, machines were disconnected and reconnected, backup batteries were prepared, and Graham Wentz was moved into the ambulance.

The back was crowded with machines, but Kate and Michelle climbed in with him. Zeke sat in front with the driver. It had been less than a half an hour since the bomb went off.

As the ambulance pulled away from the bunker, Michelle's phone buzzed. She tipped to one side and slid her cell from her pocket. It was a text from Ryan. She read it twice.

Stop. Have Kate cut the GPS tracker out of Zeke before you leave the grounds. She can show you how to get hers out. Get rid of them. I don't care how.

"Stop the ambulance," Michelle called through the window connecting them to the driver.

The driver hit the brakes and turned around. "Something wrong?"

Michelle turned to Kate. "Cut the tracker out of Zeke. You'll have to show me how, and I'll do yours."

Kate's eyes widened. She blew out a breath and nodded. "Right. Good idea."

Zeke didn't even question Michelle. He climbed down from the front of the ambulance, rounded to the back, and stepped inside.

It was cramped. Thank God the lighting was bright.

Kate scrambled to find everything she needed and set several supplies on the few inches of space near the end of the gurney next to Graham's feet. She put on a pair of blue rubber gloves, grabbed Zeke's offered arm, and felt for the spot where the GPS would be located just under the skin on the back of his wrist. She swabbed it with an alcohol wipe and picked up the small scalpel.

Michelle leaned closer, paying attention. She could do this, but it wasn't something she ordinarily did. She was an immunologist, not a medical doctor.

Kate glanced at her. "If you line your thumb up just below the location, you'll only need a small incision and then we can pull it out with tweezers."

Zeke looked a little pale, but he tucked his lips under and nodded. "Do it."

Kate made a precise cut, set the knife down, and picked up the tweezers. In seconds, she had the tracker out. It was much smaller than Michelle would have expected. "Got it?" she asked Michelle.

"Sure. You're brave letting me cut into your arm," she joked.

Kate chuckled. "I'd do it myself, if I weren't right-handed."

"Or desperate," Zeke added.

"That too." Kate set another matching kit next to the first, handed Michelle some gloves, and swiped her own wrist with alcohol.

Michelle forced herself not to shake as she thumbed the tiny tracker and made the incision. Cutting a hole in her coworker's arm in a hurry in the back of an ambulance wasn't her idea of fun.

Kate winced, but only for a second, and then she handed Michelle the clean tweezers.

Michelle glanced up to see Kate gritting her teeth. She jerked her gaze back down, pushed on the spot with her thumb, and reached into the small slit to grab the tracker. Thank God she didn't have to fish for it.

As she set it down next to the first device, she exhaled the deepest breath she'd ever held.

Zeke was holding a piece of gauze over his incision, and Kate grabbed two butterfly bandages. She handed them to Michelle who took them and calmed herself enough to put one on each of their wounds.

The second she had Zeke's on, he leaned over, kissed her

forehead, and jumped down from the back of the ambulance. He reached back with a hand. "Give me those damn trackers."

Michelle handed him the light blue paper they were sitting on, careful to make sure they were both still balanced on top. She smiled as Zeke picked up first one and then the other and turned around to launch them into the dirt. "Let's go."

It was crazy. Michelle had to close her eyes to concentrate on breathing for several long seconds. They were on the run, but no one was going to be able to track them now from the inside.

"Shit," Kate exclaimed a few minutes later. "What about Graham?" She grabbed his limp arm.

Zeke twisted around from the front. "He doesn't have one."

Michelle frowned. "Why? How do you know that?"

"Ryan got too suspicious after his parents were found in Montana. Me, Kate, Grayson, and Colton were the last group to get them inserted."

"Seriously?" Michelle frowned. "Are you positive? Everyone's paperwork indicates they have one."

"Yep. That's what the papers say." He winked at her. "Everyone was assigned a tracker. And there's a nice bag of them buried in a desk drawer. No one would have noticed it didn't really happen yet since no one has left the bunker."

"Someone's in for a rude awakening today," Kate pointed out.

Michelle nodded. "Especially if we were intentionally flushed out of the bunker in order to be tracked like caged animals." She shuddered and leaned back, rubbing the pounding spot behind her temple.

Zeke found himself surprisingly wide awake for the two-hour drive. His adrenaline was pumping so hard he couldn't have fallen asleep if he wanted to. He wouldn't be able to relax a muscle until they had Graham settled somewhere with electricity. He didn't give a single shit that they had multiple backup batteries. The entire thing made him nervous as hell.

The driver seemed to understand his need to be left in peace because after introducing himself, he'd left Zeke to himself. He never turned the lights or the siren on during the drive. Zeke was sure he'd been given strict instructions to stay under the radar.

The only reason Zeke trusted the driver was because he was Nicole Salway's partner, Pierce Titus. They were civilian police. All the ambulance drivers were. While Nicole had been working undercover at the gate, her partner explained that he'd never been far away. Surely Titus wasn't working for the bad guys. Of course, whoever was working for the enemy would be a huge surprise if Zeke ever found out who it was.

Zeke looked over his shoulder so many times, he would have a crick in his neck. Kate looked like she might vomit. Her face was even tinged green like she had motion sickness, though he was fairly certain she was just worried.

She checked Graham's vitals a thousand times while Michelle held on to the bottom of the gurney to keep from being tossed around the back. Her arm was going to be sore. And she looked exhausted.

Finally, they pulled up behind a clinic in a small town two hours south of Falling Rock. The back door opened and a woman rushed outside. She was already at the back of the ambulance when Michelle opened the doors.

"I'm Dr. Marcie Brown," she stated, her gaze focused on the patient as everyone arrived at the back of the ambulance to unload Graham.

It took only two minutes to unload the gurney, all the necessary equipment, and their luggage, and Titus nodded and took off as quickly as possible to avoid anyone in the vicinity noticing he'd ever been there.

Dr. Brown glanced around in the dark before she shut the doors to the clinic. "Welcome. I'm sure you're all exhausted. Let's get the patient settled and then I'll show you around." She smiled as she pointed at a door on the right just down the hallway.

Zeke dropped his suitcase and glanced at Michelle to find concern etching her brow. He felt exactly the way she looked. Both of them helped wheel Graham to the room and Kate went to work hooking everything up and double- and triple-checking to make sure every machine was plugged in and working properly.

Dr. Brown helped as much as possible, but they worked in silence, and Zeke knew only Kate had any idea what needed to be done.

Finally Kate blew out a breath and lifted her gaze to hold out a hand to Dr. Brown. "Thank you so much for doing this. I'm Dr. Kate Bauer. These are my colleagues, Michelle Houston and Zeke Holleran."

"Welcome. As I said I'm Dr. Marcie Brown, but please call me Marcie. I own this clinic. It's small, but I hope we have everything you might need. I got only brief information from General Levenson, but it's my understanding the patient's name is Graham Wentz and he was recently removed from a reanimation chamber?" Her eyes were wide. More than likely this was the most exciting patient she'd ever had the pleasure of meeting, so to speak.

Kate nodded. "Yes. Three days ago. The process takes two months. After four weeks in the chamber, each patient is kept under a deep coma for four more weeks to give their internal organs a chance to become fully functional. It's a gradual process after ten years of vitrification."

Marcie smiled. "Amazing. Well, anything any of you need, let me know. I live in the apartment above the clinic, and I have a spare bedroom and a pull-out couch, so whenever anyone wants to sleep, there's plenty of space. I assume you'll all want to rotate and keep an eye on your patient."

Zeke responded. "Yes. Thank you so much for your hospitality."

"I'll mostly stay with him," Kate indicated, rubbing her temples. "I'll be fine with a chair or if you have a small cot."

Marcie nodded. "Of course." She rushed from the room and returned with a fold-up cot that she popped open and situated next to the wall. "Everything is on a backup generator in here, so don't panic about electricity. Though I can't remember the last time we lost power."

"Thank you so much, Marcie." Zeke reached out to shake her hand, realizing he hadn't done so.

Michelle did also. "We appreciate everything."

"It's my pleasure. Years from now, I can tell my grandkids I was able to help out a man coming out of a cryostat."

Zeke smiled. He figured Marcie was only a few years older than him. It was unlikely she had kids running around upstairs. "Hopefully by then it will be commonplace."

Michelle rubbed her eyes. "It might take me a year to fall asleep, but I wouldn't mind trying. I've never had my adrenaline pumping for this long in my life. I'm dead on my feet."

Kate took her arm. "I'll be fine here. Go upstairs and sleep as long as you want."

"Will you be able to rest, Kate?" Zeke asked.

"Trust me. I'll sleep better on the cot in the room next to Graham than I have in weeks in my own suite."

Michelle pulled her in for a long embrace. "I understand. You sure you're okay?"

"Yes. Go." She gave her a playful shove. "Both of you. Sleep for ten hours. I don't want to see either of you until at least noon."

Zeke set a hand on Michelle's elbow and guided her to follow Marcie.

They rounded the corner to a door that opened up to a set of stairs. Zeke grabbed their bags and let Michelle climb in front of him. When they reached the top, Marcie pointed to the couch.

"It's a pull-out. Not the most comfortable, but better than nothing. The bedroom is down the hallway to the left." She rushed toward the hallway. "I'll grab pillows and sheets."

Zeke stopped her. "That won't be necessary. We'll share the bedroom."

Michelle stiffened next to him, but he turned his head to look at her, thinking, *seriously?* Was she really going to balk in front of this stranger and sleep on an uncomfortable pull-out in order to maintain some sense of propriety? He lifted a brow.

"You're right. Of course," she murmured.

Zeke faced Marcie again. "I'm sure Kate won't leave Graham for more than a few minutes at a time while we're here either, so she won't need a separate bed. We really do appreciate your kindness. There wasn't time for Temple to explain how she lined up your clinic."

Marcie came closer. "Oh, she contacted me a long time ago, and we've kept in touch. She wanted places lined up in case of an emergency. Looks like tonight is that night."

"That's for sure," Zeke added.

"Do you mind if I ask how long you all have worked in cryonics? It's so fascinating to me."

Zeke smiled. "Michelle and I don't work in cryonics. We're both immunologists. We work for the government. We just happened to be assigned to the location of the cryostats. Kate is a doctor, however. She knows more than either of us about the reanimation process."

"I can't imagine how amazing it must be to work in that facility. Your team has been responsible for so many cutting-edge developments in the last ten years."

Zeke winked at her. "Well, I can't take credit for anything that happened after 2007. I'm recently reanimated myself. So is Kate."

Marcie's eyes jumped out of her head. Her hand flew to her chest. Her mouth fell open, but no words came out for several seconds. Zeke couldn't blame her. "My God."

He smiled again. All this polite smiling was wearing him out.

"And you're totally healthy," she pointed out.

"Yep. So far no one has suffered any ill effects that we're aware of." He didn't mention Dade. There was no way in hell he would bring up that level of classified information. "It's extremely important that no one coming or going from this clinic know who we are. We're walking targets, both the reanimated and those not yet brought fully awake."

She nodded vigorously. "Of course. Temple already briefed me."

"Thank you," Michelle said. "I'm going to get some sleep." She grabbed her suitcase and slid past Zeke, who squeezed her hand before she walked by him.

He would give her a few minutes to use the bathroom and get situated. "Could I bother you for some water?"

"Of course." Marcie rushed past him and grabbed two bottles out of the fridge. "Please, help yourself to anything you can find. I'll go to the store tomorrow after the clinic closes and pick up whatever you need. Maybe you can make me a list."

"We don't want to put you out, but thank you again." How many times had he thanked her? She was saving their lives, literally. "What time does your clinic open?"

"Eight. I have a staff of six that come in about seven thirty. I'll keep the door to the exam room where we put your friend closed and tell my staff the patient is quarantined."

"Perfect. That'll work. For a while."

"We'll figure it out as we go along."

"Well, Graham doesn't make any noise," he joked.

She groaned as she scrunched up her face.

"I must be tired. That wasn't a great joke."

"Nope, but you tried. I'll let you get some sleep."

"Thanks again," he stated one last time as he grabbed his suitcase. "You're going to be tired tomorrow. If there's anything Michelle or I can do to help, let us know. We aren't medical doctors, but we have a lot of lab experience. I'm rusty after ten years in a cryostat, but I'm catching up fast."

"That's still hard to imagine." She pointed toward the hallway. "Go. Sleep."

CHAPTER 17

Michelle was under the covers of the comfortable queen-sized bed when Zeke stepped silently into the room. He had changed into shorts, so she guessed he'd already used the bathroom.

He slid under the covers next to her and immediately pulled her against his chest, kissing her forehead. "You okay?"

"Not even close." She was still shaking. All she'd done was brush her teeth and remove the scrubs she's thrown on over her shorts and T-shirt.

He rubbed her arm up and down and held her tighter. "Sleep. You'll feel so much better after you rest."

"I'm not sure how long it might take for my mind to slow down enough to do that. I'm also kind of freaked out about how poorly I've handle the last few days. I'm usually a much stronger person, able to cope with anything. Suddenly it's like I've undergone a personality transformation, and I can't recognize myself."

He chuckled. "*You've* undergone a personality transformation? I don't even know who I am." He kissed the top of her head, hoping she understood he was teasing.

She sighed. "You're right. You win. That sounded stupid. Nevertheless, I'm not myself."

"I think you're doing fine. It's been crazy. Everything that could be thrown at you has been in the last two days. You've earned the right to a bit of a meltdown."

"The worst part is that you're not seeing the real me."

"Well, we're even, because I don't know this smiling, laughing, joking guy who can make a woman moan in pleasure and lure her to come back for a second round."

She pressed her palm against his chest. "Your ex did you so very wrong."

"That's for sure."

"Honestly, she did a number on you. If I ever see her again, I'm going to punch her in the face."

"Maybe you should start working out with arm weights more often to build up these biceps," he joked as he gave one a squeeze.

She flexed. "Say that again?"

He laughed harder. It felt good. It was new for him, but damn, he could get used to it. His body shook as his chest rose and fell. He could also feel her grinning against his pecs.

When he finally stopped, the room was silent for a moment.

"I'm worried that if I fall asleep, something bad will happen." Her voice was serious.

"It won't. I'm right here." He gripped her again. "Sleep. Take several deep breaths and let your mind go. We're in no hurry to wake up. Rest."

"Will you be here when I wake up?" she whispered.

"Yes. Promise."

She sighed and nuzzled his neck, kissing his skin.

He threaded his hand in her hair and held her closer. "You're safe."

~

Michelle was surprised when she opened her eyes to find Zeke still at her side and sun streaming in through the cracks in the blinds. She hadn't moved an inch since she'd fallen asleep. Neither had Zeke.

When she lifted her face, blinking her eyes, she found him smiling at her. "Feel better?"

"Mmm. Did you sleep?"

"Yes. I woke up a few minutes ago. I didn't want to wake you, so I didn't move. Apparently I failed."

She shook her head. "I think it was natural. How long were we asleep?"

"About six hours. It's ten."

She groaned. "I'm going to feel like I have a hangover. I never sleep late like this."

"I think you earned it." He frowned at her. "Cut yourself a break."

"I'm starving. Did we eat dinner?"

"No. I'll go find us something. Marcie also said we could make her a list. She's very gracious."

"She's a godsend." Michelle moaned as she sat up and tipped her head from side to side. "Don't let me sleep like that without moving again. I'm gonna need a massage to work out the kinks in my neck."

Zeke flexed his fingers. "I don't have other plans for today."

She slid from the bed, her bladder needing attention. At the door, she turned around with her hand on the frame. "I don't remember when I've had a day off."

"It's possible we could be looking at a lot of days. I don't know what Temple might have in mind for our next move, but until she calls, I for one am going to enjoy the mini-vacation."

"Do you think the bunker's okay?" Michelle's mind went back to worrying. Two more people were awaiting reanimation. She would not be able to take the stress of losing either of them to a damn bomber.

Zeke sat up and set his feet on the floor. "The bunker is more secure now than it's ever been. Don't worry. It might take Temple a while to get ahold of everyone, but I'm positive she's safe. I wish I had been paying closer attention to who stayed behind with her."

"I assume at least a few medical doctors since there are two people left in chambers." She sighed, hating that she hadn't even said goodbye to anyone. "Temple will need people qualified to complete the reanimation of the final two members of your team." Every one of them would be stressed and anxious while they waited to reunite as a unit again.

Michelle just hoped that day came.

After using the bathroom, she padded down the hall to find Zeke in the kitchen making toast. "Coffee?"

He had a cup in his hand, and she realized there was a pot nearly full on the counter. Marcie must have made it.

"That would be great."

Zeke set his mug down and filled one for her while she plucked the toast from the toaster and took a giant bite of the bread, even though it was too hot and had nothing on it. Her stomach was rumbling.

Zeke stuck two more slices in and pushed the handle down. "How do you take your coffee?"

She glanced at the counter and found everything she would need next to the pot. "I'll fix it." After dumping in creamer and adding sugar, she found a spoon in a nearby drawer and stirred. When she lifted her gaze, she found Zeke watching her. "What?"

"Just making a mental note. We've never spent the morning together like this. I've always left for the gym before you got up. It hadn't occurred to me that I don't know how you take your coffee. I didn't even know you drink coffee. Do you not drink it throughout the day?"

She blew on the surface. "Nope. One cup. Doctored to barely resemble coffee. Usually before I even leave my suite."

"Got it." He set his mug down, took hers from her hand, and

set it on the counter next to his before he kissed her soundly. "There. That's better."

A shiver raced down her spine as he handed her the mug once more.

She was beyond rattled. They still had not discussed the future, and in a way it seemed like it was on top of them. Crowding them. Forcing them to move their relationship to a level they may or may not have been ready for. After all, for the foreseeable future, they were stuck together, sharing a bed, figuring out meals, cooking, caring for Graham, and ensuring Kate slept and ate.

"We should check on Kate," she said.

"You're right. I'll go do that."

Michelle grabbed his forearm. "I'm not sure it's a good idea to just roam into the clinic and cause eyebrows to raise farther than they already are. I'll call her."

"Good point."

Michelle headed for the bedroom to grab her cell. When she came back, already sending a text, she set it on the counter.

Zeke tucked an errant lock of hair behind her ear and cupped her face, staring intently into her eyes. She had the feeling he was assessing her mental stability. She couldn't blame him.

A text came in and Michelle leaned over to read the message from Kate.

"She okay?"

"Yes. She just spoke to Temple. Said Temple is calling us next." Before Michelle finished speaking, the phone rang, Temple's name across the top. She answered it and put it on speaker. "Hi. You have Michelle and Zeke here."

"Good. Two birds. My list of calls is long."

"Update us," Michelle said.

"I'm working with Detective Salway. She believes the incident was unrelated to anything else. The man who drove the SUV into the gate died when the bomb went off. He's been identified, and the police have already searched his apartment in Nevada. Seems he was extremely religious and didn't believe in reanimation."

Michelle cringed. Would they ever get past this insanity?

Temple continued. "It would appear that he intended to drive the SUV through the gates and then all the way to the bunker where he would have detonated the bomb, hoping to kill everyone inside.

"What he didn't count on was that the gates are far sturdier than he suspected, and his vehicle never would have penetrated them. His bomb exploded prematurely, killing him alone. Several other people were injured in the blast, but because it was the middle of the night, that number was significantly lower than it could have been in the day."

"Because most of the usual protesters were sleeping," Zeke pointed out.

"Right. Luckily Nicole was there. Anyway, I don't feel comfortable bringing anyone back here right now. This place is a target. I'd rather spread everyone out and keep each location classified."

"Makes sense," Michelle agreed.

"Kate says Graham is perfectly stable and she can't see any reason why he can't remain where he is. It will be weird when he wakes, but at least Kate is able to handle everything herself. As long as no one becomes aware of their location, my intention would be to leave him there under her care."

"Good plan," Michelle said, "but you don't want the two of us here raising eyebrows."

"No. I don't. Has anyone seen you yet?"

"No. We believe we arrived securely in the middle of the night, and neither of us have left Dr. Brown's apartment above the clinic yet."

"Perfect. I'm arranging a car for you. It will be dropped off this afternoon. I want you to head for a bunker in New Mexico. I'm sending several others to that location also. I know it's inconvenient for that facility to host guests, but they'll have to put whatever their working on aside for now until we can avert this crisis. The rest of your team will be diverted to other locations in the surrounding states."

Michelle took a long breath. So much for a day off to recuperate.

"Do you have a pen and paper handy? I'm going to give you an address. This is extremely sensitive information. Please ensure it doesn't fall into the wrong hands. Memorize it. Destroy it."

Zeke quickly found a notepad on the counter and jotted down Temple's information. "Got it," he assured her.

"Good. I need to go for now. You have my private number in case of an emergency."

"Yes." Michelle nodded at the phone uselessly. "Also memorized."

"Okay. Touch base tonight when you arrive." The call ended.

Michelle sighed. "Well, so much for lounging around as if this were a vacation."

Zeke pulled her into his embrace and set his chin on top of her head. "Consider the good news."

"What's that?" she asked his chest.

"At least for the time being, we're both going to New Mexico."

She wrapped her arms around him and held him tighter. He was right. They definitely had unfinished business. A bombing that put all their lives in jeopardy wouldn't have been her choice method of getting to spend more time with him, but here they were.

CHAPTER 18

Michelle drove the nondescript black SUV that afternoon after a bit of an argument with Zeke who insisted that, even though he technically hadn't held a license for over ten years, he remembered how to drive just fine.

Zeke was, however, playing with his phone, which she found amusing. "The GPS on this thing is spectacular. It's made amazing advances in the last ten years." He'd mastered the use of the smartphone so fast after being revived that he'd left her in the dirt, but today was the first time he'd seen the GPS in use in real time.

"Flip through the stations and pick something. It will play through the speakers in the car." She had already connected the phone to the SUV Bluetooth before they started driving.

He made a selection and eighties' rock started playing.

She laughed. "Maybe I should have made a few stipulations before I let you choose."

"What's wrong with RUSH?"

"I wasn't born yet."

He laughed. "That's right. You're a baby."

"We're the same age, old man."

"Except you can't appreciate eighties' music."

"Except for that."

Michelle had never spent this much downtime with him. Every moment of their time alone had been spent having sex. On paper, they should be the perfect match. She couldn't imagine ever meeting someone so suited for her. But what would happen if they tried to have a normal conversation about something not related to science or threats to their lives or sex? This was the test.

It was possible they both accidentally found themselves at a point in life where they had needed the release. Hell, she still craved that contact. Even driving, she was acutely aware of him next to her and the effect he had on her libido. She knew it was the same for him too because he kept shooting her a look that included dancing eyes and a grin. It wasn't aimed at the cell phone. It was for her.

What if underneath their crazed desire to scratch each other's itch, they didn't get along?

They had a lot in common. Was that a good thing or a bad thing?

She had always dreamed of meeting a man who was intellectually stimulating and challenged her. Someone with whom she could hold a conversation on a host of topics without getting bored.

Did Zeke fit that requirement?

He was also built and sexy. She loved his thick hair that she could run her fingers through. His deep green eyes that drew her in. The way he smiled only for her.

It worried her that he was accustomed to being more of an angry, bitter individual. Would he go back to that after the honeymoon period of their relationship was over?

The sour look she'd seen time and again on his face when they'd first met had made her back away on more than a few occasions. It had taken strength to put up with him without blowing a fuse.

Two things that had kept her from losing her temper and taking his shit attitude personally. One had been knowing from his coworkers that he'd woken up with the same disposition he'd had before he was preserved, so it wasn't personal or aimed at her in particular. And the second had been seeing hints of the vulnerability in him that showed her what kind of man he was inside.

It was impossible for any of them to know what he was like before he met Meredith, however. Had his ex changed him? Turned him into a bitter man who wasn't trusting? He'd hinted at as much.

If that was the case, Michelle had to wonder if the damage his ex had caused could be undone. He had been trying. But could he really trust someone completely again?

She realized she'd been in her own world for a while and turned to glance at him.

He was staring at her. "You okay?"

She swallowed, her face flushing. "Yep."

"You weren't here. I was growing worried you might drive off the road."

She furrowed her brows. "I was right here. What do you mean?"

"You were in your head. What were you worrying about?"

"What makes you think I was worrying?" she asked, nervous that he'd noticed.

"Well, it started when I asked you a question and you didn't hear me."

She frowned. *Shit.*

"Talk to me."

She should. She should tell him all her concerns. Every last one. But was now the right time? They were driving. They were stressed. She wasn't sure of anything. Not even herself. She didn't trust herself to say the right things.

"Okay, I'll start." He sat up straighter. "I'm glad you're coming with me to New Mexico for however long it might be."

"Me too." That was easy.

"You have concerns."

"Don't you?" She glanced at him, gripping the steering wheel tighter.

"Yes. Probably the same ones."

"I doubt that."

"I'd take a pretty significant bet on it. So, let me say a few things, and then you tell me if I covered it."

"Okay…" She let that word drag out to several syllables.

"You're right to be worried about my temperament. When we met, I was an asshole. I treated you unfairly and bit your head off every chance I got. As I've told you before, this had nothing to do with you as a person. It had to do with me not trusting women and finding myself attracted to you."

Damn. He did seem to have read her mind.

"On top of that, I'm used to being an asshole—"

She interrupted him. "Let's not use that word. Surly perhaps. Sour. Angry. Not an asshole."

He snorted. "Whatever. I've been *sour* since Meredith fucked me over. So, the reality is that if you ask anyone I've known for the last four years—or fourteen if you want to look at it that way—you'll find I have been this way for as long as they've known me. I was already disappointed and on the road to full-on pissed with my ex-wife before I arrived at the bunker."

Michelle pursed her lips. She didn't want to interrupt him.

"There's no question she did a number on me, and I don't trust easily. I don't need a psychiatrist to figure that out. But as you know, I've been working on that. The real question is, can I change for good? And I don't have the answer. Not yet. I'm *still* working on it."

Michelle turned her face toward him for a second. At least he was honest.

His voice was lower and he faced forward, staring out the windshield. "Something about that bomb shook me up. It scared the fuck out of me, reminding me that life is short. There are no guarantees. I shouldn't waste a moment of it."

She held her breath, absorbing his words. He was speaking from the heart with so much emotion.

He reached across and set a hand on her thigh. "I'm a work in progress. I have needed time to figure out if I can trust myself to love again. I have to work hard to school myself into something that won't disappoint you."

She shot him another glance, concerned. "That takes effort? Even now?"

He shrugged and turned to look out the passenger window for a long time. When he faced her again, he said, "No. I think I have that all wrong. When I see you, my blood pumps harder. All kinds of foreign things happen to me physically. I react to you in a way that scares and unnerves me because I never want to feel that vulnerable again."

She released the steering wheel with her right hand and set it over his on her thigh.

"Honestly, you're the first person to draw that response out of me. Meredith didn't own that piece of me. I didn't realize it even existed, so I didn't know I was missing something. I just assumed people met, got married, and lived life. I never expected her to fuck me over. But she did.

"It left me raw and burned and all kinds of messed up. Probably because I didn't have anything to compare it to."

She squeezed his hand, feeling tears gather in the corners of her eyes for this man who'd been emotionally scarred.

He inhaled long and slow. "That day in Temple's office, when I demanded something to do and she decided we should work together…"

Michelle remembered it well. She'd been furious with both Temple and Zeke.

"I already knew I was attracted to you."

Michelle flinched. "You did?"

"Yes. I think that's why I lashed out at you. I wanted to sabotage anything that might happen between us. Maybe I wanted to prove to myself that all women were bitches. Or maybe I just wanted to piss you off enough that you wouldn't like me, so I could avoid ever finding out what it might be like to date again."

Michelle lost the battle and had to swipe at a tear on her cheek.

"If I let you in, I would be opening myself up to a level of vulnerability I didn't think I could live through again. When I told you I wasn't sure if I was ready before, it was because of that."

"That makes sense," she murmured. It made a *lot* of sense. "What made you change your mind?"

"You did."

She flinched. "Me? What did I do?"

"You never fell for my shit. You took it. Day in and day out. You're strong and professional, and you didn't strike back no matter how cruel I was toward you."

"Zeke... That makes me so sad for you."

He flipped his hand over and threaded his fingers with hers. "Yeah, pathetic. But eventually I realized you weren't going to hurt me. You also weren't Meredith. You're nothing like her. I don't need time to prove that. I've known you for plenty long enough to know you're a kind and loving human being who would go out of her way to help anyone, including a jerk for a coworker who was shoved onto your team without your consent."

"You're not a jerk," she lied. He was. At first.

He rolled his neck. "Be reasonable."

"Okay, maybe a little. But not anymore."

"Yeah, so that brings us to the real question. Can I keep this up, or will I fall back into my old pattern of growling and grumbling and acting like a shit when I get frustrated with a new project? Will I withdraw because I don't trust myself? You've never seen that side of me before. I can really stoop into a very angry person both personally, and professionally, when I can't find a cure for something."

She smiled. "Zeke, we all do that."

"Maybe, but not like I'm capable of. When I look at you, I want to be better. Do better. Smile more. Take life less seriously. I want to be a man you can trust to stay by your side unconditionally. To love you like you deserve."

She couldn't breathe. In fact, she needed to face him fully and absorb this revelation. So, she pulled off at the exit and over to the side of the road. After putting the engine in park, she swiveled in her seat and faced him.

"I still don't totally know if I can be that man," he said.

"You already *are* that man," she returned, grabbing his hands and stroking the backs of them with her thumbs. "You're just you, Zeke. Don't try to be someone else. You had every right to be angry with the world after what happened to you. Anyone would have reacted the same way. What made things worse was that you didn't have prior experiences with woman to demonstrate that not every relationship is like that."

"Especially the sex." He gave her a half grin.

"Especially the sex," she agreed. "Don't get me wrong. I've never had sex like this either. Not even one time. It's awesome and amazing and out of this world. Does it scare me? Hell, yes. Anytime you have a good thing, you'll find yourself worried if you can keep it."

"That's exactly what I'm saying."

"Well, you're not alone. I'm right here with you. In the same boat. Or…SUV. I'm scared too. I want this to work. It feels so good. I've had butterflies in my belly for weeks, ever since you kissed me that night. I tried to ignore the feeling and stuff it deep down where I couldn't get hurt, but it didn't work."

He nodded.

"What I'm saying is that we don't really have a choice now."

He cocked his head and frowned. "What do you mean?"

"I mean it's happened. We're already a 'we.' We're already involved. We can't take it back. Maybe after the kiss, but not now. Not now that we've had the most amazing sex together. Not now that you've held me in the night and taken the burden from me when I thought I might lose it."

She inhaled sharply and continued. "Not now that you've smiled at me and touched me everywhere and run soap all over me in the shower and used my vibrator on me and uncovered my deepest secrets. And let me see yours."

He leaned forward, emotion filling his eyes, and then he pulled her into an awkward embrace that was hindered by the console. He kissed her neck and breathed into her ear. "You're right."

She pulled back, trying to catch her breath. She needed to say more. "My point is, we can't walk away from this. And I don't want you to worry about frowning or even lashing out occasionally. It happens to all of us. It's harder when you work with the person you're in a relationship with.

"But it happens. You're not required to be upbeat and smile all the time. It won't change how I feel about you. I love when you give me that piece of you. I love the twinkle in your eyes when you grin. But no one can hold that up all the time. And it's okay.

"So, we're going to take this one day at a time. We're going to New Mexico. We're going to figure out what we can do to help out in that facility. When Temple calls to suggest one of us move to another location, we're going to make a decision together about how to respond. If we're not finished with this, then we tell her *no*. If that's not an option, then one of us quits our job. It's simple. It's not science."

He smiled warmly and then tugged her closer and claimed her mouth. As he tipped his head to one side and deepened the kiss, she knew she'd done the right thing by speaking her mind. She melted into him and absorbed his strength and commitment until she had to pull away to breathe.

She stared at him, their faces inches apart while she caught her breath.

"So, we're going to New Mexico."

"It would seem that way."

"And I don't have to always smile," he joked.

"Well, I would prefer you do so when we're naked, but other than that, no."

He lifted a brow. "Keep driving then. I like the naked part."

CHAPTER 19

Two weeks later…

The Colorado sun was warm and inviting when Michelle pulled up to the bunker in Falling Rock and stopped the engine. She had never been happier as Zeke rounded the vehicle and threaded their fingers together.

She lifted her free hand to block the sun's rays as Temple stepped outside to greet them. Her head was tilted to one side, and she had a sad smile. She wrapped Michelle in a hug as soon as they reached the entrance. "I'm going to miss you."

"What about me?" Zeke joked.

Temple laughed. "Okay, I'll miss your expertise maybe, but not your disposition."

"Hey, Michelle has convinced me not to be so disagreeable. I'm a changed man."

Temple continued to laugh as she opened the door and the three of them stepped inside. There were two people at the front desk. The older serious gentleman with gray hair had been working there from the beginning of Project DEEP. It was always strange when Zeke and Michelle knew the same people from different decades.

He greeted them both with a nod, but he was on the phone.

Standing next to him was a woman Michelle didn't know. She came forward smiling. She was petite and slender, but something about her told Michelle she was also fierce and strong under her petite stature. Smooth dark hair hung past her shoulders. Her darker skin suggested the perfect combination of ancestors. Her dark eyes were warm and friendly. "So nice to finally meet some of the people Temple talks about." She held out a hand to Michelle. "Nicole Salway."

Michelle smiled in return as she shook her hand. "Right. Nicole. I'm Michelle Houston. I thought maybe you were a figment of Temple's imagination."

Nicole chuckled. "It probably seems that way. I've been going by the name Mary Adams at the front gate for so long, I sometimes forget my real name."

"Unfortunately, Nicole is leaving us. This is her last day."

"Oh." Zeke shook her hand next. "Zeke Holleran. Does this mean everything out front is simmering down?" He shifted his gaze to Temple as he spoke.

Nicole answered. "It's been over a week since I heard anyone grumbling about plans to thwart the efforts of the bunker or attempting to sell information about anyone on your team. You're on your own now. I've been reassigned."

"Someplace more interesting, I hope," Michelle said.

Nicole shuddered. "You would not believe it if I told you."

"Intriguing."

"Yep. I have to admit, I was getting rather bored here. Spending my days picketing out front as if I were a religious bigot is the complete opposite of my next assignment. It will most assuredly not be boring." She rubbed her arms, another shiver shaking her frame.

Michelle would give anything to hear this woman's story. Just for the entertainment value alone. If she worked undercover often, she probably had very interesting tales to tell. "Well, good luck," Michelle said.

"I'm going to need it." Nicole waved as she wandered back to the front desk.

"Come on back." Temple nodded toward the hallway that led to the offices. "Are you still planning to load your SUV and turn around and head back in one day?"

"That's our plan. It's a long drive, so we'll probably stop somewhere for the night, but we wanted to pack up the rest of our belongings. Well, Michelle's anyway. I don't really own anything." He dug in his pocket and lifted up his cell phone. "A phone. I own a phone."

Temple laughed. "Well, it's an important possession."

Zeke shrugged as he tucked it back into his pocket. "It's kind of excessive at this point. We aren't usually separated. And I'm better with the GPS. Why pay two bills?"

"Is he always this cheap?" Temple asked, glancing at Michelle as they reached her office.

"Yes. He's gotten worse now that he has a regular paycheck."

"Listen, I'm a thirty-year-old man who the government classifies as forty. I have absolutely no retirement plan and my previous saving went to pay my divorce attorney. I'll never be able to stop working and live life if I don't save now."

Temple pursed her lips, obviously deciding to stay out of this one.

He was right. And Michelle liked that personality trait a lot. She had saved the majority of her salary for the last several years. It was easy to do when you lived in government housing and had few expenses.

But it was a phone. His only expense. So, it made her roll her eyes. It had been interesting to find out he was a bit of a penny pincher. It had been even more intriguing to find out that didn't extend to how he was with her.

He'd gotten her flowers. More than once now. And he'd ordered interesting items for her from the internet. The day she'd opened a mysterious package to find a new vibrator in pale blue, she'd flushed a deep red before lifting her gaze to find him grinning wickedly at her, eyebrows wiggling.

Shaking the inappropriate memory from her head, Michelle took a seat next to Zeke as Temple rounded her desk to the other side. "Looks like things are getting back to normal around here. But it's quiet. It's never been this quiet."

"Oh, trust me, it was incredibly quiet for several years after the first team was preserved before the next team came in to resume the work here."

"Thank God Tushar and Trish's son was so insistent about reanimating us or none of us would be sitting here today," Zeke confirmed.

He wasn't wrong. All of them had Ryan to thank for their jobs and their lives. He had started this ball rolling the moment his parents were vitrified when he was only twenty years old. He'd worked his ass off to finish school and develop a cure for AP12 while simultaneously finding a cryonicist—Damon Bardsley—and convincing the government to reopen the bunker.

"Those years were long and boring. Some days I miss them," Temple joked. She had been working in this bunker and on Project DEEP for over thirty years, from the beginning.

Zeke cleared his throat. "Give us an update."

Michelle knew Zeke was fishing for information, most of which he already had, but he wanted to know what Temple knew. It wasn't that either of them didn't trust Temple. They did. Implicitly. But Ryan told them to be vigilant; a leak from the inside couldn't be ignored.

Temple sighed. "That bug we found in the conference room hadn't been there very long." She set her gaze on Zeke and hesitated before saying what Michelle and Zeke already expected her to reveal. "We think there's a good chance your ex-wife planted it."

Zeke sighed. "I guess we already suspected that to be the case."

Dade had confirmed as much to Ryan even before the bombing, making Michelle wonder if Temple was just now privy to the information or if she'd known for a while.

Temple rubbed her forehead. "She was one of the few people who had access to that conference room table in the right timeframe."

Zeke blew out a breath. "Well, it wouldn't shock me. She's greedy. If someone offered to pay her to place a bug, I have no doubt she would take the money and run."

"Yeah. I'm sorry to say that's undoubtedly the case. We'll be looking into it closer," Temple added.

"Anything else we should know?" Zeke asked.

Temple smirked. "I'm sure you already realize no one left here with a tracker in their wrist, thanks to quick thinking on Ryan's part."

Zeke smiled. "I'm clear on that. After what happened to Emily and then Tushar and Trish, no one was willing to take the chance a hacker could locate us."

Temple nodded. "In hindsight, I think it was a good idea because everyone is now safe with no chance of being located." She leaned forward, putting her elbows on her desk. "I'm not sure I like the idea of Ryan making that decision without consulting me first, but things were chaotic that night. The chain of command had gone out the window."

Zeke nodded. "We did make decisions on the fly. I'm sure everyone did."

Michelle was relieved to find Temple wasn't bent out of shape about the trackers. Why would she be? There was a good chance everyone would be in far more danger with the GPS trackers than without.

Temple straightened. "How is everyone else at the New Mexico bunker?"

Michelle smiled. "Doing well. It's weird, though. Zeke and I are back working on Myasthenia Gravis, which makes more sense now that we know there's a government employee preserved there who suffered from it."

Temple lifted her brows. "They already put you to work? I thought that research was on hold while they dealt with the influx of people from our bunker."

"Yeah, they're still shuffling us around and trying to make space, but Michelle and I felt like we were standing around doing nothing, so we put our expertise to work," Zeke responded.

Temple frowned. "There's still a lot to get up to speed on that disease. Don't get too bent out of shape if you can't solve everything immediately. A dozen people have been working on MG for years."

Zeke waved her off. "Don't worry about us. We're scientists. It's what we do. We're much more comfortable in the lab than worrying about where all the extra personnel is going to sleep."

Temple chuckled. "I believe that. How's Damon doing? Did the other two chambers arrive okay? I haven't spoken to him for a few days."

Zeke nodded. "They did. He's being very thorough to ensure they weren't damaged in transportation, and then they'll be ready for use."

Even though Michelle had known there were other bunkers for a few weeks, she was still shocked by the discovery. The idea that multiple other facilities were involved in Project DEEP was eye opening. And to find out other government officials were held in cryostats...

She took a breath to continue a rundown of the last two people who had been sent to the New Mexico bunker. "Ryan and Emily are settling into a routine. The place is significantly smaller, so we're on top of each other in the lab. We don't have enough resources to all be working at the same time yet, so it's a constant juggle for space. Good thing we don't need separate living arrangements for each of us individually because there wouldn't be room for us," she joked.

"That's helpful." Temple raised her eyebrows. "Tushar and Trish aren't happy with their son and Emily being so far away, but it can't be helped for the time being."

"Are Tushar and Trish here, then?" Zeke asked.

"Yes. They returned here a week ago." Temple didn't elaborate on where they'd been.

"Hopefully there will come a day when we can all reunite." Zeke sighed. "Those are my friends. I can't stand the thought of never seeing them again."

Michelle could hear the subtle dig in his voice. He wasn't fond of this current arrangement where everyone from both teams was now spread out into God knew how many bunkers in God knew how many states. They hadn't even had the chance to say goodbye. They were also temporarily forbidden contact with one another for everyone's safety.

Temple's voice was softer when she addressed him. "I'll do everything in my power to ensure that happens."

After a few moments of silence, Michelle cleared her throat, trying to avoid the well of emotion threatening to cause tears. "Well, we should get my stuff packed. It's a long drive back and I want to be able to see everyone who's here."

"Go. Get packed. I'll find Trish and Tushar to come talk to you while you pack." Temple stood.

Zeke took Michelle's arm as she stood. It was impressive how in tune with her he'd become in the time they'd known each other. He had a sixth sense when it came to her emotions. The look of understanding in his eyes when he met her gaze confirmed it.

Trish showed up at the door to Michelle's suite ten minutes later. After a quick hug, Michelle reassured Trish that Ryan and

Emily were fine and safe and working hard. Meanwhile Zeke moved around packing Michelle's belongings with Tushar's help. They had several boxes stacked in the hallway and were hauling them out to the SUV when Michelle's phone buzzed in her pocket.

She pulled it out and glanced at the text from an unknown number.

Get out. As fast as you can without making anyone suspicious. Say nothing.

"Everything okay?" Trish asked.

Michelle smiled as she tucked the phone back in her pocket. "Yep."

Her hands were shaking as Zeke tucked his head into the main room of the suite. "You ready? We should get on the road." His eyes were wide when they met hers, and Michelle knew he'd received the same text.

She wasn't ready. Not even close. Most of her things were packed, but she hadn't spent as much time in the bunker as she would have liked. She hadn't even had the chance to speak to anyone else working in the lab. She shot Zeke a forced smile, though. "Yep," she repeated.

In record time, they pulled away from the bunker. Zeke looked over his shoulder. "What the fuck do you think is going on?"

"No clue, but I don't like it." She adjusted the rearview mirror and glanced around, half expecting the SUV to explode. "You think the text came from Ryan?"

"I assume, but who knows. Unknown number." He twisted around to look out every window, half fearing they might be followed. "I hope we covered our expressions enough and stayed long enough that no one got suspicious."

She shot him a glance. "I hope the damn bunker doesn't blow up in a minute, killing our friends."

He cringed. "Surely the text would have been more specific if that were a threat. At the very least, if Ryan was involved in sending the text, he wouldn't leave his own parents in danger."

She nodded. "You're right. Whatever's going on has to be specific to you and me, not them."

"Agreed. Maybe someone heard we were at the bunker and intended to pay us an unwanted visit."

She chewed on her lower lip. "Well, we aren't there now, and the only way this car is bugged is if someone did it in plain sight while we were packing."

He agreed. "Unlikely. I think we're good now." He stared at the way her fingers flexed on the steering wheel. "You should let me drive."

"You should get a license," she tossed back, forcing a grin.

He scrunched up his face. "I guess I better get motivated. Will you at least share your car? Or do I have to get my own?"

She rolled her eyes. "I'll share. You get a license."

"Watch the road." He pointed toward the windshield.

She let go of the steering wheel with her right hand to take a swat at him. "Dude, if you start telling me how to drive, I'm not only going to not let you use my car, but I'm not going to let you ride in it either."

He deflected her swat by putting his arms up in exaggeration. Finally, he grabbed her hand and pulled it to his cheek. "I hate that you got yanked from your friends."

"You did too," she pointed out.

"Yeah, but no one liked me anyway. I was an asshole." He sounded like he wasn't kidding.

She frowned. "That's not true. Everyone likes you."

"Not so much. Or they didn't before we were preserved. My

best friend was Dade, and that's only because he understood me. I hate that I can't see him."

"He sounds happy," she said, "other than the fact that he's spending countless hours every day trying to solve a crime from the grave."

"Yeah. It was convenient that Blair was able to use the chaos of everyone's relocation to inform Temple he had died." Zeke cringed. "I can't imagine that phone call. She must be quite an actress. She must feel like shit lying like that."

"I'm sure she does. She worked with Temple for years. They have a mutual respect that extends far beyond the professional. It's going to be disastrous when Temple finds out that not only Blair but several of us have been lying about Dade."

Zeke sighed. "Maybe not. Maybe she'll understand our reasoning. It has nothing to do with her. Her hands are tied, however. She would have to report his existence to her superiors. As long as she's misinformed, people above her are too. And it's working. He's still alive. There have been no whispers to the contrary."

"Which means there's a good chance every insane incident is coming from higher up."

"Unfortunately, yes. And that is mind-boggling. Why the hell would someone in the government be trying to sabotage our efforts? It makes no sense."

"I agree."

They rode in silence for a while and then Michelle pulled off the highway and found a motel where they could pay in cash and get some sleep before continuing.

When they dropped into bed, mentally and physically exhausted from a long day, Zeke pulled her into his arms and kissed her before succumbing to sleep.

CHAPTER 20

Michelle awoke with a start and then a scream when she realized she'd been yanked out of sleep by a hand over her mouth. The hand tightened, forcing her scream to turn into a muffled whimper.

Her eyes went wide as she was dragged to her feet. One arm was wrapped around her middle, the other hand over her mouth. "One sound and he's dead."

She blinked, trying to see in the dark. Through the light coming in under the bottom edge of the curtain, she could faintly make out Zeke. For a second she thought he had been similarly yanked out of his side of the bed and was being held in an equally defenseless position, but then he slumped to the floor.

She screamed again, to no avail, unable to stop herself.

"Bitch. Shut the fuck up," the man holding her hissed in her ear. He held her tighter, squashing her breasts too tight.

She nodded. Her adrenaline was pumping so fast she couldn't breathe. She grasped his forearm and tried to free herself as he lifted her too far off the floor. Only her tiptoes were touching. He was tall. Large. Strong.

Focus, Michelle. Focus.

His arm was Caucasian. Dark hair sprinkled down it. No sleeves on his shirt. She twisted to get a look at him and found he was wearing a mask. Black. His clothing was black too.

He dragged her across the room and slammed her onto a chair while his partner painfully yanked her arms behind her and tied them to each other and the rungs of the chair. He was similarly dressed, but with long sleeves that made it impossible to make out his race.

She glanced at the floor to find Zeke awkwardly lying on his side, out cold.

The man holding her mouth hissed at her again. "I'm going to remove my hand. If you scream, Lover Boy is dead. Understood?"

She nodded, eyes wide again. Sweat was pouring down her face from the stress. When he released her, she sucked in oxygen. She needed to stay alert. Figure out a way out of this mess. "What do you want?" she whispered.

"Information."

"About what?" She blinked up at him. How much did he know? How stupid could she act?

The man who had tied her up kicked Zeke's body needlessly to the side. He was broader but shorter, and she thought his hands were darker in tone than the other man. Maybe he was Hispanic or black. Or just tan. It was impossible to tell.

She started to scream and stopped herself. "Stop. You don't have to do that. He's not bothering you."

The sleeveless guy leaned into her face. His exhale hit her in the nose and made her hold her breath. "Lower your voice, bitch."

She swallowed. *Think. Think think think.* "What do you want to know? My boyfriend and I are just on vacation. I don't know what we could possibly know."

The white guy chuckled sardonically. "Told you she would balk."

"She won't balk if I stab him in the gut," the darker man stated as he pulled a knife out of its sheath at his side and held it up.

Michelle panicked. *Oh my God. Fuck.* "Jesus. I'll tell you anything." She wouldn't, of course. She would tell them nothing. But maybe if she could stall or convince them she knew nothing…

"Tell us where the rest of your team is?"

"My team?" She needed to buy time. Think. She was shaking, but already she was working on the knot at her back. She also shot a grateful thanks to God that she never went to bed without shorts and a T-shirt after her freak-out night in the bunker. Zeke had teased her about it, but he also wore pants to sleep in. Blessedly they were not currently naked.

"Yes, bitch, your fucking team. Were you on the first team or the second?"

The darker man kicked Zeke again. "And what about him? Is this some sweet romance between a nurse and her patient or vice versa?" He laughed again, his voice grating on her nerves. How did these guys know so much, and who the hell was feeding them information?

"I don't know where anyone is," she stated, digging her nails into the rope. Damn, it was tight. It was also scraping her wrists brutally. But that was the least of her concerns. She ignored the pain and continued working on the knot without moving the rest of her body.

The tall, white guy leaned in again. "Liar." His voice was louder this time. "I'm going to give you about ten seconds to tell me what I want to know and then I'm going to have my partner stab your boyfriend so deep you can do nothing but watch him bleed to death."

The darker man held the knife up in the ray of the streetlights. It was huge. Zeke would not survive being stabbed with it.

"Now," the taller man hissed. "Right fucking now. I don't have all night."

"Okay. Okay." She almost had the rope loosened, but not close enough. And besides, even if she did untie it, she would be no match against these two. She didn't even have a gun with her. Neither she nor Zeke carried a gun.

Even though they were both military, they wouldn't need their own weapons when they weren't active duty. Neither of them had ever been active duty. They'd been selected straight out of their academies to join Project DEEP. They had the bare minimum of training with weapons and never owned one.

"*Bitch*." The white guy yanked her out of her mental plan to get a gun the second she got out of this mess.

"I'm serious. We were split up after the bombing." Did he know about the bombing?

"We know that. Where was everyone sent?"

She shook her head vehemently. "It's classified. We don't even know where we're supposed to go next. We aren't privy to that information."

He kicked the leg of her chair so hard it almost fell over backward. It teetered for a moment while she held her breath and then landed on all fours again. "That's bullshit," he growled. "You expect me to believe you don't even know where you're going?"

She nodded. "Yes. We don't. I swear. We get our instructions as we go. It's too dangerous for anyone to know more than they need to. It prevents us from being able to out the operation if anything like this should occur."

"Fuck," he shouted before glancing at the darker man. "Kill them both. They're useless."

Michelle sucked in a breath, trying to make a decision. Was he testing her? What difference did it make? She had no choice. There wasn't a chance in hell she would give away the location of even the few members of her team currently in New Mexico. She would sooner die, and she knew Zeke would too. If these guys really did stab them to death, at least they wouldn't have any more information than they started with.

She squeezed her eyes shut and ducked her head, digging harder to get the rope loose. Her heart was pumping fast as she experienced the worst fear of her life. She prayed they killed her first so she wouldn't have to watch Zeke die in his drugged state.

That seemed unlikely, though, since the darker man straddled Zeke and lifted the knife in the air.

Michelle screamed as loud as she could.

Suddenly, all hell broke loose. Ten things seemed to happen at the same time. The darker man spun around and lurched toward her. Zeke jumped to his feet behind the man. And a loud crash sounded as the door to the room was kicked in.

She had no idea what was happening at the door, but she threw herself backward to avoid the knife coming at her. As she landed on her arms, pain shot up to her shoulders. But she was still alive.

Zeke slammed into the darker man, sending him to the floor.

The white guy took two strides toward Zeke, a knife in his hands that she hadn't seen before.

"*Zeke*," she shouted.

It wasn't necessary. A shot rang out near the door. The white guy slumped to the floor as blood ran out the side of his head.

A moment later, several hands were on the other guy's shoulders, hauling him off Zeke and dragging him across the room. Police.

She had no fucking clue how the police had found them or how fast, but she had never been so glad in her life. Maybe someone in another room saw them break in or heard them next door. She couldn't imagine how they would have had enough time, though.

As the police were wrestling the shorter man to the floor and then securing him, Zeke scrambled to her side and lifted the chair upright. He was fumbling with the rope when a shadow filled the doorway.

Nicole.

Michelle gasped as her hands were freed.

Zeke hadn't noticed Nicole yet. He was too busy rubbing

Michelle's arms. "Jesus. Are you okay? I didn't want to act too soon. I was stalling. I waited too long. You could have been injured." He was rambling.

Michelle was staring at Nicole. "How did you find us?"

Zeke finally turned around as he hauled Michelle off the chair and pulled her into his embrace. "Nicole?"

She came the rest of the way into the room. "I followed you."

"Why?"

She pointed at the dead guy. "Because they did."

"My God." Michelle fisted her palm on Zeke's bare chest.

He was still holding her wrist, rubbing it, but she knew nothing was broken. She would be sore, but she was fine.

The police dragged the darker man out of the room and headed toward the flashing lights Michelle now noticed outside. The three of them were left with the very dead man.

Michelle avoided looking at the pool of blood forming on the carpet.

Nicole came closer, shaking her head. "When I told you it was my last day, that didn't mean I wanted you to make it exciting."

How the hell could the woman make Michelle smile? She shrugged. "We thought we'd spice it up." How the hell could *she* be joking at a time like this?

Nicole lifted Michelle's free hand. "You should see a doctor."

"I'm fine."

"I'll make sure she does," Zeke added.

"I'm *fine*," Michelle insisted again, jerking her arms free of both of them.

Nicole winced and stepped back, rubbing her temples. "The moment you two pulled through the gate, these two assholes whispered a bit too loudly to each other. I realized they were going to follow you, so my partner and I followed them."

"Does Temple know?" Zeke asked.

"Yes."

"Why didn't you stop them earlier?" Zeke asked.

Nicole cringed. "That part got fucked up. I had backup arranged all along the route. When you pulled off to get this room, these two assholes also got a room. Your superiors insisted I watch them, thinking these guys intended to follow you to your destination. I should have followed my instincts instead of orders from an unknown source I had never set my eyes on."

"We *are* still living," Michelle pointed out.

Zeke frowned. "Barely. Why the hell didn't you at least tell *us* someone was following us? We wouldn't have been caught completely unaware in our fucking sleep."

She nodded. "You're right. It wasn't my call, but I should have done something anyway. The orders I received didn't sit well with me."

Zeke jerked. "Whose call was it? What unknown source?" He held Michelle around the waist, but his body was stiff. She'd never seen him this angry. Not that she could blame him.

"I have no idea. I was connected through to someone above Temple after I called her. They've been instructing me all day. They wanted you to lead these guys all the way to your destination. They were afraid if you were informed, you wouldn't continue to act naturally."

Michelle had to grab Zeke's arm to keep him from lurching forward. She was afraid he might strangle Nicole.

Nicole's partner, Pierce Titus, stepped into the room.

Nicole rubbed her forehead. "Worst decision of my life. I didn't know who I was taking orders from, and I had a gut feeling things were going to go bad. Pierce and I have been sitting in the parking lot since you got here. Watching."

Zeke gave Michelle another squeeze. Too tight. "What the hell did you do when those fuckers came into the room? Wait for backup? They've have been in here terrorizing us for at least ten minutes."

Michelle thought it seemed longer.

Nicole shook her head. "They didn't come in through the front."

Michelle jerked her gaze to the back of the room and realized there was a window in the bathroom that was open.

"It was only because the hair on the back of my neck stood on end that we got out of the car to wander the property. When I circled your unit and saw the open window, I ran to the front."

"And the police? How did they get here?" Zeke asked. His voice indicated he was not backing down.

"They were already here. I told you I had backup. I didn't trust the situation. They were in the parking lot too. When they saw me running around the side of the building with my gun drawn, they beat me to the room."

"Jesus." Zeke ran a hand through his hair, not releasing his grip on Michelle. "That is fucked up."

Michelle twisted in his embrace. "How did you suddenly wake up?"

"I was never out. The second I realized what I was inhaling, I stopped breathing and slumped to the floor to ensure he thought he'd done his job. He's an ignorant fool to have believed I passed out. I was fucking scared out of my mind waiting for the right moment to jump up."

He looked it too. His eyes were still wild, searching her face the entire time he spoke.

The two cops came back into the room. "We need to get you folks out of here. This is a crime scene."

No shit, Michelle thought, keeping the words to herself.

One cop covered the body with a tarp while the other pointed at their suitcase. "You can take your belongings as long as nothing is part of the crime scene."

It seemed like everything and everyone was part of the crime scene. Michelle was still shaking, unable to understand what the hell had happened and why someone above Temple would have put their lives in such grave danger.

Zeke did most of the work, gathering their things and leading her out of the room. He always seemed better under pressure than her. This wasn't the first time she'd found herself dazed and having difficulty shaking out of a near trance. Good thing she'd never been sent to the front line.

After about two thousand questions from a seemingly equal number of cops, Nicole put an end to it and led them to her car.

They had been standing around, wrapped in blankets over their sleepwear. The only thing they'd done was add their shoes.

"Get in," she said, pointing at the back seat before heading back to speak to another officer.

Michelle didn't realize how badly she'd been shaking or for how long until she sat and Zeke pulled her closer. He kissed the top of her head. "Jesus. You're shivering so badly."

She nodded. She was very rattled. "We could have died."

"I know. But we didn't. I'm sorry I couldn't stop them from terrorizing you sooner." He buried his face in her hair. "I was slowly dying inside while I watched them scream at you."

"You did the right thing." She grabbed his hand and squeezed it. "You *did* stop him."

"I wouldn't have been able to live with myself if I'd failed."

"You didn't fail."

"I'm going to rip Temple a new asshole. The only reason I haven't called her yet is because I know I can't control my temper."

Michelle lifted her face to see his. "You know she didn't do this. It was out of her hands. She probably knows nothing."

He gritted his teeth and slammed his head back against the seat. "I think we're pawns in an unimaginable game so complex that we can't even fathom the scope of this operation. Maybe these guys were behind the unknown text. Maybe Ryan knew nothing about it."

Michelle stared at him. What if he was right? "What do we do?"

"We pay closer attention. We get our own personal weapons and new phones tomorrow morning." He lifted his from his pocket. "We turn these off now so we can't be traced. We don't leave the bunker again. We feed Dade every damn detail we can ascertain."

"We don't say a word to Temple about our aggravation or suspicions," she added softly.

He groaned. "That too." He nuzzled her neck and kissed her behind the ear. "I could have lost you."

She squeezed him tighter. "You didn't. And we know more now. We'll be more prepared from now on."

He lifted his head and cupped her cheeks. "We can't breathe a word of our suspicions to anyone. Not even Nicole. We have to let this go or at least pretend we did, if anyone asks. If not, we'll remain a target. Unfinished business."

"You really think someone above Temple wanted us killed?"

"I do."

Michelle swallowed, knowing he was right. Hating it just the same. "Who do we tell?"

"Ryan. Emily. Dade. This is the extent of the list of people we can trust."

CHAPTER 21

Zeke was hardly breathing easier several hours later when he finally convinced Nicole to let them go on their own. The sun was up. No one had slept. But he knew he wouldn't be able to rest until they were securely back on the grounds of the bunker in New Mexico. Michelle wouldn't either.

It would be a waste of time for them to get another room in another hotel somewhere. He wouldn't feel safe. He'd barely felt safe when they'd gone into the motel lobby to change into clean clothes in the public bathrooms. Parting from Michelle while she went into the women's room had stressed him out.

Nicole couldn't follow them. It was extremely unlikely anyone else would at this point either. The motel was still crawling with cops. She needed to stay and ensure they didn't have any more questions.

She was leery about letting them leave. She was also obviously intuitive about their predicament. They didn't exchange specific words, but she made it clear she wouldn't tell anyone she had let them leave. Not a soul. Not even Temple. She would put off calling to check in or even checking her messages for several hours and then claim she had been busy filing reports and helping the local law enforcement.

Nicole knew she'd been played. She didn't have to say it out loud.

Zeke thanked her, and then he watched as Michelle hugged her tight. "I hope your next assignment is far less exciting. I know you joked yesterday about it being more intense than this one, but I bet you've changed your mind now." Michelle's voice was light.

Nicole's face was tight. "Unfortunately, no. It will be more insane."

Michelle flinched.

Nicole smiled. "Don't worry about me. I've been doing this a while. I have good intuition. And next time, I won't let anyone try to talk me out of it. Not even my damn boss."

"I hope not. You're good at your job. Go save some more lives. Trust your instinct."

"You too." She glanced at Zeke, including him. "Both of you. Your war isn't over."

Zeke nodded. "We're aware."

"Arm yourselves."

"We will."

"Be careful." She sighed. It was obvious she hated letting them leave. Finally, she set Michelle away and opened the driver's door.

When Michelle started to get inside, Nicole met her gaze. "Why do you do all the driving?"

Zeke rolled his eyes. "Woman thinks I need a license or something." He headed toward his side of the car.

Nicole gasped, as he knew she would. "You're...?"

Zeke climbed into the passenger side and leaned over Michelle to shoot her a grin. "I last drove more than a decade ago by your standards."

Nicole was still shaking her head, stunned, as Michelle closed the door and then pulled away.

Zeke was used to that shocked look when someone found

out he'd been reanimated. It still made him laugh inside. For some reason, people always expected the revived to look different or act different. Did they expect someone more like a zombie?

"I *could* drive, you know," he said as Michelle pulled out of the parking lot.

"Yep. As soon as you get your license I'm all for it."

He took her hand, knowing he had an important job—keeping her awake long enough for them to get to the bunker.

It was late afternoon when they arrived. Michelle had never been so tense. Every muscle in her body was going to hurt the next day.

Not surprisingly, no one at the bunker had any idea what they'd been through. They took some time to explain everything to Ryan and Emily outside next to the car without going into the bunker.

It would look as if the four of them were just catching up to anyone watching, but Michelle didn't trust the bunker not to be bugged. She wasn't sure how she was going to trust anyplace anywhere at any time in the future.

Somehow she had to pull it together and pretend to play the game, though. They all four would.

They agreed there was no reason to bring Damon in on their undercover plot or the fact that they were working with Dade. Eventually, it would have to come out, but until it was necessary, the fewer people involved, the better.

"We need sleep," Michelle finally declared, slumping against Zeke. "Twenty hours of it."

Zeke snapped his head up to face Emily and Ryan. "Do you know who sent us the text yesterday?"

"What text?" Ryan asked, glancing at Emily.

"The one warning us to get out of the bunker. We figured it

was one of you at the time, but now I'm concerned it came from the same people who followed us," Zeke added.

Ryan shook his head. "I didn't text you."

"Me neither," said Emily.

"Could've been Dade too," Michelle pointed out.

Ryan's brows were furrowed as he continued to shake his head. "Not a chance. He wouldn't have done that in secret without telling me."

Zeke stiffened all along Michelle's body. "Well, someone did. And now we don't know if it was for our benefit or to put us more at risk."

"I'll make some calls," Ryan said.

Zeke glanced down at Michelle. "Let's get some sleep before we collapse." He led her across the driveway toward the row of mobile homes lined up behind the main building. Unlike the bunker in Falling Rock, this one had no inside dwellings. It was just as well. Michelle preferred being able to exit the main building at night. It gave her some separation. Perhaps it was wishful thinking, but she also trusted these outer homes not to be bugged. It seemed much less likely.

When they went inside, they each began their usual ritual of silently checking the place for any possible signs someone could be listening to them or watching. They had a small handheld device they'd purchased to scan the rooms.

Once again, they found nothing.

Finally, they both flopped down on the bed. Still dressed. They didn't even bother to pull back the covers.

"Who do you think sent that text?" Michelle asked, shuddering at the memory. "Do you really think someone was trying to warn us we were in danger?"

"I'm not sure what I think at this point. Maybe it was Dade and he didn't want those guys following us here. Maybe he didn't have a chance to tell Ryan and Emily he'd texted us."

"Let's hope. The thought of someone having our numbers and invading our phones like that makes me cringe."

It was dark when Michelle felt Zeke's hands on her body. He was tugging her shirt over her head. She moaned and blinked her eyes open.

He kissed her. "We fell asleep fully clothed," he pointed out.

"What time is it?" she asked as she glanced at the clock. "Wow. We've been asleep for nine hours." As she sat up and finished undressing, she felt more awake.

Watching Zeke shrug out of his jeans also drew her attention. By the time they were both naked, she reached for him.

He tugged the covers back between them, and they both wiggled around to get under them. The air conditioner was blasting as usual. It was hot in the desert. By silent agreement they always preferred to sleep with the temperature set low and blankets covering them. Mostly because Michelle couldn't relax enough to have sex without something over them.

Zeke never said a word. He covered them every time.

She hoped one day she would be someplace where she felt safe enough to sleep naked and have sex with the lights on where she could stare openly at his fantastic body. For now, this was their thing. They made it work.

He drew her close and kissed her gently. "Are you tired?"

"Not now," she murmured against his lips.

He smiled against her. "Good. I need to be inside you. It will make me feel alive. I need to feel your heartbeat against mine."

She moaned into his mouth as she kissed him again. It seemed he had stolen those words from her heart. "Please."

He released her mouth and tipped his head back a few inches, meeting her gaze in the dim light. His hand went to the back of her head. "I love you."

"I love you too."

"I kept kicking myself for not telling you sooner while I lay on the floor unable to move in that damn motel room."

She reached up to cup his face. "We're okay now."

"I need to feel you around me."

She nodded.

He reached between her legs and drew his fingers through her folds. "So wet…"

"Yeah…"

"I haven't even touched you yet," he whispered against her lips.

"I was wet as soon as you reached for me."

He smiled against her again. "I really love you."

She giggled. "I really love you too."

Seconds later, she was on her back, and he was sliding into her.

He threaded their fingers together and held her arms at the sides of her head. The look in his eyes as he claimed her filled her heart. They may have taken a gamble on each other, but there was no doubt the risk was worth it.

They were perfect for each other. In every way. They would protect each other. They would survive this crazy world. They would live to make love naked on a sandy beach on a deserted island somewhere.

That had to.

There was no other option.

AUTHOR'S NOTE

I hope you enjoyed book four in the *Project DEEP* series. Please enjoy the following excerpt for book five in the series, *Reviving Graham*.

REVIVING GRAHAM

PROJECT DEEP (BOOK FIVE)

"Kate?" The weak voice coming from across the room startled Kate so badly she nearly stumbled as she spun around to face her patient.

Graham Wentz. The man she had kept under constant observation for a month while his organs returned to full function as finally awake.

She rushed to close the short distance between them and set a hand on his shoulder, smiling. "Welcome back."

He frowned, glancing around the room. "Where am I?"

"A clinic in Colorado. Long story." Very long story. She knew from witnessing the reanimation of over a dozen other coworkers how confused he would be this first day. He would need time to shake the cobwebs and get his brain to fully absorb everything he'd missed.

His gaze came back to hers. "Where's everyone else?"

"Another long story. The important thing is that you're awake, and all your vitals are good. Don't rush things."

The look on his face suggested he might argue. Not surprising. After all, she'd always known him to be inquisitive and sharp.

Kate herself had only been pulled out of preservation three months ago. The first few days were a foggy memory.

Kate schooled her face, forcing a friendly smile. Inside, she was nervous. Her heart was racing and the tight ball she'd had in her stomach for weeks squeezed harder. He was back. Those pale green eyes she remembered were staring up at her. His thick strawberry-blond hair was longer than normal after spending a month in this bed. She kind of liked it.

It took every ounce of energy to keep from reaching up to smooth her hand over his hair or cup his cheek or lean in closer and set her lips on his forehead. But those hadn't been mannerisms she'd used with him a decade ago, and she didn't want to startle him. She had no idea how he might respond to her doting over him anyway.

The entire situation was crazy since she'd been nursing him back to health now for weeks. Alone. She'd seen every inch of his body. But now he was awake. It would be awkward to continue to ogle his facial features or set a hand on his arm the way she had every day.

Graham sighed and then drew in a long breath. "Start talking."

She stiffened. "How about a drink of water? You need to get your organs to fully wake up and start functioning." His organs were fine. He'd had an IV for four weeks. Everything was in working order. Nevertheless, she picked up a cup and filled it with water.

When he tried to lift his head, his eyes widened. "Holy shit. How long have I been asleep? My head feels like it's not even connected to my body."

"That's normal. Physical therapy will help. I'll get you started." She tucked her hand under his head and helped tip him forward so he could take a sip of water.

He swallowed and then dropped back down as if he'd gone for a run. He lifted one shaky hand up swipe it over his face and into his hair. His eyes were closed when he dropped his hand. "Kate. Talk to me."

She pulled a chair up closer and sat, ignoring the awkwardness and grabbing his wrist. For a moment she stared at the contrast of his lighter freckled skin against her more naturally tanned fingers. "Maybe you should try to sleep a bit longer, and then we'll talk. Anything I say to you right now will be forgotten."

He slowly turned his face toward her, meeting her gaze. He searched her face, probably trying to read her expression. "My memory has always been one of my best assets. I don't think I lost it in the cryostat." His gaze was intense, never wavering, eyes narrowed slightly.

She returned a similar stare and asked him a tough question as a test. "What was your diagnosis before you were preserved?"

He rolled his eyes as if he were bored. "Viral-onset AP12. Happy?"

Damn. He did seem sharper than she remembered feeling when she'd awoken. She realized she was gripping his wrist too tightly and eased up. Naturally, Graham wasn't the sort of person who was going to be placated. It would be easier to give him an overview now even if she had to repeat it again later today and then tomorrow.

She studied his face. She'd done so many times over the past few weeks, but he wouldn't know that. She needed to remember she didn't have the freedom to stare at him or hold his hand now that he was awake.

A new reality was descending, one in which her fantasies about Graham were about to go up in smoke. The truth was she'd been half in love with the man before they were preserved, but she'd never told him. She'd never told anyone until recently. He hadn't known her from Adam, of course, but she'd been attracted to him anyway. In fact, her last regret before being preserved had been that she'd never had the guts to so much as flirt with him.

He didn't move an inch. Not even to blink. He was staring at her, having paid more attention to her in the last thirty seconds than he had in years. He'd spoken more words to her cumulatively also.

She took a breath. "There was an explosion at the bunker about a month ago. I've been here with you ever since. We're a few hours south of Falling Rock."

"An explosion?" His body jerked.

"Yes. You're one of the last of the original team to be reanimated. The new team has been bringing us all back as fast as they can, but there are a lot of people who aren't pleased with our existence." She really wished he would go back to sleep. She'd known she would need to tell him all of this, but she hadn't counted on it being today.

He frowned. "Why?"

She sighed. "Who knows? Religious zealots think the government shouldn't be playing God. The media wants a story. You name it." She didn't even give him half of it, but good Lord, he needed to rest more.

"Did someone find a cure for AP12?"

"Yes." She smiled. This was the best part of the story. "Remember Tushar and Trish's son? Ryan Anand?"

He nodded. "He's about twenty, right?"

She chuckled. "He was. But he aged while we didn't. He found a cure and put together a new Project DEEP team with another doctor, Damon Bardsley, a cryonicist. They've successfully brought us back."

Graham licked his lips and then slowly asked his next question in a shaky voice. "How long have we been vitrified?"

"Ten years."

ALSO BY BECCA JAMESON

Seattle Doms:

Salacious Exposure by Becca Jameson

Salacious Desires By Kate Oliver

Salacious Attraction by Becca Jameson

Salacious Indulgence by Kate Oliver

Salacious Devotion by Becca Jameson

Salacious Surrender by Kate Oliver

Danger Bluff:

Rocco

Hawking

Kestrel

Magnus

Phoenix

Caesar

Roses and Thorns:

Marigold

Oleander

Jasmine

Tulip

Daffodil

Lily

Roses and Thorns Box Set One

Roses and Thorns Box Set Two

Shadowridge Guardians:

Steele by Pepper North

Kade by Kate Oliver

Atlas by Becca Jameson

Doc by Kate Oliver

Gabriel by Becca Jameson

Talon by Pepper North

Bear by Becca Jameson

Faust by Pepper North

Storm by Kate Oliver

Blade by Pepper North

King by Kate Oliver

Rock by Becca Jameson

Blossom Ridge:

Starting Over

Finding Peace

Building Trust

Feeling Brave

Embracing Joy

Accepting Love

Blossom Ridge Box Set One

Blossom Ridge Box Set Two

The Wanderers:

Sanctuary

Refuge

Harbor

Shelter

Hideout

Haven

The Wanderers Box Set One

The Wanderers Box Set Two

Surrender:

Raising Lucy

Teaching Abby

Leaving Roman

Choosing Kellen

Pleasing Josie

Honoring Hudson

Nurturing Britney

Charming Colton

Convincing Leah

Rewarding Avery

Impressing Brett

Guiding Cassandra

Chasing Amber

Controlling Natasha

Provoking Camden

Surrender Box Set One

Surrender Box Set Two

Surrender Box Set Three

Surrender Box Set Four

Open Skies:

Layover

Redeye

Nonstop

Standby

Takeoff

Jetway

Open Skies Box Set One

Open Skies Box Set Two

Shadow SEALs:

Shadow in the Desert

Shadow in the Darkness

Holt Agency:

Rescued by Becca Jameson

Unchained by KaLyn Cooper

Protected by Becca Jameson

Liberated by KaLyn Cooper

Defended by Becca Jameson

Unrestrained by KaLyn Cooper

Delta Team Three (Special Forces: Operation Alpha):

Destiny's Delta

Canyon Springs:

Caleb's Mate

Hunter's Mate

Corked and Tapped:

Volume One: Friday Night

Volume Two: Company Party

Volume Three: The Holidays

The Complete Set

Tempting Elizabeth

Club Zodiac Box Set One

Club Zodiac Box Set Two

Club Zodiac Box Set Three

The Art of Kink:

Pose

Paint

Sculpt

Arcadian Bears:

Grizzly Mountain

Grizzly Beginning

Grizzly Secret

Grizzly Promise

Grizzly Survival

Grizzly Perfection

Arcadian Bears Box Set One

Arcadian Bears Box Set Two

Sleeper SEALs:

Saving Zola

Spring Training:

Catching Zia

Catching Lily

Catching Ava

Spring Training Box Set

The Underground series:

Force

Clinch

Guard

Submit

Thrust

Torque

The Underground Box Set One

The Underground Box Set Two

Wolf Masters series:

Kara's Wolves

Lindsey's Wolves

Jessica's Wolves

Alyssa's Wolves

Tessa's Wolf

Rebecca's Wolves

Melinda's Wolves

Laurie's Wolves

Amanda's Wolves

Sharon's Wolves

Wolf Masters Box Set One

Wolf Masters Box Set Two

Claiming Her series:

The Rules

The Game

The Prize

Claiming Her Box Set

Emergence series:

Bound to be Taken

Bound to be Tamed

Bound to be Tested

Bound to be Tempted

Emergence Box Set

The Fight Club series:

Come

Perv

Need

Hers

Want

Lust

The Fight Club Box Set One

The Fight Club Box Set Two

Wolf Gatherings series:

Tarnished

Dominated

Completed

Redeemed

Abandoned

Betrayed

Wolf Gatherings Box Set One

Wolf Gathering Box Set Two

Durham Wolves series:

Rescue in the Smokies

Fire in the Smokies

Freedom in the Smokies

Durham Wolves Box Set

ABOUT THE AUTHOR

Becca Jameson is a USA Today best-selling author of over 150 books. She is well-known for her Wolf Masters series, her Fight Club series, and her Surrender series. She currently lives in Houston, Texas, with her husband. Two grown kids pop in every once in a while, too! She is loving this journey and has dabbled in a variety of genres, including paranormal, sports romance, military, reverse harem, dark romance, suspense, dystopian, BDSM, and Daddy Dom.

A total night owl, Becca writes late at night, sequestering herself in her office with a glass of red wine and a bar of dark chocolate, her fingers flying across the keyboard as her characters weave their own stories.

During the day--which never starts before ten in the morning!-- she can be found walking, running errands, or reading in her favorite hammock chair!

...where Alphas dominate...

Becca's Newsletter Sign-up

Join my Facebook fan group, Becca's Bibliomaniacs, for the most up-to-date information, random excerpts while I work, giveaways, and fun release parties!

Facebook Fan Group:
Becca's Bibliomaniacs

Contact Becca:
www.beccajameson.com
beccajameson4@aol.com

f facebook.com/becca.jameson.18
X x.com/beccajameson
⊙ instagram.com/becca.jameson
BB bookbub.com/authors/becca-jameson
g goodreads.com/beccajameson
a amazon.com/author/beccajameson

www.ingramcontent.com/pod-product-compliance
Lightning Source LLC
Chambersburg PA
CBHW070104280626
47159CB00016B/1180